SANTA FE MOJO

A Vincent Malone Novel

TED CLIFTON

Santa Fe Mojo (A Vincent Malone Novel)
Ted Clifton
ISBN 978-1-77342-053-0

Produced by IndieBookLauncher.com
www.IndieBookLauncher.com
Editing: Nassau Hedron
Cover Design: Saul Bottcher
Interior Design and Typesetting: Saul Bottcher

The body text of this book is set in Adobe Caslon.

Also Available
EPUB edition, ISBN 978-1-77342-051-6
Kindle edition, ISBN 978-1-77342-052-3

CONTENTS

1

How Did I Get Here?

Denver, Colorado: Winter 2015

"Time to go, buddy." The bartender wasn't as polite as he'd been four and a half hours ago. It was always the fate of the last drunk in the bar to get the bum's rush. The bartender wanted to go home and deal with his own miserable life—forget about the useless people whose addictions he fed for a living.

Vincent Malone didn't care. He hardly noticed rudeness, anymore. It was everywhere, broadcast in all directions without thought. He had no idea why he'd stayed in the bar for so many hours—reluctance to go home to an empty apartment, maybe. He was too goddamned old for this kind of life. He'd been downtown for a meeting with one of his clients. He'd decided afterward to stop in the bar for a quick one. Now he was headed home, wasted money, wasted time, wasted Malone.

Malone pulled out his phone and ordered a cab. He was stubbornly anti-Uber, preferring the comfort of a ratty cab and the company of an international driver. It was far better than some asshole just out of puberty who knew everything.

"Where to, pal?"

He gave his address, an apartment in the lower end of the

high-rent district, then sat back and thought—for about the hundredth time in the past week—about why his life was so shitty. Well, at least he had a little money, so he could take a cab, and he had a home to take it to rather than being out on the street, fighting that living hell.

He was wearing a heavy topcoat, mostly because it was cold as hell in Denver in February, but also to better conceal his gun. He was a big man, over six foot three, with broad shoulders, and the coat made him seem even larger. Longer ago than he cared to remember, Vincent had been an up-and-coming attorney in Dallas. He'd been married to his high school sweetheart, who was Texas lovely, with honey-blonde hair and big blue eyes. And then everything had started to go south. He'd been a drinker, which meant he hung around with drinkers. A drunk is often a lonely kind of person, so drunks gather in groups of lonely people to take the edge off their solitude. There's a herd instinct that creates a sense of belonging. Most of these people had family or friends who cared about them, but whom they ignored in order to be with people they hardly knew. Without the booze the stupidity of it would have been obvious.

The other thing about drinkers is they're all schemers. Every one of them has some idea about how to make a million, how to marry rich, how to screw the neighbor's wife, how to be something other than what you are. One night, his group was scheming their latest.

"Let me tell you, this will be the easiest money you've ever made. Have I ever steered you wrong?" Idiot Number One had an idea, which should have been an obvious sign to run in the other direction.

"Yeah, you steered us wrong a bunch." Idiot Number Two couldn't remember exactly when or how, but he knew he'd lost money doing something Number One had suggested.

"Listen, you don't get to stay a broker if you steer people wrong, and I've got a hot tip. I make millions for all those other assholes—why not *you* assholes?"

There was actually some logic buried in there somewhere. Why *not* give him money to bet on a hot tip in the stock market? What could you lose but your money? Plenty, as it turned out. For one thing, the hot tip was illegal. And the amounts were huge, attracting a lot of attention. The feds busted everybody in sight, with a few minor exceptions. Judges, for instance, fared pretty well, but everyone else had the proverbial book thrown at them.

Vincent tried the classic defenses. "I was drunk!" "He made me do it!" He didn't go to jail, but the state bar soon revoked his license. A few months later, the blonde cheerleader wife was gone, divorce in hand, taking every tangible asset with her. Vincent was left with the unpaid bills. Next step, bankruptcy.

In what seemed from his perspective like a whirlwind of confusion and liquor, he'd gone from being an up-and-coming young attorney to being a disbarred, divorced, bankrupt, unemployed drunk who slept in his brother's garage. The brother's not-so-charming wife said he couldn't sleep in the house. He scared her, apparently, and given the way he had been feeling, it had probably been a wise decision on her part.

With very little money—his brother loaned him some, mostly to get rid of him—he'd headed to Denver. He'd had no particular reason to pick Denver, other than it started with a "D," just like Dallas. Next stop might be Davenport. He'd gotten his law degree from the University of Oklahoma, and there were quite a few OU graduates in Dallas legal circles. As his life had been tumbling into hell around him, he'd called several of them, asking for referrals, and any work that might be available, in Denver. He wanted something related to law, but that didn't require a license. And he needed a character reference—someone respectable who would say that he wasn't a complete loser. He talked to maybe twenty fellow OU grads, all of whom, either implied or outright said, "Fuck you." So much for the old school bond. But one guy whom he'd only met a few times, Nick Thompson, had actually seemed to give a damn. No doubt one of the people Vincent had spent most of his life avoiding—that is, someone genuinely nice.

"Man, I've heard about your troubles—that's really tough. I know a guy in Denver who was just telling me that his firm, I think it's like two hundred attorneys, was having a hard time finding good investigators. Have you ever thought of trying something like that?"

"You mean, like a private detective?"

"You know, I'm not sure what most of that work involves. But I think it's mostly research and following up on people to locate them, and stuff like that. I don't think it's anything like what you'd think of as detective work. Might be something to think about." Nick gave Vincent a name and a contact number in Denver and wished him luck.

Being a legal investigator wasn't something he'd considered. He'd worked with a few of them in the past and had never been very impressed. They seemed sleazy to him, not exactly the kind of people you'd want representing your top-drawer law firm. Maybe his background would stand out, open a few doors. There was one major problem, though. He had no idea how to do what they did. He wasn't even sure what it was they did, but whatever it was, he didn't know how.

He called the guy, and they hired him based on the recommendation from Nick. Vincent never quite got around to calling and thanking him. The law firm, which boasted more than two hundred attorneys, wasn't interested in hiring him as an employee but rather as an independent contractor. They were looking for someone to work on an hourly basis at a specific rate. He quoted them a number. They laughed. He accepted a much lower number, and even said, "Thank you."

Over the next few months, he discovered he was naturally talented at sleazy work. And he loved it. A lot of the work required that he spend time in bars, which was something he was really good at.

That had been more than thirty years before. He'd struggled at first, learning what he was supposed to do. He was a very large man with a perpetual scowl, and a bullshitter, so he just bullied his way through. Before long, he was being praised for his work and for the insight he brought to helping attorneys as they kept their clients from going to jail, or as they worked to squeeze every possible dollar out of some deal. He abandoned all pretense of lawyerly ethics, and did whatever he had to do to get the facts or to dig up the dirt he needed to earn his hourly rate.

Soon he was doing well. By design, he was a one-man band. He had no desire to have employees—it was enough to be responsible for himself and to make a living. He had ample clients, and in a typical month had to turn down work due to time constraints. Occasionally there would be a week when he had nothing to do, but that was fine, too, once in a while.

Life rocked along. He aged. His health deteriorated. Because he was a big man, or maybe just because he was a man, he'd always felt invincible. He knew intellectually that one day he was going to die, but being sick just wasn't something he'd had much experience with or given a lot of thought. He drank a lot, ate badly, and exercised only as much as he had to so he'd be able to chase down some asshole. With all of that, he still felt great, until he didn't.

The first attack of gout lasted about a week. He couldn't walk at all for several days, and on one of the better days he only made it as far as the kitchen by using a cane. The pain was intense. He didn't have a regular doctor, so he went to the Denver Health emergency room. They quizzed him about his lifestyle, his parent's health, and his level of pain, and poked him in spots that sure didn't seem to have anything to do with his feet. After much longer than he thought it should have taken, a small, foreign-looking doctor had told him in broken English he had gout. Or at least that's what they'd thought. To make sure, they'd need to use a needle to extract fluid from his toe. He'd said no, thank you, and left with a prescription for pain medication.

The gout went away after a few days, although he kept taking the pain medication until it was gone. The pain pills lasted several weeks, but why the hell not? Life was a pain. Some of his clients grumbled about him being unreliable, but they got over their pique fast enough, and things returned more or less to normal.

Six months later he had another episode of gout, and this time he was bed-ridden for two weeks, with difficulty walking for another several weeks after that. One of his smaller clients dropped him. They needed some work done urgently, so they went with someone else. His other clients made noises about getting rid of him, so he apologized and promised it wouldn't happen again. Of course, it did.

The next episode came only three months later. He lied about it, claiming that he had a family emergency out of town, saying he'd be back soon. He was sure his wiseass clients didn't believe him. This time he was immobilized for almost a month, and most of his clients called to say "Adios." The firm that had originally given him a chance all of those years before, called and said they wanted to meet with him.

That's where he'd been before dropping in at the bar. The meeting was terse and very clear. He was fired. He offered excuses, but there was no changing their minds. Suddenly, he had no clients at all. He decided that he'd have a quick drink to soothe his nerves, but that had been hours of quick drinks ago.

The cab pulled up in front of his relatively luxurious apartment building. He paid the driver and hesitated for just a few seconds. Unemployed, unhealthy, old, defeated, alone—he'd never felt so low. When he got out, the driver said, "Good luck, mister." Anyone with sense could see he was a broken man.

He moped for a few days, then started to plan his escape. He was a few years away from a full Social Security check. He needed some kind of useless job to keep a roof over his head until he could collect that money, and just retire. Of course, that meant he needed to get out of Denver, which was an expensive place to live. He'd heard that housing in Phoenix was dirt cheap by comparison, but he decided to go to Albuquerque first, and see if he could get a job there. It was only a day's drive away. Plus, it started with an "A." His new plan was to forget about "D" cities, and go alphabetically. Of course, even thinking nonsense like that had him worried about his mental health. He put in his notice on his lease and began selling everything he could. Soon he was down to stuff that would fit into his old car. He hadn't used it all that much lately, relying mostly on cabs and the light rail to get around Denver. It was a blue 1994 Mustang, and he liked it a lot. It made him feel young again. But the damned thing sucked gas like it was free, which it wasn't, so he'd parked it in the underground lot, covered with a tarp. Once his worldly possessions had been reduced to a few suitcases and a couple of boxes, he packed and left.

The drive south on I-25 beyond Colorado Springs was long and tedious. Vincent stopped in Trinidad and got a burger and fries at a Sonic. Not long afterward, he entered

New Mexico. The vastness of the nothingness that greeted him was depressing. A few hours later, he made it to the Sangre de Cristo Mountains, which at least broke up the monotony. His plan had been to drive to Albuquerque, but as he came to Santa Fe he realized that he was nearing exhaustion. He decided to stop where he was for the night, even if it was early evening. He didn't feel safe driving any farther. He spotted a Motel 6 right off of the highway, and pulled in. After check-in, he mused that maybe they should change the name to Motel 70. It would be more accurate.

The next morning, he asked the motel clerk where the best place was for breakfast on a limited budget.

"Best place around here is The Pantry. It's just down the road on the left side. Try the breakfast burrito with red sauce— just fantastic. Or they have a breakfast special with eggs, hash browns, sausage, and toast for only three-fifty. Best bargain in town. I think they've been in business since the 1940s, and all the locals eat there."

Based on this detailed and enthusiastic recommendation, he headed to The Pantry. The special tasted good, but after you added on a buck-fifty for the coffee, it wasn't much of a bargain any more. As he was leaving, he saw a large bulletin board full of all sorts of stuff—including jobs. One in particular caught his eye. The Blue Door Inn was looking for a "mature" shuttle driver to drive guests to and from places including the Albuquerque airport. He pulled the notice from the board and asked the cashier how to find the address.

He got back on I-25 and headed back north to the Old

Pecos Trail exit.

Vincent wandered around a little before he found the entrance to the Blue Door Inn. There was a small sign, obviously new, that guided him down a rustic lane toward the most beautiful hacienda-style building he'd ever seen. Its beauty didn't matter much one way or the other as a possible place to work, but if he'd been a potential guest, he would have been impressed. He pulled into the parking area.

As he approached the entrance with the charming blue door, he wasn't sure whether to knock or just walk in. The place looked as much like a residence as it did a business. Before he could decide, the door opened, and a slightly built, bespectacled man walked out in a rush.

"Oh, sorry. Didn't mean to run you down. Hi, I'm Jerry Oliver, own the place. Can I help you?" Oliver was full of kinetic energy. He was upbeat and smiling, and in constant motion, even when he was standing still.

"Yeah, my name's Vincent Malone. Saw your ad for a driver at The Pantry. Job still open?"

There was a slight change in Jerry's manner, but the smile returned quickly. "Well, yeah. The job's still open. This is for a shuttle driver. Can't really afford to pay too much." Jerry was giving him the eye, and Vincent could almost hear him thinking. *You don't look right for this job—what the hell is this about?*

"Well, yes, Mister Oliver, I understood that the job was for a driver, so I didn't expect it to pay huge sums. I'm just kind of filling some gaps before I reach retirement. My needs are modest. I've done a lot of things, but they've almost all involved dealing with people, so I'm good at that. Might not be able to lift things the way I did in the past, but I'm still pretty strong. And I'm a good, safe driver." Vincent wasn't sure any of that mattered to Jerry, who still seemed unsure what to do.

"What sort of jobs have you had before?"

Vincent thought this sounded more like just being nosy rather than relevant, and the lawyer in him wanted to object, the way he'd do with an irrelevant question in court. *This isn't court, though*, he thought. *Might as well get it over with.*

"First part of my life I was an attorney. Some stuff happened, lost my license and became a legal investigator. Worked for a lot of years helping lawyers put together evidence for their cases. Lost my last client a few months ago, back in Denver, and decided it was time to think about something else. Saw your ad when I was having breakfast, and thought I'd see if it might fit. Apparently, it doesn't, but you have a nice day." Vincent headed to his car.

"Hey, hold on. Look, things are pretty hectic around here. This is a new business—my wife and I are just starting out. We don't have experience in this industry and we need help. We're trying to get ready for our official opening, hopefully have some guests in a few days. You seem a little overqualified for this job, but we need the help right away, so if it's okay with you, why don't we try each other out and see how it goes?" Jerry's smile returned.

"Sounds good to me. Any chance there might be a spare room where I could hang my hat for a few days until I can find someplace to stay?"

"Well—well, I'm not sure. Let me check with my wife. Probably we can arrange something." The smile was gone again.

Vincent thought Jerry was just too nice a guy to survive in business, but he did need a place to stay. "Look, if that doesn't work I'm sure I can find something."

"No, I think that's fine. We're going to have some extra rooms at the start. 'Course, that would have to be considered part of your compensation."

"Sure."

Over the next few days, Vincent handled a wide range of tasks that Jerry laid out for him. He met Cindy, Jerry's wife, and Hector and Mary Flores, a husband-and-wife team that was going to handle maintenance, yard work, cleaning and some cooking. They were the only other employees besides him.

From the beginning, it was obvious that Jerry and Cindy were nice folks who had somehow managed to acquire a very expensive piece of real estate, but who knew almost nothing about running a bed and breakfast.

As a lawyer, and later as an investigator, Vincent had developed a habit that had stuck with him, making mental notes on the events of the day before going to sleep so he wouldn't lose track of any details that he might need later. As he did it on this night, though, it felt different than it had in recent days. There was a sense of comfort and belonging that he hadn't experienced in a long time.

Not sure how this works out, but I think I found a place to heal some emotional wounds. Great people, shockingly genuine. The job is meaningless, but it's comfortable, too. At this point, a few tran-

quil days would be a blessing. Told the owner about my less than glorious past—didn't seem to faze him. Could be he's just dumb, or maybe he's actually a good guy. I'll find out soon, I guess. Try not to get too comfortable, though. Remember, bad shit is always just around the corner.

2

Fools Rush In

Santa Fe, New Mexico—Some Months Before
The realtor assured them that the price was correct.

"Why's it so much less than it should be? We've looked at other properties, and this is well below market value. Why?" Cindy was uneasy with a price that seemed too good to be true—and, to some extent, with the realtor, too.

"Believe me, Cindy, I get your concern. I have the same question. I've had two people look at the property and decide not to buy because they thought something had to be wrong with it, what with the price being so low. All I can tell you is that it's owned by a corporation out of Chicago that's involved in some kind of legal mess. I honestly think they priced it this way just to unload it. But, obviously, I would recommend a full inspection and an environmental report before you'd move forward. If everything checks out, then I think it's a real bargain."

The realtor, Sue, was a nice-looking older woman who Cindy could have identified as a realtor based only on her appearance and overly positive attitude. Cindy tended to distrust salespeople, and this one was a saleswoman, through and through.

"I think we should buy it."

Jerry wasn't usually prone to rash decisions, but the house was exactly what they'd been looking for, and apparently its only problem was that it was priced too low. If they'd been alone, he might have suggested to Cindy that if that was the only problem, they could solve it by simply paying more. But in front of the realtor, that kind of sarcasm would have earned him a dirty look from his wife.

"I think we're interested," Cindy said. "Jerry and I need to talk, but we'll get back to you in a day or so." Cindy got up to leave, giving Jerry her best "follow me" look.

Jerry waited until they were alone before saying anything. "I know you're uneasy, but let me ask you this—is it this property, or the whole idea of going into the B&B business?"

Cindy gave Jerry one of her stunning smiles. She was beautiful, about the same height as Jerry, with a model's body. It wasn't unusual for people to notice her and not even see Jerry, who was never going to be mistaken for a movie star. He was the love of her life, though. She especially loved the way he could cut to the heart of a subject and say what needed to be said—like now.

"You're right. I'm hesitating because of the property, the price, but also the whole idea. Do you really think we can make this work?"

"Look, we've been very lucky. We're lucky we found one another, and we're lucky enough to have some money so we can even think about doing this. Being together and doing something that makes us happy—that's what I want. This seems like something that can keep us engaged in life and working together, and I can't think of anything better. If we fail, we lose some money, but we'll still have a lot of cash—just not as much as before. That seems completely worth it to me. For a while, now, I haven't been doing much, and I think you'll be happier dealing with running this place than just sitting back and retiring. I say let's risk some of our good fortune, have some fun, and go back to work."

Cindy hugged him. They had found each other late in life, but they were a perfect match, and both felt blessed by it. Jerry had been a computer programmer with a small firm in Phoenix. The company had been a leader in developing software to allow universities to manage student activities and provide an integrated communication system. He had been a key member of the group and owned a slice of the company. A large rival business had offered them an unbelievable amount of money to buy them out, and suddenly, he was wealthy. He'd stayed on a few years, but he never fit well in the larger corporate structure. So, he left, and after a little time of doing nothing, he'd opened a small one-man tech consulting company. He'd met Cindy after she hired him to help develop a better tracking system for her small handbag store. She had no idea he was wealthy. And they fell in love. After a short romance, they married, and after the ceremony Jerry broke the horrible news to her that he was filthy rich. She sold her business, and they moved to Santa Fe to start a new life.

They decided to make an offer on the property, contingent upon a successful due diligence related to property inspections, environmental reports, and full and complete legal analysis of ownership rights. Within a short time, all their requirements had been met without any issues arising. They closed on the property at the end of the month.

Prior to closing, they'd identified the changes they wanted made to the property so it could function properly as a bed and breakfast. They selected a contractor who was ready to begin once they closed.

Cindy handled most of the legal work, securing the proper permits and looking into zoning issues. She'd chosen the Santa Fe law firm of Martinez, Howard and Fitch, who turned out to be very efficient at dealing with the local bureaucracy. Stephen Martinez was a long-time resident of Santa Fe and seemed to have a relative in every key department of city government. Through cousins, uncles and nieces, paths were cleared for them, and they made progress.

Meanwhile, Jerry dealt with the contractor, Ray Martin, who was a kindred spirit—he had an eye for quality, but also understood budget constraints. Ray came up with several innovative ideas for how to improve the flow of the facility, and how to enhance its public spaces. Within days of closing on the property, Ray and his crew were hard at work.

Very shortly, what had been an interesting secluded hacienda was becoming The Blue Door Inn. Cindy had a very discreet sign made for the entrance, and flyers and leaflets designed and printed. She visited the chamber of commerce and other local organizations, giving them information about the new B&B in town.

"You know," Jerry said one evening, "I think we actually could be ready for guests in a couple of weeks."

"I don't know, Jer. Having guests this soon sounds a little scary to me."

"Well, it is going to kind of defeat the purpose of having a B&B if we don't allow guests. Look, here's what we do. For a month or so, we have what's called a 'soft opening.' First, maybe around a week from now, we get a couple of guests—give them a really good deal—and we can practice on them." Jerry was itching to get the place up and running. He'd already hired two people and purchased a van, which was being painted with their logo and would be ready in a couple of days.

"Who are the people you hired? What are they going to do?"

"It's a husband and wife. They live in the area, and Ray recommended them. The guy's name is Hector, and he'll be a handyman type, plus he'll take care of the grounds. His wife, Mary, will do housekeeping and help in the kitchen. They were really happy to be able to work in the same place, and they seem like very nice people. They're going to start on Monday, help get everything cleaned up and ready for furniture delivery later in the week."

"My God, everything's moving so fast. I guess we know what we're doing, though. Right?"

"Y'know, your lack of confidence is a little unnerving. Just go with the flow. I guarantee we'll do some stupid things in the beginning, until we learn how to do them right—but it won't be a disaster. Mary's worked at several hotels and a small

B&B, and she knows how to cook and clean—she'll handle a lot of things for us. Hector will make sure we have no plumbing disasters, and that the guests get transported as needed. In a few weeks it'll all start to be routine. We can move into one of the casitas next week, and then I think it'll start to feel like our own place."

The pace didn't let up. Mary and Hector were eager, hardworking people, and they quickly took on many of the tasks that needed to be done. Jerry and Cindy picked a casita to live in. These were standalone structures, like small houses, located behind the main building. That left eight guest rooms, and one casita with two bedrooms that would be outfitted as guest rooms, plus one smaller room that could be used by an employee.

Ray's workers had completely remodeled all the restrooms. They installed new bathrooms for the new guest rooms, plus public restrooms for the new dining room and bar. A small lobby had been completely remodeled, changing the feeling of the structure so that it no longer felt so much like a personal residence. Jerry continued to work closely with Ray, under Cindy's watchful eye, as they progressed toward the completion of the construction phase. Ray had contributed many helpful suggestions, saving them a significant amount of money while still creating the ambiance they wanted.

The kitchen and small dining area only needed minor changes, and looked great. Jerry was impressed by the size and professional quality of the kitchen. He'd been working with Mary on several recipes he was considering serving once they had guests, including some sopaipilla recipes that were proving to be delicious. Combining this treat with spicy honey was going to be a staple at the breakfast table. He felt like he'd already added a pound or two while sampling his creations.

They had made some minor changes to the layout in front of the main building, adding parking spaces, but the grounds mostly just needed trimming and cleaning up, which Hector handled expertly and in short order. The property was looking great.

"I know, once we have guests, we might decide that this isn't for us. But I tell you, the way it looks now, I think we can resell and make a handsome profit." Jerry was sitting in a newly installed gazebo at the back of the property with Cindy as they examined their handy work. The view of the Inn and its newly cleaned and filled pool was wonderful.

"It's looking really good, isn't it?" Cindy sounded proud.

"Better than good. It's wonderful."

"I'm still nervous, though. What if we don't get any guests?"

Jerry chuckled. "Well, for at least a month or so, we'll live in wonderful luxury, with Mary waiting on us hand and foot while we each gain ten pounds. Then we'll put the property on the market and claim our substantial profit."

"I did have an idea about how to focus our marketing. It came to me when I was working with Stephen, the lawyer. He seems to know everybody in town. Maybe we could concentrate on lawyers, like offer some special rates and services for their clients or their fellow lawyers. Stephen told me that a lot of times during the year he'll have meetings with clients from out of town, and he'd love to recommend that they stay with us. I know he just said that because we hired him, but still—it might be a start."

"Sounds great." Jerry gave an approving nod.

"The other thing he said is that a bunch of the lawyers who work in Santa Fe live in the area across the highway. He told me he could give me a list, and then we could mail something to their homes about having accommodations near where they live."

"Makes sense. Let's do it! See, you're already figuring out ways to get guests. I'm a lot more worried about how to manage everything once we have some."

Cindy smiled. "How about we serve them mimosas for breakfast and have a free happy hour in the evening? Maybe nobody will notice we don't have a clue about what we're doing."

"Nice atmosphere, good food, and lots of booze. I'm pretty sure we'll be a hit."

3

Easy Come, Easy Go

Los Angeles, California

"Listen, you tell that lowlife bastard he better figure out what went wrong, and fast." Mark slammed his cell phone onto his desk—followed by an immediate urge to pick it up and throw it through his fortieth-floor window.

Son of a bitch! How the hell could this have happened? Mark Hamilton was having trouble breathing. He rummaged around in his desk, pulled out a bottle of scotch, poured a shot into a paper cup, and took a big gulp.

Shit, shit, *shit!* He was fucked. All of the goddamned money was gone. Mark wasn't even sure how much it was, but it had to be over thirty million dollars. He had no idea what to do. He took another swig of scotch, but it didn't help.

Using his desk phone, he called for help. "Ryan, this is Mark. We've got one big fucked-up problem—can I see you right now?" Ryan Lewis was Mark's sometime friend and lawyer. They had gone to law school together and had sweated out the final exams as a team. But Mark had moved in on Ryan's girlfriend, then married her, and their friendship had taken a blow.

"I'm pretty busy right now—can this wait until later?"

"I'm in a hell of a mess, and I need to see you now. Just give me a few minutes. I don't know what to do. All of the investment money has disappeared along with that asshole, Larry Jackson. He's fucking gone! *I need some help.*"

"Okay, give me about fifteen minutes, and then come on over," Ryan said, then hung up. His tone hadn't been exactly sympathetic. Mark wondered if he should get another lawyer—one who didn't hate his guts. He considered another drink. but he didn't want to smell of booze when he saw Ryan. Ryan had always been the moral one, Mark a little less so—maybe a lot less so.

Mark retrieved his cell phone from the floor, where it had bounced to after he'd slammed it down. Still seemed to be working. He called his wife, Ann, at their house in Santa Fe.

"Something's come up here, and I won't be flying out this afternoon. My plan right now is to take a late-night flight—as soon as I know when, I'll let you know. See you later, babe." He almost never talked to Ann directly, most often simply leaving a message. Ann was an absolute knockout, and Mark always worried when he had to leave her alone for long. She had been known to wander before, leading to angry clashes, after which Mark always forgave her.

Mark had graduated from UCLA Law fifteen years before, and had immediately set himself up as a sports agent. His only interest in the law was as a way to make money, and being a sports agent seemed like the best way to achieve that goal. He'd been a half-assed athlete in high school, playing baseball and football, although any success he had was mostly due to good genes and quick reflexes. He didn't have the dedication to train, and stopped by the time he went to college. He got to know a lot of jocks at UCLA, though, and he'd kept in touch, so it seemed natural for him to strike out as a sports agent. His big day came when an old college buddy, Buster Fisher, signed up as his first client. Buster and Mark had been sometime drinking buddies at UCLA, when Buster had held the record for the most beers consumed in one binge. Buster had become the best offensive lineman in the draft that year. Mark helped him get a reasonable contract from the Denver Broncos, which earned him a substantial fee and gave him the opportunity to meet a bunch of other football prospects. Even if he hadn't been making money, Mark would have been hooked—this was what he wanted to do. It felt more like hanging out than working.

He had done okay after adding several clients based on his work for Buster, and he was starting to be seen as a very good agent. He was probably making about the same money he could have if he'd taken a low-level job at one of the law firms in L.A., which wouldn't have given him the dream of a big payday.

Several years passed while Mark learned his trade, mostly by trial and error. Then one day, out of the blue, Dave "Hardball" Adams called, saying he wanted Mark to represent him for his new contract. He'd known Dave in high school, where the older boy had been several years ahead of him, and he'd followed his career in the majors as an ace lefty starting pitcher.

The call took Mark by surprise. Stories were going around that Hardball was going to be offered a contract for a hundred million dollars over six years by the New York Yankees.

Mark got Hardball one hundred and twenty million, with a thirty million-dollar signing bonus. Hardball was ecstatic and Mark was rich. He became *the* sports agent to hire.

Life was suddenly very good. He courted and married Ann, knowing full well that his most attractive quality to her was his money, but she was the wife he wanted—absolutely beautiful and sexy. She'd been the girlfriend of his friend, Ryan Lewis. Mark knew courting his best friend's girlfriend was below contempt, but he couldn't—or wouldn't—stop himself. He wanted her, and he was willing to lose the friendship to get the girl. Everywhere they went, she was the star attraction for most of the men and many of the women. To Mark, she was his most prized possession. Plus, the sex was unbelievable.

With his new wealth, Mark and Ann purchased a high-rise condominium in one of the newest upscale developments, just a short distance from downtown L.A. They also bought the most gorgeous house Mark had ever seen, located in Santa Fe, New Mexico. Anything and everything the nouveau riche would do, Mark and Ann did. They were shameless in flaunting their new financial status.

And naturally, along with the money and fame as the top sports agent, came opportunities to achieve even greater success. Mark was in demand, and signed up some of the top names in several sports, wheeling and dealing and on top of the world. He could do no wrong. Suddenly, everything he touched brought him more wealth.

Then, out of the blue, his old friend Ryan had called, and said he wanted to meet to discuss an opportunity. Mark had been nervous about it, since he'd heard from common acquaintances that Ryan had said on a couple occasions—usually involving alcohol—that it would make him happy to see Mark rot in hell. He'd even suggested that he might be the one to punch Mark's ticket to eternal damnation. Eventually, Mark decided that he'd go. After all, it was the middle of the day, and they'd get together in his high-rise office. It seemed far-fetched that Ryan would try to kill him.

"You might as well know; I've had fantasies about blowing your fucking brains all over your fancy office." Ryan began their meeting with a lopsided grin.

Mark wasn't sure how to respond. "Look, Ryan. I shouldn't have gone after Ann, but I was in love. I know you have every right to hate me. I think I just lost my head."

"Well, you can rest easy. I've decided not to make Ann a widow. I wish you both all the happiness in the world. She would have bankrupted me, anyway. Better she spends your money than mine."

There was still tension in the air, but it seemed that they'd both decided to move on to a more important subject: money.

"I've watched your successes. You've done some big deals, and made some major money, with this sports agent business."

"Yeah, I've had some luck. The legal skills you need to do these deals is about the level of a second-year law student. It's mostly just about making connections with the athletes.

They all seem to make their decisions on who to hire based on gut instinct, or whoever's the hottest agent at a given moment. Over the last year or so, I've been that guy."

"Well, good for you, Mark. And maybe I can help you out a little, plus help myself some at the same time. I've been dealing with a guy who I think is a financial genius. He's starting a new hedge fund, and I thought this might be a deal some of your clients could be interested in. The past returns on this guy's funds have been insane."

That was the first time Mark heard about Larry Jackson, the genius financial advisor, now the *missing* goddamned financial advisor. Ryan had introduced him to Larry, and then Ryan had become Mark's attorney. A nice, neat little package which had just been blown to kingdom come.

"Where the fuck is that little bastard? And where the *hell* is the money?"

Mark was screaming even before the door could be completely shut, and several people in Ryan's office turned at the noise. Ryan slammed the door.

"How the hell would I know where the prick is? My money's missing, too, you stupid son of a bitch."

They stood staring at one another for what felt like a long time. Then Ryan moved around his desk and sat down. Mark paced for a while, then stopped and finally took a seat on the other side of the desk. He was the first to break the silence.

"How bad is it?"

"I've talked to his staff. Looks like he disappeared sometime yesterday. The best estimate right now is that there's about forty to fifty million missing. He cleaned out five of your clients, your personal account, my personal account, and three people I'd referred to him. Why he targeted us, I don't know. What he took is about ten percent of the total fund balance he was managing. For some reason, he deliberately went after us and our connections. I have no idea why."

"Fuck. Who've you contacted?"

"I called the U.S. attorney for New York. I've dealt with him before and, on the QT, I told him what I knew. He's contacted the second in command in Larry's firm, and they're talking. The prosecutor sent me an email saying they had a full alert out for Larry through the FBI, and they're pretty confident that he can't get out of the country. So, maybe if we're lucky, they catch him and he tells them where he sent the money, and we get it back."

"Jesus, I sure hope so. At least two of my clients would kill me for a tiny fraction of what they might lose on this."

Back in his office, Hamilton made the call he was dreading. "Victor, I've got some bad news." Hamilton relayed the details about the missing money.

"We just signed a deal, and now you're telling me it's all fucked up. I hope this is some kind of sick joke. The money was transferred to you just yesterday, and you need to deliver those clients to my firm, whole and happy, right *now*. If you don't, you can return the money immediately, plus interest, or you can be dead." The man at the other end of the line hung up. Hamilton grabbed the scotch bottle and took a gulp. "Fuck."

4

We've Got Company

Santa Fe, New Mexico

"Yes, yes of course. I understand. Three doubles and two singles, absolutely. Yes, we have a van, and we can provide transportation. Yes. Yes. On the twelfth—of course. You'll be our first guests, but I can assure you, we're ready. Thank you. Yes, you can count on us. Thank you, and thank your husband." Cindy turned and smiled at Jerry who was waiting.

"What was that all about?"

"Jerry, my dear. We are in the bed-and-breakfast business. We have guests!"

"You're kidding. When?"

"Four days."

"Sonofabitch! Four days? No fuckin' way can we be ready in four fuckin' days."

"Y'know, once we have guests, you're going to have to watch your language."

"Fuck my language! There's no way we'll be ready in four days. I've only just started fixing dishes other than those damn sopaipillas."

Jerry looked at Cindy and started to laugh. He grabbed

her and twirled her, still laughing, and she joined in. Soon, Hector and Mary came into the room to see what the commotion was about, and before long, Jerry had them all dancing in a circle and laughing.

After the celebration, they all got to work with a new focus: guests in four days. Jerry and Mary were in the kitchen most of the time, working on various breakfast offerings. Mary turned out to be an excellent baker, and in no time had devised an assortment of breads she could make every morning. Jerry concentrated on a couple of quiche recipes, his favorite being a green chili-and-red pepper quiche with four shredded cheeses.

Cindy and Hector, meanwhile, finished up work on the rooms. Vincent had gone into town to pick up the new van, now adorned with the Inn's logo.

"How did these people find us?"

"It was one of the lawyers on the list Stephen gave me. They live in the area across the highway. The wife called me— Ann. Her husband's an attorney in L.A., but he needs to have a special meeting with five of his clients, and it made logistical sense to have the meeting in Santa Fe. Well, she got the letter I sent out about the Inn, and she thought it would be great to have the meeting so close to their house. Also Stephen recommended us. She seemed very nice, and apparently her husband, besides being a lawyer, is some kind of big hot-shot sports agent. I just got the list from her, all the guests with their contact info. Do you know any of these names? Dave Adams, Terry Carter, Troy Arenado, Vickie Turner, and Buster Fisher?"

"Jeez, you've got to be kidding. Do I know who they are?

Don't *you* know who they are? My god, those are some of the biggest names in sports. Well, actually, I don't know this Vickie Turner, but the other guys are pro football and baseball stars. Hell, that's fantastic. We get our first paying guests and they're famous. Sonofa*bitch*. Just fuckin' fantastic."

"I had no idea they were famous. And about that 'paying guest' part—the deal I offered in my letter was for fifty percent of our normal rate. So they'll be paying, but only half."

Jerry looked at Cindy for a moment, but decided that even at half price, it was a great deal. "That is great. Half is great! I thought you were going to say it was free. I'm excited just meeting these people. You said three doubles and two singles?"

"Yep. Three have spouses and two are by themselves. For convenience, I thought we would put them all in the main building and not use the casita. Five people are coming into the Santa Fe airport on three private planes. The other three are flying into Albuquerque and taking the shuttle, so we'll pick those up at the shuttle stop at the convention center."

"Let's hope our one van will accommodate them all."

"Hey, you're the guy in charge of logistical issues, aren't you?"

"I gave that duty to Vincent. Smart management delegates."

Cindy gave him one of her great smiles and a light punch on the shoulder.

Vincent was turning out to be about as handy as a pocket on a shirt since he'd been put in charge of transportation. He'd reached out to the private flying guests and secured ETA's.

He'd also made contact with the commercial flight guests and estimated their arrival by shuttle. Fortunately, there turned out not to be any conflicts among the various guests' arrival times, which were scattered throughout the day, and the guests seemed pleased with the extra effort made to get in touch and ensure everything ran smoothly. Jerry thought, *Vincent just might be a keeper.*

On the day the guests were to arrive, everything was ready. Everyone knew they'd prepared well, so there was no reason for concern. Of course, as in anything planned, there would have to be a SNAFU.

Dave "Hardball" Adams and his wife Linda had originally been anticipated at the Santa Fe airport at 3:30 p.m., but due to weather issues their arrival was shifted to 4:30 p.m. Terry Carter and his wife Tina had been expected in Santa Fe at 11:00 a.m., but now they were expected at 3:30 p.m. And Buster Fisher's plane had mechanical problems, so the flight was cancelled. He was able to get a commercial flight into Albuquerque and would be on the last shuttle of the day around eight in the evening. The other guests, Vickie Turner and her husband Bud, and Troy Arenado, were supposed to arrive on the same shuttle at the convention center at 4:00 p.m. One van wasn't going to be able to cover everything.

"Okay, so what's the new plan?"

"Well, we can't be in two places at once. The Santa Fe airport is more than thirty minutes away from the convention center. What makes sense is to send the van to the airport and pick up the first guests there. If they arrive on schedule, Vincent can pick up Carter and his wife and bring them here, and then make it back to the airport in time for Adams and his wife. Might be able to be at the convention center only about thirty minutes late, but if we run into any traffic or other problems, it might be worse. I think we need to send a car to the convention center for Turner, her husband, and Arenado. Hector, you can take my car to the convention center, but call the shuttle service and make sure they're actually on the shuttle. I'll stay here and help get the other guests settled. Then Vincent can go back and pick up Fisher later. Okay, everybody agree?"

These sorts of problems would likely become routine pretty soon, but for now it all felt overwhelming. They did everything to create order, but got chaos instead. Cindy had listened to Jerry explain the new plan with a silly grin on her lovely face and a tear in her eye. She seriously thought about going to her room and lying down for a nice little cry, but she knew it wouldn't be fair to Jerry.

As the day progressed, other problems arose. Jerry had placed an order for various food and cleaning supplies from the wholesaler to be delivered that day. About thirty minutes before he was expecting the delivery, he got a call saying the truck had broken down and might not be able to make it. Jerry yelled at the young dispatcher, despite the fact that the man had no control over anything, and hung up.

And Cindy discovered that the outlets in one of the guest bathrooms weren't working. She called Ray, but got his voice mail. She left a nasty message, then regretted it the moment she hung up. She found Jerry in the kitchen, slamming things and cussing. She told him about the wiring and her ugly message for the very nice Ray.

Jerry looked at her for a while. Then he smiled and gave her a hug.

"You know I love you more than anything—this whole idea was that we could be together and be doing something we enjoyed. We're doing this wrong. We need to stop being stressed. What do we really care what these guests think? If this doesn't work out, we'll cash in our chips and get the fuck out of town. We'll still be rich, and we'll still have each other. So, remember that. Let's relax and enjoy ourselves. How about a glass of wine to celebrate our first day in business hell?"

"Jerry, I love you very much."

Jerry went to the wine cooler and took out a rather expensive white wine he'd been chilling. He opened the bottle and poured them each a glass.

"Here's to our business success—or failure. Whichever it turns out to be we're going to enjoy the process, and most of all, enjoy each other." They hugged, holding each other for some time.

Mary came into the kitchen, then started to back out.

"Hey, you can't leave. It's not hanky-panky—we're just hugging because we love each other. Mary, why don't you go find Hector and give him a hug?"

Mary started to giggle and might have blushed a little. "I am not real sure Hector would hug me in public." For no reason any of them could have named, everyone started to laugh. About that time Hector walked in, and they began to laugh even harder. Hector looked confused, but decided to say nothing.

Sometimes things surprise you by working out. Both Santa Fe airport flights arrived within five minutes of each other. Vincent was able to bring the guests to the Inn and still have time to get to the shuttle drop-off at the convention center and secure the other guests. To everyone's surprise, Buster Fisher turned out to be on the same shuttle, having managed to get an earlier flight than expected. By five o'clock, all the guests were checked in and resting in their rooms. Cindy had put them on notice that cocktails would be served at five thirty.

Vincent acted as the bartender for cocktail hour. They had set up a bar in the lobby, and everyone was standing nearby, drinking and talking. All the guests seemed to know each other, or at least be aware of who the others were. For some reason, there was tension in the room. Cindy mingled, trying to be pleasant and upbeat, but the tone of the group wasn't very happy.

Jerry had prepared appetizers with Mary's help, and now brought them out for the guests. He mingled a bit, too, but the unspoken tension gave him the sense that it might be best to leave the guests to themselves.

Somewhere around six, Mark Hamilton's wife, Ann, arrived. She was a complete knockout, and very outgoing. She apologized because Mark's flight from L.A. had been delayed, and he wasn't expected until late that night. Still, she said, he'd be there in the morning to preside over their meeting.

"What's this all about, Ann? This meeting. Why all the

mystery? We all know that everyone here invested with this guy Jackson—has something gone wrong?"

"Look, Dave, you know Mark doesn't share privileged information with anyone, not even me. So, I don't know. He'll be here in the morning, and he'll answer all your questions. For tonight, just have a good time and enjoy these great accommodations." She looked toward Cindy and smiled.

"Also, I wanted to let you know I've arranged for two SUVs that you all can use while you're here. They just got here, and they're parked out front." Ann took out two sets of keys and laid them on the front desk. "The Inn has a van, and I know they will be happy to provide transportation into Santa Fe if you prefer, or there is cab service available. I'm sure Cindy can help you with any of that." Ann glanced at Cindy.

"I'll see you tomorrow," she said, wrapping up. "Enjoy your stay." And with that, Ann left, seeming to hurry just a little.

Dave claimed one set of keys, and he didn't look like he was in any mood to share. Troy and Buster said they thought they'd have a couple more drinks and some of the appetizers and then call it an evening. Terry picked up the other set of keys. He, his wife and the Turners talked about going into Santa Fe for dinner.

Cindy stepped in, offering several suggestions for restaurants where they wouldn't need a reservation.

"Did that feel a little strange?" she asked Jerry afterward.

"Oh yeah. Something's not right, and my guess is Mark Hamilton's right in the middle of it, whatever it is. I don't think

I'd want Dave Adams mad at me. Should be an interesting meeting tomorrow."

5

Meeting Adjourned

Jerry and Mary were up bright and early, preparing the breakfast menu. Jerry had made four quiche pies, and Mary had prepared sweet rolls and two kinds of muffins. They'd also made a fruit salad and had yogurt with a wide range of toppings. In deference to the male appetite, Jerry had prepared applewood bacon along with a special chorizo sausage-and-egg dish. With juices and coffee, they thought they had all the bases covered.

Breakfast was to be served at seven. Starting around six-thirty they began laying out the buffet in the dining room. They had warming plates and steam trays and self-serve dispensers for coffee and juice. Jerry placed water on each table. A little before seven, everything was ready, and Jerry thought they'd done a very professional job.

"Wow, this looks great Jerry," Cindy said. "You and Mary have done wonders. And everything smells delicious." Cindy filled a plate with quiche, bread, and bacon as she spoke. As she seated herself at the bar in the dining room, the guests started to arrive.

Everyone was polite and complimented the food, but it was obvious they had other things on their minds. Jerry thought it was too bad their first guests weren't plain old tourists having a great time. Instead they had a nervous gaggle of lawyer's clients who seemed to be dreading the news they were going to get this morning. Linda Adams was the last to arrive. She discreetly let people know that Dave wasn't feeling well that morning, but might be in later for some coffee.

When they'd remodeled the Inn, Jerry and Cindy had turned a formal dining room and sun room into a medium-size conference room. They'd estimated it could accommodate up to thirty people in classroom-style seating, or about twenty sitting around a conference table. Jerry had arranged the room the night before into a conference configuration, with ample seating for the meeting this morning. The Hamiltons hadn't requested anything in particular, so he simply arranged it in the way he thought it worked best for the room. Earlier in the morning, he'd also stocked a table with coffee and juices, then added some of Mary's bread and muffins in case someone was still hungry.

As the guests finished their breakfasts, Jerry showed them into the conference room. Ann Hamilton had said the day before that she and her husband should be ready to start at eight, which was the time now, but they were nowhere to be seen. At about eight-fifteen, Dave Adams came into the room, clearly suffering from a bad hangover. He didn't say much, just got a coffee and roll, and sat down next to Linda.

Mark and Ann Hamilton arrived at about eight-thirty. The room was full of tension, which only increased with Mark's late, nearly silent arrival. Jerry stepped out of the conference room and shut the door. He would have liked to have stayed, but since no one invited him, he decided it wasn't appropriate. Instead, he returned to the kitchen and once again congratulated Mary on the excellent job she'd done serving their first breakfast to guests, which had not only tasted great, but had also looked topnotch.

The kitchen was next door to the conference room, but the only sound they could hear was the low drone of conversation, and Jerry soon stopped paying any attention. After a while, the conference room door swung open abruptly, banging against the wall.

"Listen you goddamned son-of-a-bitch," Dave Adams screamed, "you better get our fuckin' money back, and fast, or you're as good as dead. You got that, you bastard? If my money is gone, you'll be dead!" He stormed out of the room, not bothering to shut the door, Linda followed closely behind him. Dave looked like he wanted to smash something—or someone. They went out the front door and, by the sound of it, got into one of the SUVs.

"Okay, look—I know this is horrible," Jerry heard Mark say. "I know it. Remember, the guy took my money, too. The FBI and the police are looking for this asshole. I have insurance, and I'm sure his firm does, too, although at this point I don't know how much will be covered. I know everyone's angry, but Dave blowing up and threatening me isn't going to help. I will do everything I possibly can to fix this mess, so please give me a little time. I asked you here because I knew how difficult this was going to be, but we have to work together, not fight one another, if we're going to undo what's happened. I have a handout that has my attorney's name and number, the contact information for the FBI agent who's in charge of this, and also for the federal DA in New York who's trying to find Jackson. If you can, I'd ask you to stay here a day or two, and enjoy the hospitality of the Blue Door Inn. I will be in touch with all of you, every day, to keep you up to date on what's happening. We will get through this."

"I don't understand why you thought it made sense to drag us out here." This came from Bud Turner, Vickie's husband. "So we can listen to you try and convince us not to sue your ass? Do you really think you can talk your way out of being responsible for this robbery? Vickie and I are leaving today, and I'm going to have our lawyer file suit immediately." Vickie looked like she'd rather be anywhere else, staring vacantly into the middle distance. Bud grabbed her arm and steered her from the room.

Mark said nothing. In the silence that followed, Buster Fisher, the offensive lineman now playing for the Detroit Lions, spoke up. "Look Mark. You do what you can do to fix this. You need my help, just let me know. I'm not as mad as those people, but I'm leaving, too. This is a lovely place, but I'm not going to sit here and wait on you. You have my phone number—you call me with any news." The huge man stood and left without any drama. Jerry got the impression that it was hard to make Buster mad, but that anyone who did would be in serious trouble.

Each of the remaining participants, Terry Carter and his wife Tina and Troy Arenado, said their piece, the gist of which was that they thought this was a major fuck-up, but they would stay around for a few days to see what happened. Besides, they liked the place. They left the conference room, and Mark and Ann were alone.

Ann came out to find Jerry in the kitchen. "Suppose you heard most of that. Let's just say we have a mess on our hands. Some of your guests will be staying a little while, but some are leaving today. Please do your best to help them in any way you can. We definitely appreciate what you've already done, and we won't forget this in the future. Please tell your wife that I think the Inn is going to be a tremendous success."

Then she and Mark left, too.

"My goodness, I'm just glad that no one was killed," Cindy said. "Can we be held liable if one of our guests kills someone?"

"I don't think so. Well, not unless we helped them in some way. It's interesting. The two young guys, Terry and Troy, are at the beginning of their careers, and they didn't seem that upset. I guess because they can always make more money. But the two older guys, Dave and Buster, weren't happy at all. And that Bud guy. Vickie's husband? He was really pissed, too. He seemed almost as mad about being dragged to Santa Fe as he was about losing the money. But his wife acted like she was in a fog or something."

"This is really upsetting. Did you hear anyone mention how much money is missing?"

"No, but considering who we're talking about, I'd guess it'd be millions."

"Do you think insurance will cover that kind of loss?"

"Well, I'm not sure. A sports agent is going to have some errors and omissions insurance, like a lot of professionals. But I have no idea if something like this would be covered. The guy who took the money probably has insurance since he's a broker, or whatever he is, but the same goes for him—who knows? Plus, with these sports stars, it could be tens of millions, and the insurance must have some kind of cap. One way or another, it sounds like big trouble for Mark Hamilton."

Jerry and Cindy spent the next hour or so cleaning up the conference room and kitchen. Mary was busy with the bedrooms, and Hector was handling some trash chores. Jerry had sent Vincent to town to pick up some more supplies. At this point they were not completely sure who was staying and who had left or might leave at any moment.

Vincent knew a lot about trouble. You live long enough in piles of shit, you can identify the level of grief involved just by the smell, and this smelled really bad. Based on what Vincent had heard, there was a huge problem for the money guy and the sports agent—not only financial ruin, but jail time, too. No doubt the financial guy was gone. Stealing huge sums of money from famous people almost never worked out. The authorities were notoriously incompetent, but on those rare occasions when they bothered to exert themselves and put real effort into serving justice, it usually involved people who were rich, famous, or both. The feds, the California or New York

AGs, everyone would jump all over this and go all-out to put someone in jail. So why would anyone do such a stupid thing? Something seemed wrong with the whole picture. Normally, a financial guy would steal a small, unnoticed slice of some oblivious rich person's pie, and therefore never be charged with anything. This seemed unnecessarily aggressive, with almost no chance of success. So, why?

Vincent thought through the issues as he drove to see the Inn's suppliers. Bad luck for Jerry and Cindy to have their first guests be victims of a financial fraud—they weren't going to leave the Blue Door Inn with fond memories. But why invite these people here to tell them they had been robbed? That's the kind of news you always deliver over the phone, never in person. Why have them meet? He decided that the meeting must have been scheduled for something else, and that topic had been bumped when the news of the missing funds hit. But if that was the case, what was the meeting originally to have been about? Someone would have to go down multiple avenues if they were going to figure out what was really going on. Of course, he was a driver going to pick up supplies, not an investigator. Plus, his foot hurt.

Trouble always seems to find me. Lots of hate floating around the Inn now, due to greed, or maybe incompetence. The whole thing stinks of bad news to me. Probably head out in a day or so—last thing I need is to get caught up in someone else's legal problems. I've had all the cop contact I can take in one lifetime. Feel sorry for the Olivers, though. You mind your own business, just trying to be happy, and in pops the ugly fuckin' world to slap you in the face.

I'm not sure they're ready to handle a real problem very well—they don't know me from shit, and even so, I can tell they want me to help them fix it. I really don't need to get sucked in by nice people who can't seem to take care of themselves.

6

Death Comes Calling

The phone rang, waking Jerry and Cindy.

"Yes?" Jerry listened, then abruptly stood up. "What? Oh my God. Okay. I'll be at the front door in a minute. I just need—I just need to put on some clothes." He hung up.

"What's going on?" Cindy sounded sleepy.

"Sheriff's department, a detective. Said Mark Hamilton has been killed, and he wants to talk to our guests. He's outside, waiting."

Cindy sat up. "Killed? Seriously?"

"Yeah."

"It's four in the morning and he wants to talk to our guests?"

"That's what he said. Sounded like he meant it." Jerry got up and found his pants and a robe. He went into the bathroom. "I'm going to wake Vincent and ask him what I should do."

"Vincent? Why ask him?"

"He used to be an attorney."

"You didn't tell me that." Cindy sounded annoyed.

"Yeah. Well, I guess I didn't think it mattered. But I'm not sure what to do, and maybe he can help." Jerry left.

"Vincent. Vincent." Jerry knocked lightly, not wanting anyone else to hear.

The door opened.

"What's goin' on?" Vincent asked, and Jerry explained. "Go let them in. They can do damn near whatever they want, so don't get defensive. I'll get dressed and be right there."

Jerry opened the front door and saw a short, balding man emerge from an unmarked car. He seemed to be the only one around.

"Sorry to get you up so early, Mister Oliver. My name's Tony Sanchez, I'm with the Santa Fe County Sheriff's Office. As I said on the phone, Mark Hamilton's been killed, and I believe that some of his clients are staying with you. I'll need to talk to them."

"Hello, Detective Sanchez." Vincent stepped around Jerry. "My name's Vincent Malone, I'm an employee of Mister Oliver's. Can I get you some coffee?" He smiled, extending his hand.

"No, thanks."

"You know," Vincent continued, taking the reins. "I'm not sure we know who is here and who left after the meeting yesterday. I can go see who's in their rooms. You want them to come out here and meet with you?"

Sanchez was giving him a look, like he was trying to figure out how he fit into the picture. "That'd be great. Ann Hamilton said there were originally eight guests, but she wasn't sure if some had left already or not. So, whoever's here, I need to talk to them." The detective's manner had become more official, and Vincent could tell he made the man nervous. He glanced at Jerry, then went to wake the guests.

Cindy came into the room, and Jerry introduced her to the detective.

"I think I'd better go make coffee," she said.

"How was Mark Hamilton killed?" Jerry asked once she'd gone.

"Not giving out the details, but it was no accident. He was murdered. Maybe a blow from a baseball bat."

"Jesus, how horrible. That just doesn't sound like something that should happen in such a nice neighborhood. It's so—well, terrible."

Sanchez nodded. "Ann Hamilton told me they had a meeting here yesterday, and there were some angry words exchanged between her husband and some of the other people. Did you witness any of that?"

"Yes. I wasn't in the meeting, but when it ended and they opened the door, I heard them yelling."

"I understand that some of your guests left at about that time. Do you know when they came back?"

"Not really. We're not like a hotel. We lock our doors at night, and each guest has a key to the front door. They come and go as they please. We don't monitor when they go or come in."

"So, that's what your man meant about not knowing who was here. If they left, how would they go? Were they driving your vehicles?"

Jerry was starting to feel uncomfortable about being asked

so many questions.

"No. The SUVs they were driving were provided by Mister Hamilton as a convenience to his clients. We have a van we use to shuttle people around town, or to the Santa Fe airport, or even the airport in Albuquerque. But no one used the van last night."

Jerry heard indistinct sounds down the hallway as Vincent roused people. Someone yelled, "Tell them to go to hell—I want a lawyer," followed by silence. Soon Vincent returned to the main room. "They're getting dressed. Looks like all eight guests ended up back here last night. So, you'll have a full house, Detective Sanchez."

The detective was poking his head into some of the rooms in the public area.

"You think I could use that conference room so I could meet with each person alone? The rest of the folks could wait in here."

"I guess." Jerry wasn't sure what to say, so he defaulted to agreeing.

"I'm sure that'll be fine, detective," Vincent said. "We'll set up some coffee, juice, and a bit of food for the guests while they wait." He smiled at Jerry and nodded.

"Right, okay. I'll go get some muffins started," Jerry said, leaving.

Detective Sanchez looked at Vincent. "What do you do here?"

"Whatever Jerry or Cindy need done. Mostly driving the van."

"How long have you worked here?"

Typical cop bullshit. Chat away like it's a casual conversation, knowing full well it isn't.

"Not very long."

Before the detective could ask his next question, people started wandering groggily into the room. Within a few minutes, all eight guests had arrived. They were obviously tired, and some glared at the detective.

"Look, I don't know what's going on here, but you can't just roust people from their sleep and tell us nothing. I want to know what the hell's going on, or I'm going back to bed and getting out of this hellhole first thing this morning." Dave Adams was a little less loud than he had been the day before, but not by much, and he was clearly still in a foul mood.

"My name's Detective Tony Sanchez. I'm with the Santa Fe County Sheriff's Department. Sorry for waking you. What's going on is that Mark Hamilton has been killed." Sanchez paused for effect.

Linda and Tina gasped. No one else seemed to react. Vincent noticed Troy Arenado and Terry Carter eyeing one another, then quickly looking away.

"Dead, huh? Well, I don't give a shit. I'm glad the bastard's dead. He stole my money, and deserved whatever happened to him." Dave Adams seemed bent on getting himself arrested, although Vincent didn't think it was a premeditated strategy—more likely just stupidity.

"It's Mister Adams, right?" Sanchez knew perfectly well who he was.

"Yeah."

"I don't blame you for being upset. Mrs. Hamilton told me about the missing money. Said her husband had lost money, too, but I can sure understand that you would hold him responsible. Did you see Mark Hamilton last night after you left the meeting?"

"I'm not answering any questions, got it? You want to arrest me? Go right ahead. But I'm not telling you anything about anything until I have an attorney." Adams got up and grabbed his wife, surprising her. She tripped and fell to the floor. Vincent and Sanchez bent down to help her up.

"Leave her alone." Adams seemed out of control.

"Dave, please. It's okay. I'm okay. Just calm down." Linda managed to calm her husband a little. She got up, took his arm, and they left the room.

"I know everyone's upset, and having the police show up is a shock. I'm not here to arrest anyone, no matter what Mister Adams may think. I'm just looking for information so we can get to the bottom of this. I know some of you want to leave, and I can't stop you, but you should know that we have the legal authority to question you if we believe you have information that's critical to our investigation. Which means we can come to wherever you live and question you there, most likely at the local police station. I'd think that would be a lot more disruptive than taking a few minutes this morning and telling me what you know. I'd like to talk to you one at a time, which I think will only amount to ten minutes or so with each of you. So, we can take the harder path, or just get it done this morning while we enjoy some good coffee. And muffins, too, I think I heard." Sanchez was doing a decent job of calming everyone's nerves, although having Adams out of the room helped.

Troy Arenado stood up. "I'm ready to tell you what I know, which isn't much, if it means I can go back to bed." Sanchez showed him into the conference room. Jerry came into the room to leave re-heated muffins. Vincent went back into the kitchen with him.

"What do you think's going to happen?" Jerry was obviously nervous.

"Sanchez will talk to everyone, although probably not Adams. Then he'll go. I have no idea what sort of forensics they discovered at the crime scene, but based on his dash over here and getting everyone up, he had a good reason to think that someone here was involved. He can't keep these people from leaving unless he arrests them. I'd bet a big five-dollar bill he's planning on arresting someone this morning. So I think he leaves, but comes back, either with an arrest warrant or a search warrant—and the obvious choice is Adams."

"Yeah, he threatened to kill the guy yesterday, and today he's dead. Do you think Adams will try to make a run for it?"

Vincent chuckled.

"Sanchez would anticipate that, so my guess is the place is sealed off. Nobody's going to leave unless Sanchez says it's okay."

"Man, what a way to start our business."

"At least the murder didn't actually happen here."

"What are you two talking about?"

Cindy had dressed and was ready to begin her day. She seemed like a person who took whatever was thrown her way and made the best of it.

"Murder."

As Vincent predicted, the detective interviewed everyone except the Adamses and left. The guests all returned to their rooms. Cindy and Mary were preparing breakfast while Jerry took a walk outside. He spotted several sheriff's deputies and patrol cars—it made him instinctively uncomfortable.

Buster Fisher and Terry Carter returned to the common area dressed for the day. They got themselves some coffee and sat together, talking quietly. Soon they were joined by Terry's wife, Tina.

Vincent grabbed a coffee pot and offered them a refill.

"D'you think they'll let us go today?" Terry Carter asked him.

"Legally, they can't stop you from leaving unless they arrest you, so you can leave whenever you want." Strange how people will trust someone they don't know, who's serving them coffee, to give them legal advice.

"We want to leave this morning, if we can. We were wondering if the Inn could give us a lift to the Albuquerque airport and we'll just get on the first flights we can, and head home."

"I'll have to ask Jerry, but I'm sure that'll be fine with him. Depending on where you want to go, might be best to call the airline you think is most likely to head your way, and see what they have. Didn't you come in on a private plane, Mister Carter?"

"Yeah, we did. That was a charter, though, not our plane. They're scheduled to come back for us in a few days, but now we're thinking we don't want to wait. No offense to this place, but we were thinking we just want to get out of here."

"Sure. Let me go talk to Jerry." Vincent understood the desire to skip town, but thought Sanchez might try to delay them somehow, legal or not.

Sanchez entered just then, accompanied by two uniformed sheriff's deputies.

At the same time, Adams and his wife walked into the common area. Dave saw Sanchez and flinched. Vincent hoped Adams wasn't carrying a gun. He saw the deputies tense, their hands moving just slightly toward their weapons.

"Mister Adams, we have an arrest warrant charging you with the murder of Mark Hamilton," Sanchez said, looking directly at Adams.

Two other deputies entered the area on Adams' left. Dave looked angry, glaring at Sanchez, but he extended his hands. The two deputies stepped forward and brought his hands behind his back, and he was handcuffed.

"You're wrong. I wanted to kill him, but I didn't."

Vincent stepped forward and looked Adams in the eye.

"Mister Adams wants an attorney."

"Yeah, I want an attorney." He gave a slight nod to Vincent.

A deputy read Adams his rights while Sanchez walked up to Vincent.

"You some kind of lawyer or somethin'?"

"Nah. You didn't want him sayin' anything, anyway, before you read him his rights. Just helpin' you out."

Sanchez chuckled. "See ya later."

Time to leave. Rich people found dead. No doubt murdered by other rich people. No way this is a good thing for me. The head cop is already giving me the eye—wants to lock me up for something. Give him enough time, and he'll find somethin', or just make some shit up. Need to head on to Phoenix. Too bad—thought I might stop here for a while. No rest for the wicked. I know it's because I just don't belong. Seems like I haven't really belonged anywhere for a long time. What a fuckin' crybaby.

7

Dave "Hardball" Adams

Phoenix, Arizona—Many Years Earlier

Dave Adams wasn't the smartest person in the state, nor was he the most likeable guy around. But he was the best damn baseball pitcher most anyone had ever seen at Northwest High School in Phoenix, Arizona—or anywhere, for that matter. In his senior year, Dave added a changeup and a nasty curveball to his ninety-seven-mile-an-hour fastball, becoming almost unhittable.

Every game Dave pitched in his senior year was attended by four or more pro baseball scouts. The scouts saw an athlete who was not only a great pitcher, but also had the aggressive, take-no-prisoners attitude of a player who was ready for the major leagues. Nobody went from high school directly to the majors, but many scouts thought he might be ready his second year in pro ball—an almost unheard-of situation.

No matter what happened, Dave was ready to be done with high school, with teachers, and with his idiot classmates. He was eager to get started on his pro baseball career. For as long as he could remember, he'd worked toward being a baseball player. His father had been a so-so semipro player who always thought he should have made the big leagues, but never did. He transferred much of his frustrated ambition onto his son and began pushing him, hard, from a very early age. Dave mostly hated his dad, but he was too intimidated to complain much. Then, when Dave was in the ninth grade, his dad was found shot to death in a downtown alley. How and why he'd died was never determined, but everyone knew it was something connected with his dad's secret life. His mother never talked about it, but Dave had always thought his dad was connected to organized crime in some way. His mother was devasted at the loss of her husband. Dave was sad, but mostly surprised—it was hard to believe that someone so strong could actually die.

He thought about quitting baseball after that. His mom didn't care—she thought all sports were stupid. But pitching was the only thing he was good at, and without the pressure from his dad, he began to like playing baseball. By his senior year, he was already big—almost six-foot-five, and close to two hundred and thirty pounds, pretty imposing for a high school pitcher. And his normal expression was a scowl that seem to suggest that he'd like to punch you in the face. He was intimidating on the mound, and in the rest of life, his silent manner, huge size, and foul disposition made him someone most people avoided. Dave had no friends to speak of. In the ninth and tenth grades he'd had a good friend, Timmy Jones—but Timmy's family had moved away, and Dave had mostly been alone since then.

As Dave grew older, be began to realize that much of the

energy he put into pitching came from his suppressed anger at everything and everyone around him. He seldom saw his mother, who had discovered free and easy sex after his father died. The constant stream of lowlife men passing through his mother's life disgusted him. They all seemed to be the same guy—weak and easily dominated by his mother. He was sure it was some kind of reaction to the torment she'd put up with while living with his good-for-nothing father, but he didn't think about it too deeply. Mostly he just ignored the whole thing and stayed in his room.

By the time graduation was near, he'd received twenty-two offers to play college ball. He knew he wouldn't be able to do the academic work, but most of the college reps said he wouldn't have to worry about it—he'd be taken care of. Dave hated them all. He'd already made up his mind that he was going pro. The draft would be in June, just a month or so off, and then he could start making some money and be on his own.

Dave Adams was the number one draft pick by the Los Angeles Dodgers. They offered him a signing bonus of one and a half million dollars, a record at the time, and a half-million-dollar-per-year contract for three years. He signed.

Dave left home the day he signed his contract. His mother wasn't around at the time, so he left her a note. He was headed to the AA farm team in Bakersfield. He was frugal by nature, mostly because he'd never had much money, so he walked to the bus station and bought a one-way ticket to Bakersfield, California. The other reason was that he didn't have any cash. At the contract signing he'd taken the check and stuffed it into his pocket. The team officials and lawyers couldn't believe this kid didn't have an agent or an attorney. They were hesitant about just handing over the check, but he gave them one of his *I might just kill you* stares, and they relented. Once he got to Bakersfield, he was going to have to find a bank.

Dave was rich and playing ball—life couldn't get much better than that. Within a few months he was the star pitcher for the Bakersfield Dodgers. On the days he pitched, the crowds were three times bigger than they were on any other day. He was becoming known, both in Bakersfield and in baseball. Also, as a complete surprise to him, he began to attract groupies. He'd never had a girlfriend, but now there were very attractive young women following him around, asking him if he wanted to screw. Dave was embarrassed and shocked. He mostly ignored them, trying—without much luck—to avoid them altogether.

One of the girls, Linda, was especially aggressive. Dave stayed at the Hilton in downtown Bakersfield and took a taxi to and from the stadium. He'd never owned a car and wasn't a very good driver, so it made sense to him to let someone else drive. Plus, he was sure he'd be moving soon—he was just too good to stay in Bakersfield—so he wasn't going to make any big purchases or put down roots. As he got into his cab one day, Linda jumped in the back with him. She was the most attractive of the girls who'd been hounding him for weeks. She gave him an alluring smile.

"Hi."

"Hi. I don't mean to be rude, but I think it would be best

if you got out."

"Come on, Dave. I've been trying to get your attention for weeks. How about I just go back to your hotel with you and we can get a drink or something?"

"I don't drink."

She turned toward him on the seat, showing off an amazing set of legs. Her skirt rode up and Dave's face turned red.

"Okay then, *I'll* drink and *you* can watch." She slid closer.

Dave was embarrassed, but aroused. Linda had her way with him that day—and every day for the next week. His only bad pitching was that week. The boy was exhausted.

Linda became Dave's regular companion. The relationship was based on money and sex, but they also seemed to care for each other. He definitely enjoyed the sex, but it was also comfortable having her around. They spent a lot of time talking, and what amazed Dave was that Linda was a real fan of the game, and knew a lot about baseball. It wasn't the usual bonding process for a couple, but for the time being they each seemed to enjoy the other.

After about five months in Bakersfield, Dave was sent to the AAA affiliate in Oklahoma City. He had a long debate with himself about what to do about Linda, but decided he wanted her to come. The two of them set up house in the Skirvin Hotel in downtown Oklahoma City, just a few blocks from the ballpark. They'd slowed the sex down a little, realizing that exhausting a pitcher before the game started was no formula for success.

The AAA hitters were better than any Dave had faced. It

took him a couple of outings to get his sea legs, but once he did, he quickly came to dominate in OKC. The minor league season was about over when, in an unusual move, the big-league club called Dave to L.A. The Dodgers were in the playoff hunt, and one of their best pitchers had just injured his foot sliding into second base. Unlike the American League, with its designated hitters, the National League required pitchers to hit, and there was nothing worse than losing a star pitcher to some freak accident while he pretended to be a hitter or a baserunner. The accident meant Dave was in the bigs in his first year in pro ball. Only a few players had ever done that.

"Are you nervous about being called up?" Linda sat next to Dave in the first-class area of a Delta flight from OKC to LAX. She was sipping champagne. Oh, the joy of money.

"I guess I am, but not a lot. You know, it might sound arrogant, but I can pitch to these guys just as well as to the Triple-A guys. I don't want to get cocky, but the truth is that I'm eager to go up against big league hitters. The Double-A guys were way too easy. I hardly ever had to use all of my stuff. The Triple-A guys were a little better, but when I focused, there were very few who were a real challenge. I've been pitching since the sixth grade, and my dream was to pitch in the major leagues. So, I'm a little nervous, but mostly I'm just excited." He gave a sly grin.

Linda squeezed his large arm and cuddled a little. She'd pursued Dave because ballplayers had a lot of money, and she'd had very little. But as she'd gotten to know him, she'd surprised herself by falling in love. Her pattern had been to find a new ballplayer every year, but Dave was different.

The landing was smooth, and within a few minutes they were entering the terminal to find a significant contingent of team officials waiting for them.

"Hey Dave, my name's Logan. I'm an assistant to the president of baseball operations. We're all really excited to have you joining the big-league team. You may not have heard this, but another one of our pitchers was injured yesterday in an auto accident. Looks like he's going to be fine, but he'll miss his next assignment. Morgan, the manager, has decided he wants you to start. That's tomorrow night against the Giants. How about that—ready to play some ball?"

Dave just stared at the guy. This was the type of bullshit asshole he hated—big handshake, big mouth. Starting tomorrow night, though—that was absolutely fucking perfect.

"Sounds good, Logan. Who do I see about getting a uniform?"

It was Logan's turn to stare at Dave. These were two people who would never be on the same page. Both of them saw it, but fortunately, neither cared.

The team entourage transported Dave and Linda to one of the luxury hotels downtown and got them checked in. Someone told them that the manager wanted Dave at the ballpark. Linda stayed at the hotel while one of the team's people drove Dave. Dodger Stadium—or Chavez Ravine, as some call it—was large and impressive, although Dave thought there was a plainness to the area. Still, he'd never been very particular about the aesthetics of the place where he played.

The manager, Jack Morgan, was like a lot of managers in baseball, which is to say, tired. He told Dave gruffly that it hadn't been his decision, no matter what any asshole said, to start him the next day. It was "a bunch of bullshit coming down from upstairs." He mumbled something about the assholes not knowing a damned thing about baseball. Then he apologized in an offhand way and told Dave that he should just do the best he could, and if it got too bad, he would pull him early. With those uplifting words he left, mumbling something about the world containing more shit than he could hope to deal with.

Dave got his equipment and uniform and was assigned a locker. He was told to dress before going on to the field to find the pitching coach, Paul Thomas. Paul was the opposite of the manager.

"Sonofabitch, it's great to finally meet you, Dave," he announced cheerily. "I've heard nothing but good shit about you. Can't wait to see you pitch. Understand you can go as high as a hundred miles an hour on that fastball—fuckin' great!"

Dave immediately liked Paul, and didn't bother to correct him about the fastball. He spent the next few hours practicing pitches and meeting the catchers. He also decided to take a few laps around the park to get limbered up after the plane ride. He wasn't officially on the roster until the next day, though, so he couldn't stay in the dugout for the game. He could either use one of the boxes to watch the game or go back to the hotel and get some rest. He chose the hotel. He definitely needed some rest, but first he was going to enjoy Linda's awesome body for a little while.

The next day, when Dave showed up at the ballpark, everything seemed different. Everyone knew him now, and greeted him in a friendly way.

"Lots of luck, kid."

"Go get'em, Superman."

"Hey, Hardball, give 'em hell."

Dave hadn't seen it yet, but the morning paper featured an article on the front page of the sports section describing Dave as the next superstar pitcher in baseball. And they'd nicknamed him "Hardball." When he found out, he simply ignored it all.

The game was against the San Francisco Giants; the Dodgers' prime rival in their division. Either the Giants or the Dodgers were almost always expected to win the NL West Division, and that was the case again that year. The Giants were a game and a half behind the Dodgers, with ten games remaining in the season, three of which would be head-to-head matches. Those three would most likely decide who would win the division title. And Dave, a nineteen-year-old kid just out of high school, was the starting pitcher.

The first batter Dave faced hit his first pitch into center field for a single. You could hear the collective groan of the crowd—quite possibly for miles. Some kid pitching his first game, just barely out of high school, in the biggest game of the year? What the hell was the goddamn manager thinking?

Dave wasn't fazed. It was the major leagues, and he'd just given the guy a minor-league first pitch—right down the middle of the plate—and he wasn't going to repeat the mistake. He went on to pitch a three-hit ballgame, completing the game as the Dodgers won five to zero. He was proclaimed the next great pitcher of the Dodgers organization.

The press, meanwhile, was something he couldn't wrap his head around, as if each reporter was some kind of alien life-form. Dave answered the dumbest questions he'd ever been asked, over and over again. It was as if the sportswriter standing right next to the guy who'd asked the previous question didn't hear him ask it, or Dave's answer. He mostly gave monotone, nonsensical responses to the nonsensical questions, which worked just fine, because that's what all the ballplayers did.

The Dodgers won the division and lasted until the League Championship Series, where they lost to St Louis. Dave was a hero. In two playoff series, he pitched four times and won all his games. Even though the Dodgers ultimately lost, many people said he should be named MVP.

That was the beginning of a twelve-year relationship between Dave and the Dodgers. He signed three contracts with the team, each one with a significant increase in money. He could have opted out as a free agent, for even bigger increases, but he had more money than he needed, and he liked L.A.

Dave and Linda were married on their fifth anniversary; by which time they'd become extremely close. She was really the only person Dave had ever come to trust. While they seemed like an odd match to most people, for them it was perfect, and they were happy.

8

Staying and Going

Before Dave Adams was taken away by the deputies, he asked Jerry to call an attorney for him. The only lawyer Jerry knew was Stephen Martinez, who'd helped them with the legal work on acquiring the Inn. Martinez told Jerry he would handle everything. He actually sounded excited at the prospect.

It's not every day you got a call to represent a famous baseball player, especially in Santa Fe. And on a murder charge? Unheard of. Stephen had met Mark Hamilton several times at charity events, and knew quite a bit about him. He was definitely aware that he was a rich sports agent who mostly lived in L.A. It would have been a big case anywhere, but for Santa Fe, it would be a blockbuster. Albuquerque television stations and national news organizations—from newspapers to the major broadcasting networks—would all descend on the quaint, unusual capitol of New Mexico.

Santa Fe's population was about eighty thousand, but on most weekends there could be an additional hundred thousand tourists, or more. This odd mixture of residents and visitors created an outsized feeling of activity and bustle. Traffic jams, parking woes, crowded sidewalks—Santa Fe was blessed with all the problems common to a big city, although it wasn't one. But it also had some of the best restaurants in the country, with several famous chefs staking out spots in one of the most unusual dining scenes in the nation. The cultural mix ran from high-end art galleries attracting buyers from around the world to sidewalk vendors hawking trinkets and baubles of various qualities. The community had the usual problems, like drunkenness, petty crimes, and street violence, but that didn't include having one of its upper class murdered.

The county and city shared a downtown jail. This jointly managed detention center also housed the serious crime unit of the sheriff's department. Martinez entered the jail only a short time after Adams had been brought in. He asked to see Adams, and was told he was being processed. The clerk, who—like most clerks in most jails—was not terribly friendly and offered only limited information, said the process could take several hours. Martinez thought of several smart-alecky comebacks, but decided the clerk wouldn't appreciate his sense of humor. He asked to see Detective Sanchez, and was told to wait.

"Hey Stephen. You have some connection with Adams?" Sanchez knew Martinez. They'd both been in Santa Fe for years, living in the same neighborhood. Their kids had been on the same sports teams at various times, too. They were acquaintances, but they'd never been close friends.

"My connection is with the owners of the Blue Door Inn. They retained me to deal with the purchasing of their property. Apparently Mister Adams asked Jerry Oliver to contact a local attorney as he was being arrested, so, here I am."

Martinez had had dealings with the sheriff's department before, but usually on much more routine matters involving things like domestic disturbances, real estate issues and parking problems. He knew the department had a reputation for being overbearing, starting with the notoriously pompous Sheriff Matias Ortega, who was well known for his hatred of the lifeblood of the area—the tourists. Martinez had family connections with the sheriff, and didn't believe all the rumors about the man. He thought the sheriff was just protective of his community, and that was okay with him.

Ortega had been known to hassle many a famous person who while visiting Santa Fe had had the ill fortune of running afoul of him. He was one of a small band of locals who thought the tourists, and the businesses that catered to them, were destroying their hometown. Due to the strange election laws in New Mexico, he'd nevertheless somehow managed to be reelected for as long as most residents could remember, winning a whopping thirty-five percent of the vote. Most residents hated him, but that meant in every election there were three or four people running against him, splitting the opposition, so he only had to win a small proportion of the available votes to beat out a crowded field of candidates. Locals had tried for years to get the structure of the local election changed to a runoff between the top two candidates, but had been unsuccessful.

"Makes sense. Come on back."

Sanchez led Martinez through a maze of small hallways to his tiny, cluttered, windowless office. Martinez felt like he'd been sent to solitary.

"Guess you stay out in the field a lot," he said, glancing around at the untidy, claustrophobic office.

"Yeah. I asked for a bigger office with a window once, and was told they would have to cut my pay—my choice. Been here ever since." Sanchez gave him a wry smile, suggesting that might or might not be true.

"Asked if I could see Adams, got a vague response from the clerk out front. When do you think I can see him?"

"Those jail people seem to operate in their own world. They even scare me a little. Until they decide he's all settled in, you won't be able to see him. How long that'll take is a mystery. I know he's scheduled for an appearance before a judge in the morning, first thing. If he hasn't seen you by then, the judge will give an order that he either meets with an attorney or the court will appoint one. So, worst case, you'll see him after his hearing in the morning."

"That's not right. I should be able to see him and appear with him at the hearing. I want to request bail so he can be released."

Sanchez shrugged. "Right or not. My guess is you won't see him until the morning, after the hearing. Pretty sure the DA will ask for no bail on this one. It's murder, plus Mister Adams is a very wealthy man, with his own airplane and no connection to Santa Fe. I'd say he's a flight risk if I've ever seen one."

"He's a world-famous baseball player—where the hell is he going to hide? Just because he's not a resident of Santa Fe is no justification for keeping him locked up." Martinez was starting to get angry.

"Look Stephen, you don't practice in this arena very much. I'm just telling you what will happen. You can fight it, but you won't win. Everybody in the legal system here has a real complex when it comes to these famous people who come here to play, or even live part-time in their million-dollar haciendas. The DA isn't letting anyone just walk away with a murder charge hanging. I'm not a lawyer, and I wouldn't presume to argue the law with you. I'm just telling you the reality of what goes on."

"Well that sucks!"

"Yeah, probably."

Vincent helped Carter and Fisher load their luggage into the van so he could take them to the Albuquerque airport, where they hoped to be able to get a flight. They hadn't said where they were headed, and of course, it was none of Vincent's business.

The airport—called the International Sunport, for no obvious reason—was in the southern part of the city, and would take a little over an hour to get to. Before they left the Inn, Vincent had checked with the other guests to see if they might want to go along. Troy Arenado was the most vocal, saying that he thought he'd stick around for a while and see how things went for Dave Adams. Bud Turner said his wife wasn't feeling well, and they wouldn't be traveling until she was better. His arm was in a sling, and when Vincent had casually asked him how he'd gotten hurt, Bud had given him a withering look and said that he'd bumped into a door—then slammed the door in Vincent's face.

Vincent got his three passengers settled in. He had positioned the massive Buster Fisher on the opposite side of the van from the driver's side to help distribute the weight. They headed out.

This was Vincent's first trip to the Albuquerque airport. He was interested in the scenic drive and amazed by the amount of traffic. He hadn't given it much thought, but Santa Fe was the capital, after all, with lots of government offices. No doubt many people who worked there lived in Albuquerque, the largest city in the state. Plus, there would be a lot of people who would have dealings with the government who would drive in from there. As a result, the traffic was heavy most of the way. His passengers seemed lost in their own thoughts or stared at their phones. There was very little conversation.

Buster put his phone down. "Hey, Vincent. You seem like a smart guy. How did you end up a van driver for a Santa Fe B and B?" Buster was leaning forward some.

Vincent was a very large man—not Buster's three-hundred-pound large, but maybe linebacker large—and knew riding in a cramped van for an hour or so couldn't be comfortable for someone even bigger than him. He figured the question had more to do with Buster wanting to move around a bit than actually caring about the answer. "Life is full of surprises. I'd been in Denver for a lot of years, and the cold was starting to cause me more misery than I wanted. Thought I might head to Phoenix. Stopped in a diner and saw an ad for a driver at the Blue Door Inn. Why not? Ever do anything crazy like that yourself?"

"Nah, all I've ever done was play football." There was melancholy in Buster's voice. "Not sure what I'll do if I can't play anymore."

"Maybe coach, or something else to do with the game."

"Yeah, maybe. Although I've never really studied the game much. One of my weaknesses, according to my coaches, is that I don't play smart. How's that for a nice way of calling me stupid?" There was an unmistakable edge to Buster's voice. "I was thinkin' about quitting this year. Now, with all of my money gone, I don't know what's going to happen." Vincent wasn't an emotional man, but if he hadn't been driving, he might have given the big man a hug. Sounded like he needed one.

The remainder of the trip was uneventful. Vincent made a wrong turn into the airport and had to backtrack to get into the passenger drop-off area, but his passengers didn't seem to notice. They'd gone back to their cell phones.

Despite their recent financial losses, both men were generous with their tips. Vincent thought about not accepting the gratuity, but then decided it might insult them, so what the hell—he pocketed the money. The drive back was a lot more relaxed without passengers. He thought about life, its ups and downs. Financially, it seemed like a lot of people went through periods of success and failure. He sure had. Maybe it was rare to go through your entire life without a setback, but that didn't make it any easier to take. Having huge success thrust upon you as a professional athlete must be an amazing experience. Most of these people had been born with incredible physical gifts. To be rewarded with money just for being who you were—that had to be dizzying, unreal. Becoming a millionaire before you were twenty-five, for playing a sport you loved. And then the money's gone. From a dream to a nightmare.

Vincent was a good investigator, and he knew you couldn't know something was a fact until every alternative explanation had been eliminated. And he didn't know all the possibilities about who might have wanted Hamilton dead. It could be someone who had nothing to do with his being a sports agent. But based on what Vincent did know, he sure thought it was one of the five guests—or maybe, he should say, one of the eight guests who'd stayed at the Blue Door Inn.

Murder in paradise—sounds like a book, or maybe a movie. But what it feels like is shit falling on my head. Does trouble just find me, or do I seek it out somehow without meaning to? Plus, I have a lot of pain in my foot. Need to get my prescription filled— means I need a doctor. God, I hate that bullshit. Some know-nothing pill-pusher will ask me if I smoke (a little), if I drink (used to, a lot), and if I have any other complaints—well, my doctor's an idiot, that might be one. But if the gout gets worse and I can't walk, then I need to leave. These poor people are so nice that they would try to take care of me, and that'd just piss me off. Nice people trying to help me. I'm a miserable old man.

9

Everyone Will Be Tested

After Dave Adams's short and largely meaningless hearing, he was put into a small conference room and Martinez was allowed to see him.

"Mister Adams, my name is Stephen Martinez. I'm a local attorney. Jerry Oliver called me and asked me to see what I can do to get you out." They shook hands. Adams seemed in a daze.

"Can you get me out?"

"Not right now. They're holding you for now, but they've scheduled a bail hearing in two days. At that point we can make our case, argue that you should be allowed to post bail and be released. A murder charge, in itself, doesn't mean you cannot be released. What I've been told is that the main issue for the prosecutors is they're afraid you'll leave the state, maybe even leave the country. You have your own plane and lots of money, and they're going to argue to the judge that you're a flight risk."

"Jesus! What does that mean? I have to stay in jail until the trial?" Adams looked frightened.

"We'll make the case to the judge that you can't adequately

prepare your defense while you're locked up, but that's not going to be enough by itself. What the judge is really concerned about is the possibility that you'll take off. So, we'll let him know, first of all, that you've lost access to most of your money due to a financial fraud. Being rich is one of the things that makes the judge think you'll run, so the less money you have available, the better. Plus, we'll offer that you wear an electronic monitor. That way the police will know immediately if you try to leave. Those two things together might do it."

"I didn't kill that sonofabitch. I saw him, but when I left he was alive." Adams put his head in his hands and looked like he was on the verge of tears.

"You saw him that night?"

"Yeah. We left, my wife and I, after that fiasco of a meeting, and eventually I started drinking. Linda, my wife, got mad because I was being loud in public—probably an asshole, too. I took her back to the Inn and left again. Found a bar and drank some more. Eventually I went to Hamilton's house. I was outside yelling at him when he came out holding a baseball bat. He seemed to be drunk, too, like I was. He yelled back at me and threatened me with the bat, and he said I was a dumbshit, and it looked like the feds had recovered most of the money. Well, I don't know, but suddenly I did feel like a dumbshit. What was I going to do, kill him? I got back in the car and left. Went back to the Inn and passed out."

"Mister Adams, my guess is that someone saw you, or they have you on security video, or something putting you at the scene. You threatened to kill him in front of witnesses, and now they can put you at the scene of the murder. That's definitely enough evidence to charge you, and probably enough for a judge to be reluctant to set you free."

"Isn't there some legal way to force them to release me?"

"Not really. They can't hold you without cause, but it sounds like they probably have that. You have a right to a speedy trial and proper legal representation, but you don't have an absolute right to be out of jail before your trial. The bond hearing will determine if the judge is inclined to release you, and what conditions he'll put on that release if it happens, but there's not much we can do except make our strongest arguments and hope for the best."

"Goddamn. They're not going to let me go. Why would they? I'm screwed."

"I'll be glad to help you in any way I can, but you need to know that this isn't exactly my forte. I'm just a local lawyer who mostly does real estate stuff. I can give an out-of-state attorney a local presence, but you need someone who knows how to handle this kind of thing. I don't even know who that is, but you're going to be contacted, very soon, by a whole truckload of publicity-seeking lawyers. You need to hire someone who has experience with this type of trial. If you want me to ask around, I can."

"Look, you seem like a good guy, and Jerry said you had all kinds of local connections. So, for now, can you represent me?"

"Sure. I'll get a representation letter to you. But ethically, I'll have to bow out at some point because I'm not qualified to be lead attorney in a murder trial. We need to find someone else. And you'll need to hire an investigator to find out, if possible, what really happened. I know that seems like something the police should do, but if they think you did this, they stop looking for anyone else."

"Do you know anyone who could handle that?"

"No. I'll ask some people and see what I can find out."

Peter Tucker was, at one time, one of the most notorious defense lawyers in the country. Now he was approaching seventy, and he was still active every day, although it had been years since he'd had a big case—well, any case. When he'd started, he'd had one goal in life, which was to make as much money as he could. He'd represented people based on two factors: did they have a lot of money, and would the trial get him a lot of publicity. He was either cashing in on or adding to his national reputation, or both. He'd defended evil people and good people. Some were innocent, some were not. None of that mattered. Tucker cared about one person, and that was himself.

He'd had a brilliant, tremendously successful forty-year career, and he'd become both famous and rich, but he'd remained always alone. There had never been time, or room, for anyone else in his life. He'd had a lot of sex, but never found anyone to love apart from himself. With no family to comfort him in his golden years, he'd become more and more reclusive, tucked away in his mansion in southern Tulsa.

As a result of his narrow focus on what he considered ideal cases, he'd defended quite a few clients associated with organized crime. During the seventies and eighties, he'd become known as a Mafia fixer. He was involved in five high-profile mafia murder cases and was successful in having his clients found not guilty, when anyone with common sense knew they were guilty as sin. Most were tried in New York City, and Tucker became a Big Apple media darling. The tabloids and television, especially, were always looking for larger-than-life characters, and they fawned over Tucker, with his abrasive manner and his unprintable, can't-say-that-on-TV vocabulary. The rest of society shunned the now famous, very rich attorney.

His fame started to become a liability. Judges reacted quickly when he showed up in court to limit his public statements. Gag orders became the norm. He was fined several times, due to slight missteps, and he was once threatened with jail if he spoke in public again about a case. The great charismatic media machine was being throttled. Then several highly visible cases went horribly wrong.

In one, Tucker had been able to get a real goon found not guilty in a case that started out looking like a slam dunk for the prosecution. The local DA hadn't taken it well, and had said in a press conference that Tucker was evil, a monster who would do anything for money. His comments sparked a war in the media between the two legal eagles, each accusing the other of unethical behavior. And just as this verbal battle began to quiet down, Tucker's client, the goon, was in a shootout with the cops. He was killed, but he shot and killed two young police officers. The DA said that Tucker was as guilty as anyone involved in the shooting. The press turned on him. He was no longer a media darling.

The next bit of bad luck involved an evil hitman who the authorities suspected had killed at least six people, but who'd never been charged. He'd finally made a mistake on his most recent job, by leaving a witness alive, a twelve-year-old girl. During Tucker's cross-examination of the young girl, he was particularly brutal, and the judge had to admonish him several times. At one point the prosecutor actually threatened Tucker just to get him to stop bullying the witness. The judge called for a recess. Before court could resume, the girl had a breakdown and couldn't return to the stand. Tucker immediately called for all charges to be dismissed. He was actually booed by members of the public who were in the courtroom. Normally, with an outburst like that, a judge would call for the court to be cleared. This time the judge simply sat, staring at Tucker, with his arms crossed. A mistrial was declared, the girl's parents refused to allow her to testify again, and the hitman went free. Tucker had done his job brilliantly, but he was demonized on TV and in the press.

People were being arrested every day, but the calls to his office stopped. Even the bad guys thought he'd gone too far, or at least they worried about how his reputation might affect their cases. He was entering his sixties, and he had serious health issues. It was during this time that he'd purchased his hideaway in Tulsa. After a few years of low visibility, most people assumed he'd died.

It had been years now since he'd been in court, but he still read most of the major newspapers of the day and kept up with the law reports. Every day his routine began with the newspapers. He was looking for that perfect case, the one that would allow him to come back in a big way, and beat the shit out of the system. He knew he needed something special, not a run-of-the-mill mob killing or street gang assault. He needed something that would give him a real stage on which to rise up again, to once again become the great defender of justice he'd once been, at least in his own mind.

One early morning, sipping his strong coffee, he started his morning journey through the papers. The *Albuquerque Sun* was among those delivered to his home every day. Gathering the papers and laying them out for him was one of the regular chores handled by his staff. He owned a special cart, which one of his people would wheel out to the gated entrance to collect the twenty or so papers each morning. Most of the people who worked for Tucker thought he was mad, but he didn't care. The papers had to be laid out in the same order every day, otherwise the offender would suffer a loud, profane dressing-down for "fuckin' things up." Once Tucker entered the dining room with his coffee and notepad, the staff person who'd arranged everything would hurriedly leave the room.

Every day he would circle articles and make notes about things he found interesting. At one time he'd telephoned people he knew who lived in the towns where the cases were located to talk about how he might get involved, but these days most people didn't return his calls.

"Well sonofabitch, look at that. Goddamn baseball buddy got his ass locked up for murder." He broke out into laughter, then yelled for his staff.

"Somebody get me a plane ticket to Santa Fe—*right now,* you assholes. I want to leave immediately."

Nobody within earshot was going to disagree. They wanted him gone, too.

The Blue Door Inn was quiet. There were still four guests. Linda Adams was in her room and had told Jerry she was going to take something to help her sleep, and that she shouldn't be disturbed. Vickie and Bud Turner were also in their room, but they hadn't said anything to anyone about their plans. The staff assumed Vickie was still not feeling well. Troy Arenado had gone for a walk some time ago, and hadn't returned.

Vincent was helping Mary put away dishes from the dishwasher when Jerry spoke behind him. "Got a minute, Vincent?" He was standing in the door.

Vincent followed him into the main dining room. "Just got off the phone with Stephen Martinez. He's the lawyer I called when Dave Adams asked me to contact someone. He said it looks like Adams won't be released on bail, at least, not right away. He also said he was going to have to find someone to represent Adams, that he isn't qualified to handle a criminal case, especially murder. I was wondering if there was anyone from Denver or Dallas that you might recommend."

Vincent had lost all trust in people, but it was clear that Jerry still believed in basic honesty and goodness.

"He's going to need some top talent to represent him. Once it gets out that a famous baseball player has been accused of killing his agent, New York and L.A. attorneys will be knocking themselves out trying to get him to retain them. Won't even matter that he's lost his money. These guys are looking for media cases. They'll do it for nothing, if they have to."

"Well that's something else Stephen said. Adams told him that Hamilton said the feds had recovered most of the money, although he hadn't seen it yet."

"Seriously? That would be awfully fast. You know, Stephen shouldn't be telling you stuff like that. He needs to get back to real estate law really quick, before he gets himself in trouble."

"Probably. The main reason I wanted to talk to you is he said Adams wants to hire an investigator to look into the murder. He doesn't trust the Santa Fe cops to keep looking now that he's been arrested. Is that somethin' you would want to do?"

"Firing me already, Jerry?"

Jerry looked a little embarrassed.

"We both know you weren't planning on driving a van for long, but you're welcome here as long as you want. Might be more interesting, and lot more rewarding, to do some investigative work on the side, don't you think?"

"Yeah, it might. I know it would sure make Sanchez's day. As soon as the legal vultures land and Adams picks one,

I might approach them about doing some snooping. Who do you think did it?"

"All I know is that it was not me or my lovely wife. Everybody else is a potential suspect." Jerry grinned at his own joke.

"Does that include me?" Vincent didn't smile. It made Jerry pause a bit.

Murder and some big-time asshole lawyer falling into my lap. I should run—I know it. I'm a good investigator, but I'm supposed to be hiding from the world. I quit already. I have no desire to solve anything apart from my own damn health problems. Maybe I should start drinking again and just drink myself to death. Great, glorious ending to a lousy fuckin' life. Why are these people so nice? It's getting on my nerves. And they're way too trusting. Don't they live in the same world I do? A guy accused of murder, no doubt with a bunch of evidence pointing to him, and he hires a real estate attorney to represent him? And this, in a town where he's just visiting—a town that has some kind of grudge against famous people who just drop by to ruin the peace and quiet. Jesus. This should turn out great. I'm not responsible for these people. Run, now.

10

Family and Friends

Dave Adams was shown into a small conference room—the sign on the door read "consultation room." He was shackled and felt heavy-hearted as he entered, expecting to see Stephen Martinez.

"What the fuck are you doing here!" Adams glared at the old man.

"Good to see you, too, asshole. I'm here to save your ass. I thought you'd be pleased."

"I don't want your help. I thought you were dead." Adams felt his anger rising. He loathed Peter Tucker for what he had done to his mother, Tucker's sister.

"Don't be stupid, Dave. You need help, and this is the kind of shit I can handle—maybe better than anyone."

Adams wanted to yell at him to leave, but he hesitated. Peter Tucker *was* exactly what he needed. A ruthless, asshole lawyer with no ethical constraints. He would make a mockery of the so-called justice system, and no doubt enhance his tawdry reputation. And Dave was scared and didn't know who else to turn to. "I wasn't just being a wiseass. I really thought you were dead."

Peter could read people easily after decades of practice, and he knew immediately that his nephew had weighed his options and decided he really did need his long-dead uncle's help. "Well, I *sort of* died. Dropped out of the world. Had of run of bad luck, so I decided to just hide for a while. That turned into years. I followed your career, though. Guess *you're* the famous one in the family now." Tucker wasn't good at chit-chat. "Did you kill the bastard or not?"

"Not. I was angry and drunk. I'd pissed off my wife, and she said she was going to bed. It felt like all of it was Hamilton's fault. Of course, a lot of my anger was that my career was probably over, and baseball was all I had. I was scared. And then, to lose the money? It was too much. I left the Inn, and found a dive bar just outside of town, sat there for a while, drinking and stewing. I know now that it was dumb, but I decided I had to yell at Hamilton, maybe punch him a couple of times. Never was going to kill him. I left the bar and drove to his house."

"What time was that?"

"I'm not real sure, probably about nine. I rang the doorbell and he came to the door carrying a bat. He was even drunker than I was. He looked awful. We yelled at each other for a minute or two. Then I thought he was going to use the bat, and we struggled for the thing. Somewhere in there, I'm pretty sure the bat hit him in the head. I'm bigger than him, but he had some real strength and he seemed a little out of his mind. I took the bat away from him and threw it into the yard. I felt foolish about the whole scene by then—I'd sobered up a little. Hamilton looked crazy. I left. He was alive."

"Other than calling you names; did he say anything?"

"Yeah, he told me the money had been recovered, but mostly he was just yelling obscenities."

"So, you got your money back. Have you heard from the FBI, or whoever recovered the money?"

"No. Of course, I've been in jail. And I guess Hamilton could have been lying for some reason. I just want to get out of jail. What are the chances of that happening?"

"It can be done. The biggest problem is your fame. To some judges, that means you'll be an upstanding citizen and show up for court. But to others, it means you're a spoiled rich guy who'll skip town in a New York minute. I think if we offer the judge a place for you to stay in Santa Fe that'll be secure, and if they can monitor you, that'll go a long way toward getting you out. Where were you staying when this happened?"

"The Blue Door Inn—my wife is still there."

They discussed what had happened with Stephen Martinez and how Tucker could get hold of him. Dave filled him in on what Martinez and he had talked about. Martinez had been told by the sheriff's deputy that there would be a bond hearing in two days before Judge Nathanial, who the sheriff's deputy described as a tough sonofabitch. They also talked about an investigator and what to do about money.

"Until you know for sure that your money has been recovered, I'll cover any costs. And don't worry about it—I literally have more than I could ever spend."

"Did you have my dad killed?"

"Jesus Christ. That's horseshit. When he died, your mother lost her mind and decided that I was somehow connected with his death. I had nothing to do with it, I swear. It broke my heart when your mother banished me. She was wrong, but she was so heartbroken, she would never listen to me—just completely shut me out. But I'm telling you, I had nothing to do with what happened."

"I hope not. If I thought you were involved, I'd have to kill you."

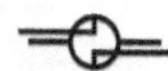

"Vincent, I need you to run downtown to the La Fonda on the Plaza to pick up a new guest." Jerry referred to the note in his hand. "Man's name is Peter Tucker. Stephen Martinez was the one who called about this. Apparently, this Tucker guy is a big-time lawyer and is going to represent Adams. Not sure why he is moving out here from the La Fonda, but I guess it's always good to have another guest."

Vincent knew the name and he wasn't sure it was good. He headed to the famous plaza in the middle of Santa Fe. As he pulled up to the front, he noticed a short, older man standing outside with luggage. Vincent parked the van.

"Are you Mister Tucker?"

"Yes. Thought you were supposed to be here ten minutes ago. That's no way to run a railroad—or a B and B." The annoying little man got into the van and Vincent loaded his luggage.

Traffic around the plaza was slow, and it took a few minutes to escape the congestion. Vincent concentrated on his driving to avoid hitting pedestrians.

"Understand you're some kind of investigator. I need someone local to help me gather information on what really happened here when Hamilton was killed. I'm going to be representing Adams. Can't really believe some guy driving a van has any idea about how to investigate a murder, but maybe there's nobody else. Guess you must work cheap."

Vincent took a beat before he said anything to calm himself.

"Understand you're some kind of asshole attorney who made all his money representing Mafia monsters by exploiting the media and tricking juries into believing up was down. Whether I would work cheap or not is irrelevant—I won't work for a prick like you."

Vincent half expected an explosion, but there was only silence. Then Tucker spoke in a new tone.

"Guess you know I can get you fired for that little speech."

"If that was true, I wouldn't want the goddamn job."

The remainder of the trip passed in silence. When they arrived at the Inn, Vincent opened the sliding door, gathered Tucker's luggage from the back, and took it into the front room. Jerry came out and greeted Tucker and began the process of getting him registered. Vincent moved the van to the parking area and went around back to have a smoke. He thought it might be a good day to fall off the wagon and have a drink. Jerry came out.

"Strange little man. Sure hope for Adams's sake that he knows what he's doing. Not a very friendly guy."

"Did he mention our little exchange?"

"No. I asked him how the ride was, and he said, 'Fine.' Never said much more than that. He did say he'd need a ride downtown in the morning. What was the exchange about?"

"He wanted to hire me, I think. To do investigative work. But the man is a rude little prima donna. Not sure I could work for him. He knew I had done investigative work—how did he know that?"

Jerry blushed a little. "Sorry, Vincent. I told Martinez. I was going to tell you, but I forgot. That was when I thought he was going to try and represent Adams, and I thought Stephen would need help. Sorry."

"Oh, it's okay. I don't know this Tucker guy, but I know about him. At one time he was one of the top criminal lawyers in the country, but his reputation is that of a street fighter. Not sure that's what Adams needs, but it might be. For all we know, Adams actually killed the guy."

"Yeah. I thought about that when I called Stephen. Well, I'm sure having Tucker is better than having a real estate lawyer representing you in a murder case."

Vincent laughed. "Yeah, he's got to be a notch or two above that."

"Look, we've only known each other for a short time, but I rely on you and your judgment. Cindy and I both trust you, and you're great with the guests. I know you're not going to hang around long in this job, but you're sure welcome to if it works for you. And if something like this investigative work comes up, we're comfortable with you taking that sort of thing on. It works for us to have you around."

"Well, thanks, Jerry. I don't know what my long-term plans are, but I like it here. So, I guess we can just play it by ear, and see what happens. You have many bookings lined up?"

Jerry smiled in a funny way. "Yeah, I guess that's relevant to this conversation, too. At this point we don't have any. Zero. So, who knows? In a couple of months, we might just shut down and sell the place. We probably have more unknowns than you do. I guess the best plan is to not plan at all, and just see what happens."

"Sometimes that's the only way to go."

They were becoming friends, which from Vincent's point of view was good and bad. Connections lead to pain, to sorrow.

"Okay, we got off on the wrong foot. My fault. I know I'm abrasive, can't seem to help that. I don't know you, and there was absolutely no reason for me to be rude to you yesterday. I apologize. And you're right, I'm an asshole attorney. For most of my life, that was actually my goal. The more people who were angry with me, the better. It's hard to adjust from that kind of life. So, again, I'm sorry I was so rude."

Vincent wasn't sure how to respond. The guy he'd met yesterday, he could understand. But this kinder, gentler Tucker was confusing.

"Don't worry about it, Mister Tucker, I'm a pretty thick-skinned guy. It's already forgotten."

They traveled in silence a while, toward the courthouse. Vincent wanted to ask Tucker why he was staying at the Inn when it made much more sense to stay in one of the many hotels downtown, but he didn't. His instincts still said Tucker was a hired gun, and not to be trusted to do anything except enhance his own fame and pocketbook—and if that happened to be good for Dave Adams, too, then so be it.

"I've talked to some people about you," Tucker said, breaking the silence again. "I've been told you might be one of the best investigators in the whole damn country, when you're not drinking. If that pisses you off, too bad, because that is what people are saying. And I've been told you have some medical problems that limit your mobility from time to time."

"That doesn't piss me off. It's the truth. I was a damn good attorney until I drank away my future, my wife, my money, and all my friends. I'm a good investigator because I know what's actually useful to a lawyer when they're in court, plus I know how to handle people—gently or not. But I don't do that anymore. I'm very comfortable driving this van."

"You may not believe this, but I completely understand. I was a broken man. I've been hiding for years in a big, cold mansion in Tulsa, afraid of everything. I failed, and I didn't know how to cope with it. Just coming here was harder than anything I've done in a long time. Facing my faults, my age, my own medical problems—an old man, body dying, mind dying. But I'm still better than most lawyers, and Dave Adams is my nephew. He hates my guts. His mother, my sister, cursed me before she died. But, Mister Malone, he's the only family I have. And if there's one thing I know how to do, it's defending a murder charge. So, I'm here, pissing you off along with many other people, I'm sure. But I need help. I think I need your help. The way you came back at me yesterday was perfect. I need someone who won't take any bullshit, including from me. That does me no good at all, and it does Dave Adams no good. If you'd consider working on this case, it would be a real benefit to me and my nephew."

Two assholes on one team, how could they lose?

"Did he do it?"

"No."

"Will I get paid?"

"I have more money than God."

"It's a deal."

Well, might have just made a deal with the devil. If he's not the devil, he'll do until the real thing comes along. Got to admit though, I'm a little excited. This could be fun. This old asshole of an attorney will shake things up in Santa Fe, which could be interesting to watch. Adams might not like the old bastard, but compared to the real estate guy, he's a godsend for anyone accused of murder. And maybe this is good for me, too. I really was thinking that maybe I should just hang out here and be a driver and help in the kitchen, but that's probably nonsense. I'm good at what I do, and if I'm not doing something useful, I might as well be dead. Plus, I'm lousy in the kitchen. Guess it's time to do some real work.

11

Investigate What?

Vincent's normal approach to investigating a serious crime had always been to contact some of his drinking buddies at the police department. A couple of nights of shots and beers, which suited him just fine anyway, and he would usually have spent an impressive amount of his client's money while also getting the inside story. He'd have information no one else could get, and the client would be happy. That was Denver, though, and this was Santa Fe. He had no drinking buddies—no buddies at all.

He had some contacts, if just barely. One was Tony Sanchez, the Santa Fe County Sheriff's Office detective. Vincent knew the detective had major concerns about him because he didn't fit in, and no detective liked that. He didn't belong at the Inn, and he was definitely not your typical van driver. Vincent knew how the detective's mind worked, that he was asking himself who Vincent was, really, and whether he might be connected to the murder. Why was he in Santa Fe? Was it just a coincidence that he'd turned up just before the murder? The question had to be nagging at him. Vincent could practically read his mind, thinking about how convenient it would be to have this nobody, this person who didn't belong, be the killer. They could throw him in jail, and pretty much no one would care.

The first thing Sanchez would do is gather background information. By now he'd know that he was mostly a loser, but one who might have connections. He'd know that Vincent had been an investigator, and therefore could be a real pain in the butt. Sounded like a good time to drop in for a visit.

His gout was acting up, but only slightly. He hadn't been taking medicine, even though he knew it was available—he just hated going and seeing a doctor to get a prescription. He decided the slight limp the gout gave him added to his overall image, which in his mind was that of a pirate. Vincent had no close friends, so—fortunately—he'd never discussed this strange personal quirk with anyone.

"Mister Malone, I was just thinking about you. Come into my office. Something wrong with your leg?"

"Old age and poor health habits would be my guess."

Vincent gave Sanchez an I-can-be-clever smile. It was one he used a lot. They settled into Sanchez's closet-sized, windowless office and stared at one another for a minute.

"Still not sure why you're working at the Blue Door Inn as a driver."

"It's Jerry's cooking." Vincent knew that if this were the old west, Sanchez would be threatening to run him out of town about now, because he looked like trouble. "Look, it's not a mystery. I'm on the verge of retiring on Social Security. I was headed to Albuquerque, looking for cheaper housing and saw an ad for the Inn. Suddenly, I'm in charge of transportation. No conspiracy, no hidden agenda."

"Did you know any of the guests, or Mark Hamilton, before you started at the Inn?"

"Not really, other than what I'd heard about most of them because of their sports careers. Not a huge sports fan, but I do read the sports page, and I'd seen most of their names. I knew nothing at all about Hamilton. You don't think I have anything to do with this, do you?" Vincent dropped the smile and gave Sanchez a harder-edged look.

"Just askin', that's all. Why did you want to see me?"

Sanchez also had dropped all pretense of hospitality.

"No doubt you've checked me out. You know that I used to work as an investigator in Denver, mostly for attorneys. Peter Tucker's going to represent Dave Adams, and he's asked me to assist him in preparing for trial."

"No shit. I heard the rumors about Tucker being here because of Adams. You know he's mostly known for representing Mafia types. Not somebody I'd want to associate with." Sanchez's expression suggested he'd suddenly caught a foul odor.

"Well, we're not getting married. It's just a job. You arrested Adams pretty damn fast. What was the key evidence?"

"Malone, I'm sure you know I'm not telling you anything. From this point on, the case'll be handled by the DA. He'll decide what the defense gets according to the normal evidentiary rules, subject to court oversight. I'll tell you, though, that we're comfortable with the charge and our evidence. One factor in arresting him so quickly was the risk of him bolting. That's no secret—we were concerned he'd head out of the state, maybe even out of the country."

"That must mean you have been able to place him at the scene of the crime."

"No comment."

Sanchez's smile had returned. All hints regarding the arrest, even minuscule ones, were clearly over. Malone debated whether or not to ask the detective if he'd like to get a drink, but realized the man would say no, and that it was actually Malone who wanted a drink. So, he left with nothing.

He decided to take a walk around the famous plaza. Its center was a public park with a large gazebo. Surrounding that were two-story buildings with a variety of retail shops, bars, and restaurants. Several people—homeless, by the look of them—sat or stretched out on the park benches in the bright sunshine. The sidewalks were busy with a mixture of tourists, locals, and street people. No one in this eclectic assortment seemed concerned about the mixture of classes, and most folks appeared to be in a good mood. A number of bars facing the plaza had upstairs seating on balconies, where patrons sat, drinking and people-watching.

The aptly named Plaza Cantina was Vincent's choice as a venue to test his current resistance to alcohol. The motif was mostly bright, not his personal norm, which was a dark bar with moody jazz. This was a tourist hangout, where everything was overly colorful and cheerful. He found the bar and took a stool. The bartender came his way.

"Welcome, what can I get you?"

"What's your specialty?"

"Best damn margarita in Santa Fe, on the rocks, no salt."

"Perfect."

He was pretty sure he'd never been drunk on margaritas—the amount of sugar alone would surely kill you before you could get half-bombed. The bartender placed the drink in front of Vincent. It was a large vessel full of lime green concoction. He sipped. He smiled. "Haven't tasted all of the margaritas available in Santa Fe, but this is the best damn margarita that I, personally, have ever had."

The bartender nodded his appreciation and moved on to tend to the next customer. After some time spent sipping—it was a huge drink—Vincent was feeling no pain. Realizing that it would be folly to order another, he finished his monster drink and headed outside. It was a cool day in Santa Fe, and the mountain air seemed to engulf him. He found an empty bench in the plaza and took a seat. He needed a plan.

Hamilton had been murdered at his house, and his wife had been at home at the time, but apparently she hadn't heard anything. Now the wife had gone back to L.A. It seemed an odd choice to Vincent, but maybe it had something to do with work, or children left behind, or a dog. There had to be some reason to leave town so quickly and suspiciously after your husband was killed. He needed to ask Tucker if he would spring for a trip to L.A.

He also needed local gossip. Even in Santa Fe, there was bound to be a dive where the local cops, sheriff's deputies, and whoever else hung out and bitched about the stupidity of their bosses. Local law enforcement always congregated somewhere. It was safer to drink in the place where other cops hung out, but if you asked them where "their" bar was, you'd get a blank stare—outsiders weren't welcome. Still, one source of information about cops was the people they dealt with every day. Street people knew as much as anyone about the folks whose job it was to hassle them. Street people—at least the ones that weren't too crazy—knew plenty about a community. They observed while mostly going unnoticed themselves, and they talked amongst themselves. But they were as mistrustful as the cops. The only way to get information from them was with money—they always needed money.

He went back to the bar and asked the bartender where there was a community center or rescue mission for the homeless. The bartender directed him to an area west of downtown, where there was a clinic and a homeless shelter. The bartender, being wise and discreet—like all bartenders—didn't ask why Vincent wanted to know, just took the twenty dollars he was offered, and smiled. Vincent's first Santa Fe connection: Jake the bartender at the Plaza Cantina.

He could have walked, but with his foot hurting, he decided to drive. He knew he was in the right area when the number of people congregating on the sidewalks increased. He parked around the corner from the clinic and walked back. He went in, looking around for someone in charge. An older man with a white beard was either an early arriving Santa Claus or the person running the place. As Vincent approached, the man, who sat at a small desk, looked up.

"What kind of cop are you?"

He still looked jovial, fortunately. Vincent smiled. "Private."

"Don't get too many private cops snooping around in Santa Fe. I had you figured for some kind of federal agency, maybe something to do with health."

Santa's smile vanished and his expression was cautious.

"I do investigative work for attorneys. Looking into the murder that happened over the weekend up in the foothills."

"Rich people killing rich people. Don't think that has much to do with my group."

"Lots of good gossip on the street, though. Thought maybe there was somebody who always knows the latest."

Santa Claus smiled.

"Yeah, there are a couple of people who think they know everything. Why would they talk to you?"

"Money."

Santa Claus chuckled. "I guess you know that lying for money is no different than telling the truth for money around here."

Vincent smiled. "I'll take my chances."

"Biggest know-it-all is Tito. Haven't seen him today, but he's about. Hang around for a while and I'll put out word he has a customer. He'll find you."

Vincent got a cup of coffee and put a twenty in the donation jar. He winked at Santa and went out front to wait. He found a bench around the side of the building and took a seat. There were people milling about, but Vincent wouldn't be hard to pick out.

After a short wait, Vincent noticed a tall man walking his way. He seemed deliberate, with a manner that was almost regal. He was in his late thirties or early forties, with a neatly trimmed beard. He had a confidence that seemed out of place on the street. He sat down next to Vincent.

"Information is expensive in Santa Fe, sort of like downtown hotels. It's part of the town's charm. Hundred bucks, and I will tell you what I know."

"Tito, I assume?"

"Yeah, that's me."

"My name is Vincent Malone." Vincent took out two one-hundred-dollar bills and gave them to Tito. The extra hundred was a bonus so Tito would remember him. He would need to get reimbursed by Tucker, quickly. "Who killed Mark Hamilton?"

"Don't know. That's not street crime. Whoever killed him is not part of my world. The word is that it was one of his clients staying at the new B&B out there. What I *can* tell you involves his wife. She was having an affair with Stephen Martinez, the attorney."

"How the hell would you know that?"

Tito gave a mischievous grin.

"How doesn't matter, I just do. If the murderer wasn't one of the clients, then Martinez might be a suspect. Also, you should know that the cops think you have something to do with it. Big tough guy shows up in town, takes a nothing job, and in a few days, someone is killed. They think you're a hired killer."

Vincent wasn't surprised. He already knew that Sanchez was suspicious of him. Someone who showed up where they shouldn't be will always get an extra-long look by the cops. It gave him a certain level of confidence in Tito's information.

"Where do the cops hang out around here?"

"Crown Bar on San Francisco Street. I'd be really careful in there. They don't like strangers—meaning anyone who's not a cop."

Street people are an odd lot. Some of them seem like they should be successful at something—and maybe they are. Not sure I could survive the life they live—each day must be a series of struggles. It was good to get out and about, start working out how I can get the information Tucker's going to need. Re-engaged my brain a bit. Did smoke a couple of cigs—not good. Also had a huge margarita. No chance I'd become addicted to those things—it tasted good, but it's no drink for a drunk. It's good to feel useful. This Tito guy is very strange. Something about him doesn't add up—he knows a lot more than he's giving me. Need to follow up with him and stay in touch with Santa Claus.

12

Memories and Thoughts

When Buster Fisher was in the sixth grade, he was fat. When he was a freshman in high school, he was fat. When he was a senior in high school, he was an all-state offensive lineman on the state championship football team—and he was also fat. He had friends, even had a couple of dates, but only because he was a football player. He seldom studied, but got a B in every class, including ones he never attended. And in his senior year, he was offered a full scholarship to UCLA. Without football, Buster probably wouldn't have existed. He thought about nothing else. He wasn't sure what he would do if he couldn't play football—maybe die.

He had learned a great deal at UCLA about how to be a good offensive lineman. In high school, he'd just relied on his size and gotten in people's way. In college *everyone* was big, and much quicker than him. His first year was a disaster. He was reduced to being the third-string offensive guard, and played very little. A coach, Jack Myer, took him aside and said that if he wanted to play football beyond college, he would need to learn the game. He would have to lose some fat and put on muscle. And he would have to learn how to move his feet, how to pull on certain plays. What he needed was to learn how to play football. Of course, Buster had believed he was the best, so it was an adjustment to realize he was not even very good. During the off-season, Myer took Buster under his wing and worked him hard. Buster actually worried at times that he might die of a heart attack. But he became stronger and quicker. With guidance from Myer, he was a much-improved player by his second season. He actually started the last two games of the season, and he was an honorable mention as a PAC-12 all-star.

His confidence grew, and he worked doubly hard in the off season. At the start of his sophomore year, he was a starter. Pro scouts started to pay attention to him. As the year progressed, it became clear that he'd become one of the best offensive linemen in the country. Buster Fisher had turned into a star, and he no longer felt fat, though no one would have called him slim.

He continued drinking large quantities of beer all during this period, though, and he was a leading member of a legendary clandestine society of beer-swilling college athletes. He earned a new kind of fame the night he consumed the largest number of beers ever recorded. One of his drinking buddies—a second-rate athlete who would graduate that year from law school—was Mark Hamilton. He and Mark had hung out many a night at an off-campus pub that was a favorite of the less well-known jocks.

In his senior year, Buster was an All-American, and it was even rumored that he might go in the first or second round of the NFL draft. He contacted Mark, who had recently gotten his law license, and asked him to be his agent. There were other options, even better options, lots of them. But Buster liked Mark, and trusted him.

Buster never questioned Mark. He just signed where he said to. He was drafted by the Denver Broncos at the beginning of the second round. They offered what sounded like a huge sum of money, and he and Mark agreed it was generous. Buster later found out it had actually been pretty ordinary, but he still trusted Mark.

Vincent had collected contact numbers for all the guests from Cindy. She was hesitant, and asked Jerry, who said, "Sure, give him the numbers." Vincent assured her he wasn't going to annoy anyone, that he just wanted to ask a few questions. Cindy still wasn't completely sure it didn't violate some privacy law, but she shrugged and gave the information to Vincent, anyway. The list was complete, phone numbers and email addresses. Cindy was nothing if not efficient.

Vincent left a message for Buster at his Denver number. "Mister Fisher, this is Vincent Malone, I'm the van driver from the Blue Door Inn. Doing a little part-time work for the attorney representing Dave Adams. If you have a minute, give me a call." He left his number.

He was taking out the trash when his phone rang. "Vincent Malone."

"Vincent, this is Buster. What can I do for you?"

"Thanks for calling me back, Buster. As I said in my voice mail, I'm working with Peter Tucker, who's representing Dave Adams. He's asked me to make contact with all the guests who were at the Inn. Just a couple quick questions. You were one of Hamilton's first clients, is that right?"

"I was the very first. I was his only client for almost a year. I knew Mark in school, we used to drink at the same bar. I liked him, and I didn't want one of the suits who were chasing me. They seemed slimy. Anyway, he became my agent and worked out my first contract with the Broncos."

"You two get along?"

"Oh, sure. If you're asking me, did I kill him, the answer is no. We had kind of grown apart the last few years. He hit the big time, got married to Ann, who I think thought I was a jerk. And they traveled in the high-society circles, not with my kind of people."

"Any reason someone might want to kill Mark, other than this latest financial fiasco?"

"Well, some people didn't like him much. He'd become kind of snooty, so most of his old friends didn't have much to do with him anymore. Ryan Something—sorry, can't remember his last name—was a guy who worked with Mark. In fact, I think he was the one who introduced the financial guy to Mark. Anyway, they used to be pals, but Ann was Ryan's girlfriend, and when Mark and Ann became an item, I think their friendship hit the skids."

"When you say 'the financial guy,' you mean the one who

took the money?"

"Yeah, I met him once. Larry, I think. I got the impression that whole thing was Ryan's doing."

"Ryan live in L.A.?"

"Yeah. He and Mark had offices in the same area downtown. You might as well know that the rumors I heard said that Ann and Mark were both having affairs. Like I said, he and I weren't buddies lately, not the way we were at the beginning. But I heard stories that they were living pretty high on the hog."

"What about the other clients at the Inn? Do you know them very well?"

"Nah. I've seen them at one thing or another, but none of them are pals. I've followed Terry Carter's career, just because we both play football, and I see him at football-related events. But the others I really don't know."

"Do you plan on coming back to Santa Fe?"

"Not unless they make me. I'm sorry Mark was killed, I'm sorry poor old Adams is in jail, but there's not much I can do about it. Mark left me in a bad spot, did the same thing to Terry. He convinced both of us to take an incentive-based contract because it would mean more money. Of course, if we got injured it would be a disaster. The SOB shouldn't have done that. I always trusted Mark, but he wasn't doing right by a lot of people toward the end."

"I didn't know you were injured."

"Yeah, got a serious problem with my knees. Too much weight. Not sure I'll be able to play next year, and I was out a big chunk of money this year. Made about half of what I would have if I hadn't taken that incentive contract. But it sounds like the FBI has recovered the stolen money, not that I've seen shit yet. So, maybe I'll be okay. I got to go now. I hope you can find who killed Mark and get Adams off, because I don't think he did it. He has a temper, but I don't see him as a killer."

"Thanks for talkin' to me, Buster. Good luck."

He hung up.

Vincent looked at his list and called Terry Carter's number. There was no address listed, and he didn't recognize the area code, so wasn't sure exactly where he was calling. The phone rang and rang, never answered and never going to voice mail. Eventually, Vincent hung up. When he looked up he saw Troy Arenado sitting alone in the gazebo. He debated on approaching him. He had obviously picked the spot to be alone.

"Mister Arenado, sorry to interrupt. Got a minute?"

Troy stared at Vincent a little too long, no doubt debating how to tell him to get lost. "Not interested in being interrogated."

"Not my job. I'm just gathering a little background information for Peter Tucker. If this isn't a good time, maybe later?"

Vincent gave him his best, rarely used, I'm-really-a-good-guy smile.

"I didn't kill Mark, and I don't know who did. So, I can't help you get Adams off." Troy was clearly annoyed.

"Well, okay. Were you and Mark friends?"

"It's easy to look up, which no doubt you already have—I was suing the bastard. Guess he's no longer a bastard now that he's dead, but he sure was when he was alive. And we weren't friends. He screwed me long before this latest financial scam."

"Sorry, Troy. I really didn't know," he lied. "What was that about?"

"I'm a free agent this year—my big chance to get life-changing money. I didn't want Mark to represent me. I didn't think he handled my last contract very well, and I didn't really trust him anymore, so I was going to hire someone else. He said if I did that, I would owe him two million dollars. I had no idea what he was talking about. But in our last agent contract, there was a penalty clause if I cancelled. I'd never heard of such a thing, and I sure as hell didn't know it was in my contract—when I signed, he told me it was just a standard rep agreement. I told him right then, I was quitting, and there was no way I was paying him anything to fire his ass. Also told him I wanted all the money he was managing for me transferred back to me right away. We got into a little exchange, and I hit him. The whole time he's yelling at me that I'm a bastard, that he's made me millions. I told him I was going to throw his ass out of his office window—and his office is pretty high up. He was bleeding from a cut above his eye where I hit him. He got to the phone and told someone to call the police. I left."

"What did you do then?"

"Hired a lawyer. He looked at the contract and then he called Mark, with me still sitting there, listening. Told him he could get him disbarred for writing a contract like that. They argued back and forth, and Mark told him that he would void the contract, and slammed the phone down. A few days later, my lawyer got a letter from Mark voiding the agent contract and cutting off all relations with me. But he still hadn't sent me my money he was holding, so I had the attorney file a lawsuit to recover it. A couple days after that, Mark called me and said he was going to get my money, but he wanted us to part friends. He asked me to come to Santa Fe, said he would pay for everything. Said the money was safe, but it would take a day or two to get everything set up so he could transfer it to me. Supposedly it'd all be done by the time I got to Santa Fe. So, I came here."

"I guess you were surprised to see the others."

"Yeah, you could say that. I have no idea what he was trying to do. But I think he'd asked the others to be here before he knew the money was missing. It was going to be some kind of bonus for being loyal clients, or something. Maybe he thought I wouldn't kill him if other people were around."

"I know this isn't really my business, but why are you still here?" Vincent tried to sound disinterested, but he was curious.

"Good question. Funny thing happened. I hired a new agent, and I hate the guy. He's all corporate and it's so goddamned annoying. I was supposed to meet with him in Orlando, but I cancelled. Said I had to stay here, which wasn't true, but I just made it up on the spot, as an excuse. So then I stayed, basically just because I'd lied to the guy." Troy chuckled, but he didn't look happy. "I really didn't kill him. I wanted to a couple times in the last month or so, but at one time he was my best friend. It hurt when he tried to screw me out of money, it really hurt."

Could it be my first guess was right, that it was one of the clients staying at the Inn? Of course, it could be something completely unrelated to his sports agent business. Maybe he owed somebody money for fixing his car and refused to pay. How did this Mark guy turn out to be such an asshole? Oh, well. Not my job to figure out why people are assholes—that's for a higher power to worry about. I need to get with Tucker and give him what I know.

13

Plan Your Work, Work Your Plan

Vincent sat in the conference room at the Inn, waiting for Tucker. He'd covered quite a few bases in a short amount of time, and was ready to give Tucker his first report. His tasks had included a visit to the murder site, along with gathering some gossip around town, and some computer time, doing research.

"Morning, Vincent. Let me get a cup of coffee and I'll be right with you." Tucker was dressed for court, and somehow maintained a regal bearing even as he slumped into his chair. The hint of what he had once been was still visible.

"So, who did it?"

Vincent chuckled. "Can't say at this point, but there sure are plenty of suspects. Of course, we have the guests at the Inn. Every one of them, with the possible exception of Bud and Vickie Turner, has a reason to be unhappy with Hamilton. Apparently, he was getting very rich off his clients, but still wanted more. Some of his dealings were questionable at best, maybe even illegal. Hamilton's need for cash seemed to drive a lot of his actions. At the heart of that need might be his wife, Ann. According to rumors, and some press reports, she spends a lot of money. Very socially active in L.A., and a big spender in Santa Fe. She went back to L.A. almost immediately after her husband's death. I think it might be wise to fund a trip to L.A. I can see if she'll talk to me. You agreeable?"

"Sure. Any chance she's involved in his death?"

"I'd say there's a chance. But I have no direct evidence, mostly just the sudden departure, which seems odd. Something else that's weird is that she's linked to your co-attorney, Martinez. Again, this is something where I don't have definitive proof, but they've been seen out and about in Santa Fe at some social functions."

"Your best guess?"

"I'm getting some street talk about her as maybe not the most loyal wife in the world, although it's limited to Martinez, as far as I know. I've seen her, and she's a gorgeous woman. Might be hard for a guy to resist."

"Well, we need to get that nailed down immediately. Can't have my co-counsel carousing with one of the crime suspects—doesn't look good in court." Tucker actually grinned, though it looked like he didn't get much practice at it. "Can you talk to Martinez?"

"I'll visit with him before the hearing. I went by the Hamilton house. Still lots of crime-scene tape. One deputy was on duty, seemed like a good guy. We chatted a bit, but he wasn't about to let me past the police tape. Still, even from where I was, I could easily spot at least four cameras on the exterior of the house. If the guy was killed in the front yard, the cameras would have captured it for sure. So, it looks like either the cameras weren't working, or for some reason they didn't capture the murder, because if Detective Sanchez had video of it, he wouldn't have been screwing around with questioning the guests at the Inn. He would have just gone and arrested whoever was on the video, immediately. But something made him focus on Dave. My guess is that the cameras captured the exchange with Dave and Hamilton, but didn't show the actual killing. The other possibility is that someone saw him there and told the cops, but I think the video is the most likely reason. Witnesses aren't reliable. Sanchez knows that, but he's acting like this is a slam dunk. Ann was at the house when her husband was killed. She was supposedly out cold from some sleep medication she took, but there's no actual evidence to back that up. Maybe she turned the camera off for some reason after Dave left."

Tucker was silent for a moment, apparently thinking about what Vincent had said, then spoke up. "I filed a motion setting out the reasons why Dave should be released on his own recognizance. I imagine the DA, a guy named Nick Carlton, will file his own motion saying that Dave is a flight risk and there should be no bail at all. I said in our motion that Dave would stay at the Inn and would agree to wear an ankle monitor, and that he'd surrender his passport. And I've argued that he needs to be out of jail so he can participate in his defense, but I'm not sure that'll be anywhere near strong enough for the judge to rule against the DA. Find out anything on the judge?"

"Not much. He seems to be an outsider. He's not a prosecutor's judge, but it appears he's not on the defense attorney's side, either. He rules based on facts and lets the chips fall where they may. He's not liked by law enforcement because he's made some pretty candid comments in court about the ineptitude of the sheriff's department. According to my source, Sheriff Ortega hates him. Which reminds me: some of my information is the result of a little excessive tipping at a couple of bars—bartenders know everything about everything. It would be very helpful if I could get reimbursed."

Tucker frowned at Vincent. "How reliable is this stuff, if you're paying for it?"

"I'm only going to pass along what I believe to be reasonably true. But most informants don't come with a money-back guarantee."

Tucker reached into his coat pocket and pulled out a wallet. He handed Vincent ten one-hundred dollar bills.

"That's a lot of news in a very short amount of time. Maybe you're as good as you think you are." He pulled out a credit card in the name of Tucker and Associates. "Use this for your travel. You decide what's reasonable, but don't travel like you're damned royalty. Keep it reasonable and we'll get along fine. Thanks for your help."

Tucker got up and left the room. Vincent picked up their coffee cups and went into the kitchen.

"Vincent, do you have time to run some errands today?" Jerry seemed engrossed in whatever he was making and didn't look up.

"Sure. What's that you're making? Smells great in here."

"Pumpkin bread. Already got one in the oven. I think I'm

getting to be pretty good at baking." He smiled.

"Won't get any argument from me."

"On another topic," Jerry said, "I need to ask you something. Mister Tucker asked me if we could accommodate Dave Adams and his wife for a while. My first reaction was that it's always good to have paying guests, so I said I thought so. Well, Cindy's not really happy with that. Tying up a couple of rooms for Adams and Tucker will limit any group bookings, but I think the bigger issue is the whole idea of having a murder suspect and his infamous attorney staying here. I know how that sounds, but I think Cindy has a point. We're just starting, and this probably isn't the kind of publicity we need. What do you think?" Jerry's happy baker smile was gone.

"You and Cindy have every right to be concerned. This is very low-key right now, but that's about to change. This hearing coming up will be the start of a lot of media attention. If Adams is released and stays here, you'll have to increase security just to handle the media people, and then reporters will start asking if you have rooms available. How are you going to handle that? On the other hand, my guess is there's about a fifty-fifty chance Adams won't be released at all. The decision comes down to the individual judge, and how that judge happens to feel about public figures and flight risks in general. Most judges believe a defendant has every right to be out of jail so they can participate fully in their defense. But no judge wants to be accused of coddling someone rich and famous, especially if that person ends up taking off. So, until the hearing we won't know if Adams will even be out. I'd wait until you know if it's going to happen to say no to Tucker. If he's released, let him stay a few days, and then I can talk to Tucker and see if it wouldn't make more sense for Adams to be in one of the big hotels downtown. If there's a media mob camped out here, it's going to be hard for Adams to have any privacy, whereas in one of the hotels they can rent a whole floor and be secure. Money won't be an issue, so it's very possible Tucker will figure out for himself that they need a more secure place to stay, and you won't even have to get into it."

They discussed the list of errands Jerry wanted Vincent to handle. It was a welcome distraction for Vincent, who needed time to think through everything he'd learned and what to do next.

"Looks like we'll have some more paying guests in a week or so. One of the big galleries on Canyon Road is hosting a famous artist from France—I think they're from France, anyway. They asked about rooms. It's the artist and some other people, a total of three rooms for about two weeks. Plus, they want to hold a couple of events here. We're not even sure how they ended up coming to us—Cindy didn't do any marketing focused on the art community."

With that new information, Vincent understood the concern about Adams better. Artsy folks and an accused murderer could make for awkward seating arrangements.

"That sounds good. I think that very soon, once you've had more people stay here and word-of-mouth gets going, you'll have more demand than you can handle. You and Cindy have done a great job creating a unique place to stay, and it's exactly what people think of when they think of Santa Fe."

"Thanks."

"Sometime in the next week or so, I'll be gone for a couple of days. Going out to L.A. to interview Ann Hamilton. What was your impression of her?"

"Well, my first impression was she's one beautiful woman—like, movie star-level beautiful. Plus, she was so perfect, she didn't seem to have a single flaw. Her looks, makeup, clothes, hair—everything about her seemed just so. In an odd way, even when I was standing next to her, she didn't seem quite real. She might be someone who's easier to look at than actually live with."

"That's a great insight." Vincent hadn't meant to sound so surprised, and he went on quickly, hoping it wouldn't be noticed. "How did she seem around her husband?"

"It was only that one meeting, in the morning, when they were together. He was definitely in charge, but sometimes I saw him looking at her in a way that suggested there was tension between them. I don't know why. I mean, it could have just been the meeting itself and the topic they were going to have to address. He seemed nervous, she didn't."

"Have they paid you for the rooms?"

"She paid for three days for all guests in advance. With some leaving early and some staying longer than expected, it's about a wash right now. Do you think there'll be a problem getting paid?"

"Not sure. Just curious if she's the type to handle those kinds of details."

"I only talked to her for a few minutes, but she seemed not only gorgeous, but smart, too."

"This is gossip, so best not to spread this around, but I've picked up on some rumors about Martinez and Ann Hamilton. Would you have any information about that?"

"Our Martinez? The lawyer?"

"Yeah, him."

"What do you mean, 'rumors?'"

"Having dinner, going to social events together—stuff like that."

"Wow. Cindy will shit when I tell her this. Ann Hamilton and Martinez? No, we had no idea."

"How did the Hamiltons hear about the Inn?"

"Martinez."

It's too Zen for me, but it's weird how everything was over in my life just a few weeks ago and now I'm more connected with people than I have been in a long time. Not sure I even want it—people are a pain in the ass—but, there it is. Even this old fart, Tucker, seems to trust me. Why? Maybe it's the altitude in Santa Fe—higher even than Denver. Does thin air reduce intelligence? The feeling of belonging here is starting to bug me—and worry me. Time to visit the cop bar and restore my lack of faith in humanity.

14

Heard At The Hearing

Vincent dropped Tucker and Linda Adams off at the courthouse, then went down a couple of blocks to Martinez's law office.

"Here to see Stephen Martinez. My name's Vincent Malone. I was sent by Peter Tucker."

The receptionist absorbed this info, then talked quietly on the phone.

"You can go in." She indicated the door with Martinez's name.

"Hello, Malone. I know who you are, but I don't believe we've actually met." Martinez was a good-looking man with a friendly face. He shook Vincent's hand. "How can I help you? I was just headed over to the courthouse for the hearing."

"Mister Tucker asked me to talk to you about that. We've picked up some uncomfortable information about your relationship with Ann Hamilton, and wanted to ask you about it."

Martinez looked blindsided. He went around his desk and sat down.

"Shit, I knew I should have told Peter about that. What does he want me to do?"

"Were you having an affair with Ann?"

"Well, yeah, I guess I was."

"You guess."

"You don't have any right to question me." He gave Vincent a dirty look. "Get the fuck out of my office." He stood up.

Vincent didn't flinch.

"You need to calm down. I'll leave your goddamn office when I'm ready." He moved toward Martinez, not away from him as the lawyer had expected, and now stood in front of the man's desk—a very big man with an ugly scowl. Martinez sat back down and looked nervous.

"What do you want?" he said softly.

"First, don't go to the hearing this morning. The judge more than likely won't notice or care. But, just in case, we need the name of another attorney in your office who can be our local connection. After the hearing, Peter wants to talk to you about your relationship with Ann. He or I will call you and schedule something at the Inn. Got all that?"

"Yeah." Martinez handed Vincent a business card with another lawyer's name. "If it comes up, you can use this name."

"Good." Vincent left.

Judge Walter Nathanial had been appointed by a term-limited liberal Democratic governor whose one great pleasure in life involved thumbing his nose at the entrenched establishment that existed at all levels of government. Nathanial's appointment was for the one year remaining in the term of a judge who'd died, after which he'd have to run for reelection for a six-year term. He'd been appointed by the governor because he'd been recommended by the dean of the University of New Mexico School of Law, where Nathanial was a well-respected, but not particularly well-liked, professor. He knew the law better than most, but had difficulty with his people skills. He'd earned his law degree from Notre Dame with honors. His first teaching job had been at his alma mater, but he'd almost immediately become controversial because of his opinions—which he spoke about frequently and publicly—regarding the administration of the school. After a loud shouting match with the Dean of Law, Nathanial resigned. The UNM position was several layers below his previous one, but it was a job. He'd learned his lesson about publicly criticizing your bosses, and mostly kept his head down and did his job, teaching future lawyers the law. But even while trying to keep a low profile, he quickly became known as the smartest, rudest, and most difficult professor at the school. The Dean had recommended him to the governor mostly to ensure that he left, and the governor had accepted the recommendation because the dean had said that Nathanial would drive the establishment in Santa Fe fucking crazy. Everybody was happy except Nathanial. He hated Santa Fe. He thought it was a silly, pretentious place, mostly full of hustlers.

Shortly after Nathanial's appointment to the bench, he became ill, resulting in a serious case of pneumonia. While he was still sick, he made the decision to run for a full term, mostly because he couldn't afford to lose his insurance. He did no campaigning and made no public statements. He'd spent very little time on the bench and had gotten to know exactly no one. Due to the appointment, and the good, but vague, recommendation from the UNM Dean, he ran unopposed.

Once he was healthy again, he began his full term on the bench of the First Judicial District Court. Within weeks, he had pissed off almost every person who had appeared before him. He'd also offended the sheriff by saying that several of his deputies appeared to have no knowledge about what they could and couldn't do when apprehending suspects. He threatened them and Sheriff Ortega, with contempt of court. It suddenly became obvious to anyone paying attention that the new judge was going to be a problem, and his six-year term had only just started.

Most criminal charges carry a specific bail bond amount. Petty offenses are usually set at no bail, with the accused being released on their own recognizance, while more serious offenses would sometimes require five hundred dollars or more. Serious felony charges could be scheduled for five thousand and up. Murder had no specified amount—it was up to the judge at the bail hearing to decide if bail would be granted, and if so, in what amount. All of this meant that a typical bail hearing was mostly procedural, and would last only a few minutes, while the bail hearing in a murder case was far more formal and would take however long it took.

Judge Nathanial was a tall, lean man. Some said he looked like Abraham Lincoln, but it wasn't meant as a compliment.

What most people didn't know was that Walter Nathanial was a huge baseball fan. He probably knew more about Dave Adams than just about anyone else in Santa Fe, other than Dave's wife.

"Please rise." The bailiff said, announcing the arrival of the judge. "The Court of the First Judicial District is now in session, the Honorable Judge Walter Nathanial presiding." The judge took his seat and addressed everyone present. "You may be seated."

The court clerk introduced each party, and the judge acknowledged Tucker, who spoke first.

"Thank you, your honor. As we have set out in our filings, Mister Adams isn't a flight risk. He's a celebrity throughout the world because of his success as a baseball player. He cannot sneak across the border or hop on a flight without being recognized, but more importantly your honor, Mister Adams is a law-abiding citizen who has never before been accused of any crime, much less convicted. He's not a risk to society. A person like that shouldn't be punished simply because he's well-known and rich. Those factors do not support the idea that Mister Adams is a flight risk—in fact, the exact opposite is true. He's not going to run away to hide in some shantytown. He will appear in court as directed to defend his innocence. We do recognize the seriousness of the charge, of course, and we offer more than just his assurance that he'll appear in court as directed. He will turn over his and his wife's passports, and he will submit to wearing an electronic monitoring device, and he agrees to remain in Santa Fe for the duration of the trial.

If Mister Adams is held in custody for the amount of time it will take to reach a trial date and a verdict, he will suffer undue punishment. Famous people are not treated well in jail, which would probably mean that Mister Adams would have to be separated from the general population, which will cost the state more money and will unduly punish my client further by subjecting him to isolation. And a vigorous defense will require Mister Adams to participate in the planning of that defense, while being in jail will impede that process. It is our belief that justice demands that Mister Adams be released on his own recognizance with the conditions we have laid out. Thank you, your honor."

"Mister Carlton?" The judge showed no emotion.

"Your honor, much of what Mister Tucker has said is true. However, we are talking about murder, the most serious charge possible. Even a famous person might risk everything to avoid a trial in which he could be found guilty of such an offense. This isn't some frivolous charge. It's one based on facts, with one big fact being Mister Adams threatened the victim just hours before he was found dead. While there may have to be special accommodation for Mister Adams in custody because of his fame, that's not a reason that he should be allowed the liberty that might tempt him to leave the court's jurisdiction— possibly never to return. Mister Adams is famous, it's true, but as Mister Tucker said, he's also rich. Money can make a lot of things happen, including a flight from justice. We believe, as stated in our filings, that Mister Adams should be denied bail and held for trial in the Santa Fe County jail. Thank you, your honor."

The judge made some notes, then appeared to be in thought. He looked out into the court with an unusual calm. It was clear at this point that he'd made up his mind.

"Every accused person has a right to be presumed innocent until proven otherwise. However, no person has the absolute right not to be held for trial where their guilt or innocence can be determined. If the trial was in a matter of days, I wouldn't hesitate to hold the accused until trial, but our system cannot function at that speed and find true justice. It takes time. The longer the time, the more unjust it is to hold someone in jail. We use bail as an inducement to have a person return for their trial, unless they represent a risk to society. I do not believe Mister Adams poses a risk to society. But if a person has the means to leave our jurisdiction, even maybe leaving the country, we cannot release that person without some assurance that they will not flee. I agree the suggestions Mister Tucker has made regarding electronic monitoring and a requirement to stay in Santa Fe until the trial would offer the protections the state needs to ensure that Mister Adams will return for his trial. As further inducement, I will order bail at one million dollars. Once bail requirements have been met, Mister Adams will be released to pre-trial services, who will install and monitor the electronic device. Mister Adams will be required to make regular contact with them as they stipulate. Thank you all. Court adjourned."

The judge rose and left.

"Can I be released today?" Dave sounded desperate to get

out of jail.

"Probably not. I'll post the bail today, but more than likely it'll be tomorrow before you're released. I'll request that you be placed in a private cell. Just stay calm, and you'll be out tomorrow, I'm sure."

Dave still looked very nervous. Deputies came, handcuffed him, and took him back to jail. Linda cried quietly.

"Why don't you take a cab back to the Inn? As soon as I know anything, I'll call you." Tucker comforted Linda as best as he could, but he had limited practice at being nice.

Vincent thought adding the million-dollar bail was excessive, and probably motivated more by the desire to avoid criticism rather than having any real impact on whether Adams ran or not. But since Dave's uncle had millions to spare, it was more of a hassle than a barrier. Tucker had gotten most of what he wanted, and by his expression it was clear that the DA felt like he'd lost. Nonetheless, he could see in Adams' eyes that he was about to explode. Jail is simply not a place for people who aren't used to it.

"Congratulations." Vincent nodded to Tucker.

"Yeah, I guess so. He'll be out pretty soon. Sure thought that judge was going to let him go without bail, though. Minor delay, but Dave is really getting jumpy. I need to get him out, pronto. I'm headed downstairs to arrange bail. Not sure how long it'll take. Are you sticking around?"

"Going to be in the neighborhood. When you're ready to leave, give me a call."

It seemed a good time to visit the local cop bar, given that it was close by. The Crown Bar was more upscale than Vincent had expected. He entered through an impressive ornate wooden door, and once his eyes adjusted he could see the room was large and well-appointed. The actual bar was a massive slab of wood that would have felt right at home in an old western movie. The place was very clean and well-kept. Vincent had been in a lot of bars that had a neglected, rundown feel to them, but this one had clearly had a lot of care, far from the dive atmosphere he'd been expecting. There was a large dining area, too, and since it was approaching noon there were a number of people having lunch. Vincent half suspected he'd been given bad information about this being the local cop hangout.

He grabbed a spot at the massive bar. The bartender noticed him and came over. She was a middle-aged, attractive woman with what he took to be a mischievous gleam in her eyes. Not your normal bar, not your normal bartender.

"What can I get for you today?"

"How about a Coors Light, on tap?"

"You bet." She turned, and very efficiently filled his glass.

"Looks like you do a pretty good lunch business. Must be good food."

"Well, I think so. 'Course, I own the place, so I might be biased." With that, Vincent found himself on the receiving end of a very nice smile. "You have to be some kind of cop. New in town?"

"Why do I have to be some kind of cop?" Vincent gave her his best smile back.

"Instinct."

"Private kind of cop—I'm an investigator. Looking for information. I was told this bar was a favorite for law enforcement."

"Yeah, probably is. My husband was a cop before he was killed, and a lot of his friends still stop by. What kind of information you looking for?"

Vincent gave her a brief version of his history and said he was working for the Adams defense lawyer.

"My name's Vincent Malone."

He extended his hand and she accepted it, shook it.

"Nancy McAllen. Nice to meet you." Her eyes seemed to suggest that maybe it wasn't all that nice. "Let me know if you need another beer."

She returned to the other end of the bar and he watched her go, then got his head back in his work. He was going to have to visit later in the day, see what the evening crowd was like. His phone rang—it was Tucker.

"Ready, I'll be out front."

"That didn't take long."

Vincent had pulled up in front of the courthouse, where Tucker stood waiting.

"No, it didn't. I think posting a million-dollar bond wasn't a normal transaction for the clerk, but she was polite and efficient. I suppose there's some chance he could be released today. Just have to wait and see."

"Do you want to head back to the Inn?"

"Yeah. They said they would call once he was close to being released. The bond lady said the most likely time was in the morning, since he has to go through pre-trial services. Might as well wait at the Inn."

"What did you think of the judge?"

"I liked him. He seemed very engaged in the process. I've been in front of judges before who I swear must be on some kind of drugs, not even paying attention. This guy was on the ball. The bail surprised me, but to be honest, I'm not so sure I wouldn't have done the same thing in his spot. He knew the bail could likely be met by using a bail bondsman anyway, so it was more a gesture to avoid looking like he was doing exactly what I asked. Smart move."

They rode in silence for a while as they both thought about what had happened. Tucker's phone rang as they were pulling into the Inn driveway. "Yes." Tucker listened for some time. "Okay, thanks. We will be there in just a little bit."

"Good news?"

"Yeah. He'll be released in about an hour. The call was from the bond clerk. She said the judge got involved and made sure everything was processed this afternoon so Dave wouldn't have to spend another night in jail. I don't think that means he's on our side, but it definitely means we need to be careful. He's smart, and he'll be really involved in this case. I'll have to limit some of my shenanigans so as not to irritate him, but I think I can do that."

"Let's go get Mister Adams. Should you call his wife and let her know?"

"Yeah. Let's leave first, otherwise she'll want to go with us. I'm not really good with emotional people."

Okay here's an odd thing, I was attracted to Nancy McAllen. What the hell is that? Hadn't thought about a woman in a long time, but there was no doubt an instant attraction, something about her eyes. Probably should stay away from that bar, although, of course, I have to do my job, so I have no choice but to go back. Good rationalization. And this Tucker guy is starting to seem like an actual human. His whole image of being an asshole seems to be slipping. No doubt it's old age—some kind of mental impairment. If this guy really wants to be an asshole, he should be allowed to stay in his comfort zone. Cindy even said he'd offered to pay for all the rooms while they were staying at the Inn, presumably so no one else would be there to disturb their privacy—but still, it was thoughtful, in a way. It's disappointing, actually. You meet a true blue asshole, someone who seems to have the courage of his lack of convictions, and in a matter of days find out he's really nice. Very disturbing.

15

Night Life

The atmosphere along San Francisco Street after dark was different from the daytime tourist frenzy. Fewer people, and a certain air of mystery among the old buildings. The Crown Bar looked closed, but once you passed through the massive wooden doorway there was an active, even boisterous, crowd. These people fit better with the image of the dive Vincent had been expecting. There were a few who were still in uniform. Most were in civilian clothes, but that did nothing to dilute the cop vibe. Vincent headed to the bar like he'd been summoned.

Once seated, he waved over the bartender on duty and ordered a Diet Coke. The time for discipline had arrived—he didn't want to turn into an old drunk. He couldn't quite bring himself to admit that he was giving up booze, but he was going to try.

"Well, Mister Malone, you're back soon." Nancy McAllen gave him a questioning look.

"Nancy, you have a nice bar. How could I stay away?"

"Don't cause any trouble in my bar, Mister Malone. These people are here to relax and forget work—they don't want to be spied on."

Malone gave her a gesture of innocence. "Not interested in causing any problems. And, please, call me Vincent."

She left to help a customer but was smiling as she parted.

"I've heard about you," said a guy on the other side of him.

"How's that?"

"I'm not a cop. I work in city government, I'm an accountant. I don't have any inside information about murder. My biggest secret would be a fifty-dollar discrepancy in the animal control office's petty cash." The man cackled at his own joke—a laugh that made it clear he'd had a few too many. "I've heard your name. Some people think you're the killer. I don't think so, though." He slurred a little, and he'd begun to lean into Vincent as he talked. "Why would the killer be so visible? Just hanging around, waiting to be arrested?" He dropped his voice to a stage whisper. "Don't let them hear you say it, but these cops aren't as bright as they think they are."

"Jimmy, think it might be time to go home," Nancy cut in. She was smiling but her voice was stern. "Don't want that new wife of yours to get upset."

"Yeah, maybe so." Jimmy looked like a kid who had been scolded. "Pay you next time." He got up and left.

"You know all of your customers?"

"Well, it's a small town. And a lot of them are regulars. Jimmy's actually a cousin. Just got married a few months ago to the nicest girl you could ever want to meet. What the hell is wrong with men who will sit at a bar and talk to some stranger about bullshit when they have the loveliest wife in the world waiting for them at home?" Nancy didn't look happy.

"I don't have the answer to that, but it's a common problem." Vincent knew all about the affliction. "Do you think I'm a hired killer?"

Nancy grinned.

"No. You're just a guy who's out of place. I have no idea who killed that guy, but I'll bet you dollars to donuts that it has to do with sex or money, or both. This is an emotional crime, which means the person who did it was involved with the person who died. A wife, a girlfriend, a boyfriend, or some guy who got cheated out of a lot of money."

"Yeah, hired killers are pretty rare. On the other hand, lust and greed are very common, even in a small town like Santa Fe." Vincent put some bills on the bar. "You have a nice bar, Nancy. If this was during my drinking days, I'd probably be a regular. Good night."

Vincent walked out into the fresh night air. It was going to be cold. The free clinic was in the area, and he decided to drop by and see if Santa Claus or Tito were there and had anything to say. As he approached, there seemed to be a commotion. Two men were arguing, and he recognized them both.

"Fuck you. If I find out you're spreading rumors about me, I will kill you." That was Stephen Martinez, and he was threatening Tito Alverez. Martinez stomped off in the other direction without noticing Vincent.

"Good evening, Mister Alverez."

Tito turned and glared at Vincent. "Thanks a lot, asshole. Now Martinez thinks I gave you information about him and that Hamilton woman."

"I didn't tell him anything. Why would he think you were gossiping about him?"

Tito continued to glare. Vincent recognized his building anger, a need to hit something or someone. "Look, Tito, I don't know what's going on between you and Martinez, but I didn't tell him where I got my information. That said, he had to be told that we knew. He couldn't be co-counsel any more, and there was no way to explain that without telling him why. But he must suspect you because of something going on between you two—I never said jack to him."

"Yeah, maybe so. He and I go back some. We're not good friends, might even say we hate each other. Anyway, I should be more cautious who I tell shit to."

Vincent held up his hands, palms out, pleading innocence. "Wasn't trying to cause trouble." Tito turned and headed to the backroom of the clinic. Vincent found a chair and sat to wait a bit. He didn't see Santa Claus, and after a while he got the feeling that Tito had left through a back door.

"Well, Mister Malone, looking for a free meal or a flu shot?" Nancy was standing behind him.

"Following me, are you?" Vincent didn't know why she was there, but he knew it wasn't because she was following him.

"Nope." She smiled. "Surprised to see you here. Not exactly on the tourist maps. You investigating someone here?"

"Just general snooping. I'm a very curious person. And I'm surprised to see *you* here."

"My uncle runs the place. I brought him his dinner." She

held up a to-go bag. "Maybe you've seen him, guy with a long white beard."

"Santa Claus is your uncle?"

Nancy laughed.

"Yep that's him. A lot of people call him Santa Claus, and he doesn't mind. His real name's Butch Collins. He's my dad's brother. He raised me when my parents died. I was ten, and without him I wouldn't be here today. So, you be nice to Santa." She smiled that great smile, though her eyes still held sadness.

"Are you related to everyone in this town?"

"No. But my family and my husband's family have lived here for a lot of years, so there are lots of connections. Might not be related to everyone, but I bet I know someone who knows someone who's related. Most small towns are like that. That's why you have to be good, otherwise someone will tell on you." She gave him a sly smile that he hadn't seen before.

Butch came out of the back and walked briskly toward them.

"Thanks, Nancy. See you've met our new town investigator, Mister Malone."

Butch didn't sound happy, and Vincent suspected it had to do with Tito and Martinez.

"Tito thinks I did something I didn't do. He can be angry at me if he wants, but I'm not the one who created his problem."

"What are you two talking about?" Nancy was concerned.

Butch took the to-go bag and shrugged. "Oh, not much. Guess Tito gave Mister Malone some information and now thinks that was a mistake. It's nothing to worry about." He was smiling, obviously wanting to move the conversation on to a new subject.

"Think I'll call it an evening. Nice to see you again, Nancy." Vincent looked at Butch. "Tell Tito I didn't do anything with the info he gave me other than what I already said. He's got no reason to be mad at me—neither do you, for that matter. See ya."

Vincent left, but he could feel the eyes on his back.

"What happens now?" Dave Adams was sitting in the dining room of the Inn with his uncle—or his lawyer, depending how you wanted to look at it—sipping a large glass of Crown Royale. He'd spent some time with his wife after he was released, and was feeling a little better, although he was still upset.

"There will be several court hearings over the next few weeks. In one of those, a trial date will be set. My guess would be about two months out, although it all depends on the court docket and availability. A murder trial takes a lot of time, so they'll have to have a large block of time, or move things around." Peter Tucker had trouble feeling comfortable around his client. He wasn't comfortable with most people, but in this case their troubled personal history added to his difficulties. He tried to be very careful with what he said to Dave, and wanted to keep him calm.

"Shit, months? I can't stay here for months. I'll go nuts.

We need to go home. Linda's a wreck. She won't last two months—she'll just leave."

"Dave, I really do know this is difficult. But you and Linda need to stay calm and try to relax. We've got Malone working on finding new information so, hopefully, we'll be able to point the sheriff's investigator in a new direction and end this before a trial."

"Malone—the *van driver*? My god, is that the best we can do? I thought you were some kind of fuckin' hotshot lawyer, but the best help you can get us is the fuckin' van driver?"

"Why don't you just yell at me, Dave?" Tucker snapped. "I'm sure that'll make everything better."

"Okay. Yeah, okay. I shouldn't yell, sorry. But really, is he the best we can do? What do we even know about him?" Dave took a gulp of his drink. He knew he was on edge, because he was scared. He felt trapped in a nightmare.

"I checked him out. I know it's unusual, but he really is good, as long as he's not drinking. He's already found out some things that might help us. I can bring in other people, but right now I think he's our best shot at finding something that could point to an alternative suspect."

"Well, someone killed him. Why do the cops think it's me?"

"Are you serious? You threatened him in front of a whole mob of people. You had motive and opportunity—you were *there*, at his *house*. Vincent thinks they got you on the security video arguing with Hamilton. He was alive when you left, so obviously the security camera won't show you killing him. If they had that, you'd still be in jail. So, something happened to the security equipment, someone either turned it off or tampered with it. Something happened after you left, and then Hamilton was killed, but the cops have no evidence who that was, so you were their best bet. They arrested you, and now they're not looking for anyone else."

"What has the ace detective found out?" Dave's words were a little slurred.

Peter gave him a stern look.

"I'm not your enemy, and neither is Vincent."

He told Dave about Stephen Martinez and Ann Hamilton.

Dave started to laugh. He laughed so hard he was soon coughing.

"So, my local lawyer was having an affair with the wife of the man I supposedly killed, and he isn't even a suspect. How did Vincent uncover that gem?"

"I'm not sure, but when Martinez was confronted, he confessed to the affair."

Dave poured another drink.

"Has anyone talked to the wife? Is she still in Santa Fe?"

"She left town almost immediately after her husband's body was found, and went back to L.A. Vincent is going out there to interview her in the next day or two." Peter paused. "Getting drunk is not going to make things any better." He wanted to help his nephew, but he could also see that he was not an easy man to like. Maybe it was genetic; ran in the family.

"Well that's what I'm going to do—get drunk and pass

out. Otherwise I might actually kill someone." Dave grabbed his glass and headed to his room.

Peter turned off the lights and sat in the dark. Dave was going to be hard to defend. If he put him on the stand, the jury might dislike him. Whether it should or not, that kind of thing could affect a verdict. He had no idea yet how to nudge the outcome in the right direction, and it worried him. If they—and that mostly meant Vincent—couldn't find a better suspect, Dave could easily be found guilty. He poured a large drink for himself and decided he would get drunk, too.

16

Give 'Em Hell

Vincent was in the kitchen helping Mary with breakfast—or, more accurately, watching her make breakfast. Her breakfast burritos smelled delicious.

"Where are Jerry and Cindy?"

"I think they went to town to buy some supplies. And to meet with a new attorney."

"Have you seen any of the guests this morning?"

"Both the women were up early and had coffee and muffins. Mrs. Turner went back to her room, and Mrs. Adams went for a walk. The burritos are for the men, if they get up. I think Mister Adams and Mister Tucker stayed up pretty late. There might have been some drinking, too, based on the glasses they left out." Mary finished rolling up a couple of burritos and offered them to Vincent. He didn't hesitate, and took them outside to enjoy the cool morning and wonderful food.

The first burrito disappeared in a flash—it was very good. If Jerry could ever get this place organized and running like a real business, it could be successful, he thought as he sat down at one of the small patio tables. He looked up and saw Arenado sitting in the gazebo, just where he'd been the other day.

"Got an extra burrito—want one?"

Vincent wanted it for himself, but it was a good way to open the conversation.

"No, thanks. Not real hungry." He was obviously agitated and didn't seem to like having his private thoughts interrupted by Vincent yet again. "Think I'm headed out this afternoon. Can I get a lift to the airport in Albuquerque?"

"Shouldn't be a problem. Jerry's out running some errands this morning. I'll check with him as soon as I can, but I'm sure it'll be okay. Headed home?"

"Nah, think I will go to L.A. There's a new training center there that I hear is really something. Lots of high-tech stuff I want to check out."

"Did you know anyone named Ryan who's connected with Hamilton?"

"Sure. Ryan Lewis was his attorney."

"Were you around Ann Hamilton much?"

Troy chuckled.

"You're really something. Look, I didn't kill Mark, and I wasn't screwing his wife. Go find someone else to annoy, okay?"

Troy got up and walked away—he never did say whether he was around Ann much. It had just been a wild stab, but it seemed like Vincent might have hit something. It seemed safe to assume Mrs. Hamilton had a very active sex life, and he'd delayed the inevitable trip to see her long enough. He went inside and called the airline.

⎯◯⎯

"Hey, Vincent. Just chatted with Troy Arenado, says you're a real asshole and he's leaving. He also said those two things were not connected, and he wants you to take him to the Albuquerque airport." Jerry tilted his head, as if trying to see if Vincent really was an asshole.

"Sorry about that. I hit a nerve I wasn't aiming for. He was already leaving before I annoyed him. I'll get the van ready." Vincent gave Jerry a shrug as he headed out.

Once Troy's luggage was loaded, they started out.

"Look, Troy—sorry if I pissed you off. I wasn't implying anything, I'm just curious about Ann. Seems so odd she left almost immediately after her husband was killed."

"It's okay. She's the most beautiful woman I've ever seen, but it's all on the outside. Inside, she's not lovely at all. She came on to me, and I was actually shocked. I considered her and Mark good friends at the time, and I told her I didn't approve. She gave me one of those evil smiles of hers and went and told Mark that I'd attacked her, damn near raped her. He and I argued, but did not come to blows. After that, I stayed away from them. I don't know if that had anything to do with him trying to cheat me on that contract—all I can say is neither one of them was very nice."

They traveled the remainder of the trip in silence. Alone on the way back, Vincent opened the window and smoked. He knew it was going to kill him, but there were days he just didn't give a shit.

When he pulled into the driveway of the Inn, he saw Detective Sanchez leaning up against his car. Vincent parked and walked over.

"Detective."

"Malone. Got some news for you and Tucker. Saw Jerry and he said you'd be back soon, so I just waited. Guess I wanted to make sure you came back." Sanchez didn't smile. "The financial guy who supposedly stole all of the money was found dead this morning in New York. Hit in the head with something heavy. Still had all his possessions; nothing stolen. He was in an alley in a neighborhood you wouldn't just wander into. They think maybe he was meeting someone, and the meeting didn't go well."

"Must be karma."

"Yeah, I'm sure. I'm getting word that you've been snooping around. When I told you I didn't want you doing any investigative work, I meant it."

Vincent tensed—what total bullshit. He'd been in this same situation too many times to count, and one of these times he was going to pop.

"Still a free country, even in Santa Fe. I'm gathering information for my client, who's representing a man charged with murder. I'm sure the judge would be interested to know that you don't believe a guy in his client's position has a right to a defense."

Sanchez nodded while giving Vincent the eye. "This case will be over soon. I'd advise you to not stay in Santa Fe after the trial."

Vincent edged a bit closer to Sanchez. He was a very big man—Sanchez was not.

"Detective, fuck you."

Sanchez's face lost color, and he pulled back. "You're asking for trouble. This isn't some big city with big-city games. This is my town. And if I have to, I'll nail your ass to the wall." He seemed to think that he'd regained whatever face he'd lost, he turned and left.

Vincent took a deep breath before going into the Inn to find Tucker. He spotted him in the dining room sipping a drink.

"Vincent. Come in and have a drink, and tell me what you know."

The lawyer seemed to be in a good mood, or maybe he had already had a couple.

Vincent passed along the info about Larry Jackson being found dead in New York, and gave Tucker a sanitized version of his conversation with Sanchez.

"Well, well. Looks like someone is taking care of loose ends. Who do you think that could be?"

"The first name that jumps out is Ryan Lewis. He was Hamilton's attorney, and he was the one who recommended the financial guy. So, he seems the most vulnerable to some kind of lawsuit, other than Hamilton. But, of course, no matter what the police think, it could be just random. A guy's in the wrong place at the wrong time, and some shithead kills him for whatever reason—maybe for nothing at all."

"I know it happens, but I'm not a big believer in things being random."

"Lewis was also Ann Hamilton's boyfriend—that is, before she decided that his best friend was a better catch. Lots of tangled webs there.”

“Where is he?”

“L.A.”

“Okay. Well, you need to visit the widow and Lewis, ASAP.”

“Already got my ticket. Headed out late tomorrow. I’m going to call Ann before I go. Any legal reason she should talk to me?”

“Nope. In fact, she probably shouldn’t talk to us.” Tucker paused. “Tell her if she doesn’t meet with you, we’ll get a court order forcing her to come to Santa Fe for a deposition. Whereas, if she cooperates, we might be able to get by with just a discussion.”

“Is it true?”

“I don’t know. If she’s telling the truth, then she didn’t know what was happening that night because she was doped up. But for some reason she seems to be at the center of things, so she may hold a key to all this. I don’t know what—yet. Just bullshit her a little, and see if she’ll meet with you. If not, I’ll request that we depose her. Since she has a home here, I think we can make sure it happens here in Santa Fe. What about the Lewis guy?”

“If he has an office, I’d prefer to just drop in. In my experience, if you give a lawyer warning that you want to see him, he disappears.”

“Sounds about right. Half of all attorneys are lowlifes and the other half are worse.”

"How's Dave doing?" Vincent worried about Adams staying sane while he waited for his trial.

"If it wasn't for Linda, I'm not sure he could hold it together. But she's been great. He's a lucky guy to have such a supportive wife."

The old unmarried loners sighed in unison.

Vincent broke the silence. "Sanchez didn't come all the way out here to let us know about Jackson. He wouldn't get out of his office chair, not to help us. He came out here to give me that warning. The thing is, I don't think he actually cares enough to do that—not on his own. Which means someone sent him."

"The DA or the sheriff?"

"The sheriff. The guy thinks he runs an old west town, told Sanchez to run me out of town. Most likely, he'll make more trouble before this is done. I think it's critical that we get discovery, including exculpatory evidence, now rather than later. I really don't trust the people here to preserve all the evidence. We need that security video so we'll have some idea what was captured and when the system stopped working."

"I've already filed for discovery. We'll have a status hearing the first of next week. My plan was to raise hell if we haven't got discovery by then, but you're right. I need to raise hell now. They haven't given us anything, and I'll make it a point that we want the security video immediately. Thanks for pushing me. I used to have a staff to keep me on my toes, but no more. I'll e-file my request right now, and maybe we can get something before you leave tomorrow." Tucker gulped the remainder of his drink and gave Vincent a wave as he headed to his room.

Vincent filled a glass. He was having trouble understanding why Sanchez had been waiting for him to deliver his stupid message.

"What's going on?" Jerry stood in the doorway.

"Just thinking about the day's events. You should know, Jerry, that Sanchez suggested I get out of town. Pretty sure this has to do with me snooping around, but in some ways, it doesn't make sense. I think I've hit a nerve around here. But I don't know what I did, exactly."

"Could be they just don't like your looks." Jerry was smiling.

"Well, it's true there could be very little thought behind the whole thing—just an instinctive reaction. The part that doesn't seem to fit is that they know I'm working with Tucker and they still tried to strong-arm me. They must know that's like waving a red flag in front of Tucker. He's going to come charging. So, I guess my question is: why do they want him pissed off?"

"I wish I knew more about this town so I could help you, but Cindy and I are new here, like you. It's not like we have any inside information. Although our contractor, a guy named Ray Martin, told us—when he found out we were using Stephen Martinez as our attorney—that Martinez was part of a group that runs the town. He even told me, all hush-hush, that we should be careful how we deal with Martinez. When I asked him what he meant, he said to just be careful. Never did find out anything more specific."

"Well I definitely pissed Martinez off the other day. Maybe that's what this is all about." Vincent hadn't even thought about Martinez being a mover and shaker. "How about a drink? I'm buying." Vincent smiled—it was Jerry's liquor.

"I'm fine. But you go ahead. Have I even paid you anything?" Suddenly Jerry looked concerned.

"Well, not exactly, but based on my free room and board—and other considerations," Vincent saluted Jerry with his glass, "it could be I owe you money."

Way too many damned suspects. And that's just the ones I know about. Could be hundreds more who wanted Hamilton dead for reasons that have nothing to do with Santa Fe or this particular group of clients. Got to get the list whittled down, figure out who definitely didn't do it. Get down to a few likely people and concentrate on them. Is Martinez one? He was having an affair with the available and gorgeous Ann. But why would he kill Hamilton—was he jealous? Did Hamilton even know about Martinez? And how was Tito connected to Martinez? Too many players. Maybe I should start with Dave Adams—is he really innocent? Got to get that security video. One more drink, then I'm off to bed.

17

Who Knew What and When

The pounding on his door sounded angry—not his favorite way to wake up. Vincent glanced at the small clock, which read six a.m. Early, but not absurdly early.

"Just a minute." He grabbed his trousers and pulled on a robe, then paused for just a second to let the dizziness subside. He jerked open the door, ready for a confrontation if one was waiting for him.

"Shit and goddamn it, we've been played for amateur fools. Just look at this!" Tucker stormed into Vincent's tiny room without invitation, a space that Vincent felt was crowded even when he was alone. He examined the document Tucker had handed him.

"Fuck, you've got to be kidding. Have you talked to Adams?"

"No, had to calm down first. I might kill the bastard." Tucker was visibly shaking—not a good sign for an old man.

"Did this just show up?"

"Not sure when, but apparently it was delivered sometime during the night, left on the porch. Jerry just found it." Tucker sat on the bed looking light-headed.

"You okay?"

"Let's go into the dining room. I think I need some water." Tucker was ashen and a little wobbly, but they made it into the dining room and Vincent got him a glass of water.

"So, they're sandbagging us. Any idea why?" Vincent got some coffee and joined Tucker at the small table.

"I think the security video is in with the stuff they delivered. That might answer some questions."

Vincent got up, retrieved the box from the hall by the front door, and brought it back to the dining room. "Yep. We got a thumb drive, that'll be the security video and some other goodies. I'll get my laptop, and we can watch the video."

By the time he got back, Tucker was looking better. Vincent brought a bottle of aspirin and offered it to Tucker. "It'd be real disappointing if you died before the trial."

Tucker took the bottle and got a pill. "Wiseass. Get the video working."

Vincent inserted the USB drive and started the video. The image wasn't high-quality, and the lighting was bad, but they could make out the front yard of the Hamilton house. The camera must have been triggered by movement, since it began as soon as someone entered the frame: Dave Adams.

"No bat," Vincent commented, as the image showed Adams ringing the doorbell. After a moment, Hamilton answered holding the bat. There was no audio, and no way to read their lips with such poor picture quality, but it was obvious they were arguing. After only a few minutes, Hamilton threatened Adams with the bat, Adams reached up and grabbed the bat as they tumbled out into the yard. Adams took the bat from him, and in the struggle the bat hit Hamilton in the head. He seemed stunned, but he continued yelling at Adams, who at that point threw the bat out into the yard and left the camera's field of view. Hamilton got up holding the back of his head and went inside, then shut the front door. The video ended.

Vincent looked at Tucker. "Why would they let us think he was killed by the bat?"

"Don't know. Could be something as stupid as that they thought it was fun."

Tucker was thinking. Vincent grabbed the police report that he'd first looked at in his room.

"It says he was shot. It was in his front yard but they can't pinpoint the time in relation to the video. The gun was recovered and it was registered to Dave Adams." Vincent glanced at Tucker. "Now, here's the real problem—there were no prints on the gun. That's the cause of a lot of the bullshit we're dealing with. They think they have their man, but why would he wipe the gun down and leave it there?"

"Here's another big question: why the hell would our client not tell us that he took a gun when he went to visit Hamilton?"

"I think the obvious answer to that is that he didn't tell us because he *didn't* bring it to Hamilton's. Dave's a pain in the butt, what with his temper, but he's not stupid. If he'd taken a gun there, he would have told us—unless, of course, he actually shot Hamilton. But, even then it wouldn't make sense to leave the gun behind if it's registered to him, prints or no prints. The answer has to be that he wasn't the one who took the gun there. Someone else did."

"Time to wake Dave up and ask him."

Vincent held up his hand, palm out, to indicate that he would go and get Adams. He went down the hall, returning in a few minutes. "He's getting up. Wasn't happy about it, though. Sorry, Tucker—nephew or not, the guy's a bit of a dick."

"I know. I have no idea how he missed out on my natural charm."

The wisecrack didn't require a response, and they waited in silence.

"What the hell's going on now?" Adams more or less growled the question.

"The police report says that Hamilton was shot," Tucker said. "That's what killed him. He had a minor injury to his head from the blow with the bat, but that happened before he was shot. The gun was found at the scene and it's registered to you. Did you have a gun with you when you went to see Hamilton?"

"What the hell? I thought he was killed with that bat."

"No, he was shot with your gun."

"Fuck, no. My gun is in my room. I didn't take it with me—I wasn't about to shoot him, for Christ's sake."

Vincent chimed in. "Unless you have more than one handgun registered to you, I don't think the gun is in your room."

Adams jumped up and headed down the hall. Vincent and Tucker waited in silence.

"Shit, shit, shit. It's not there. My god, they're going to hang me, aren't they?"

"Tell us again what happened that night."

"It's the same as before, nothing has changed. I've already told you!"

"One more time." Tucker spoke softly, as if to a small child.

"I was drunk, so everything is a little fuzzy. I went out to his house, and rang the doorbell. He came to the door carrying that stupid bat. We argued, I called him names. I think he was drunk, too, and he called me names. He raised the bat, and I grabbed it. We struggled over the bat, and I pulled it away. He might have hit his head or something, but anyway, he fell down. I tossed the bat out into the yard, called him some more names, and left. As I was leaving, I saw him get up and go back into his house. That's it. He was alive when I left, and I didn't go back."

"We just watched that on the security video and it hap-pened exactly the way you described it. Then the video ended. The cops didn't give us any more video, so either there is none, or they're hiding it." Vincent didn't bother with the soft, kiddie voice. He was getting sick of the guy making a scene. "Who knew you had a gun with you?"

Dave took a deep breath.

"Well, Linda did, of course. And that first night, I was talking to a some of the guests about security, with all the crazy fans and everything, and I said that I'd started carrying a gun when we didn't fly commercial. I really don't remember who was in that group—might have been all the men."

Tucker spoke up. "Have you said anything to the detective or any deputies about anything to do with that night?"

"No. Anytime they asked me, I said I wanted you present. So, we never had any conversation. I kept expecting them to try to pressure me into it, but it never happened."

Vincent thought that was odd. Adams had a right to have his lawyer present, but the cops also had a right to question him. They didn't— just charged him, anyway. Very odd.

Jerry came in. "Fresh coffee, and we'll have some muffins in just a little bit." He glanced at Vincent, refreshed the coffeepot, and left.

"I just remembered something. This may be useless, because I was drunk and very mad. But when I walked back to the car, I had a feeling there was someone there, in the trees. There was movement or something that caught my eye. But when I looked over that way, I didn't see anything. I was sure there was something there, though."

Vincent nodded to Adams. For whatever reason, Vincent believed him, probably because he'd already decided Adams hadn't killed Hamilton. If he'd been going to kill him, he would have just done it when they fought, consequences be damned, video camera be damned. That's what most people do. They don't think about consequences when they kill. They just do it on impulse, emotionally. So, another person being there actually made sense. If Dave hadn't done it, someone else must have been around—but who?

"Dave, I believe you. Someone else did this." He gave

Dave a reassuring look. "But it had to be someone who had access to your gun. That's one issue. The other big issue is this: I don't think the cops are protecting some murderer who was caught on tape just so they can frame you. That means there actually isn't any video of the murder—at least if it happened there, and the cameras were still working. Someone turned them off or messed with the recordings, and either way, they'd need access to the house. We need to go over everything the cops gave us, and see if there's anything that might point to how the security system was disabled."

Linda came in, looking worried. Dave took her into the small meeting room and shut the door, presumably to give her an update on what was going on. When they re-emerged, it was obvious Linda had been crying, but she was also ready to fight.

"I'm a pretty detail-oriented person. If I can help in any way, going through that stuff, then I want to do it."

"Thanks, Linda, we can always use your help." Tucker said. Then he stood and gave her a hug. She seemed shocked—so did Tucker.

Vincent pulled him aside and got things back on track.

"Think I'll postpone that trip to L.A. Ann hasn't called back yet, so I don't even know if she's actually there. And the more we can learn here, the better my chance of getting something useful out of the meeting when I do see her."

"I agree." Tucker nodded. "Although, if you can't get her to return your call in the next few days, I want to start the process of legally compelling her to come here for a deposition.

So, keep me posted."

"Since we're having trouble with the sheriff's department and DA screwing us around on the discovery, I think I'll run into Santa Fe and go to the cop bar. See if I can't get a handle on whether this is just normal for the small town good ol' boys, or something special, just for us."

With a slight salute to Tucker, Vincent headed to the kitchen to see if Jerry or anyone needed something while he was out.

"No, I think we're okay. I know you can't tell me what's going on, but it looked like some bad news out of that front-porch box."

Vincent smiled at Jerry's curiosity. "Obviously, I can't discuss details about the case. But, you're right, it wasn't good news. The sheriff's department or the DA kept some critical information from us, which isn't playing by the rules. So, we've got some things to figure out and to try to explain. What have you heard about the sheriff's department since you've been here?"

"Nothing, really. Ray Martin once told me that the Santa Fe Police Department and the sheriff's department seemed to always be in some kind of feud. But he thought it was just the leaders—that the actual cops were pretty good."

"Interesting. Thanks, Jerry. See you later."

As Vincent drove to the Crown Bar, he chuckled at how stupid newcomers can be. He hadn't even known there *was* a Santa Fe Police Department. And since everybody else knew, they assumed you knew, too, so they never bothered to tell you.

He tried to remember if he'd seen police cars with different markings and realized he had, but hadn't really paid attention. A trained professional investigator overlooking the obvious— maybe he wouldn't bring that up to Tucker.

Now, if there was a police department, there had to be a police chief, and it seemed like that was someone he should meet.

18

Sheriffs and Chiefs

Vincent left the van at the Inn in case it was needed, taking his Mustang instead. Besides, the old car needed a few miles on the road to keep it limber. He parked on the street just down from the Crown Bar, and stepped out into a cool drizzle. There weren't many tourists out, given the light rain. It was okay with him, though—it fit his mood.

"Well, look who's back. Mister Malone. What can I get you?" Nancy was smiling, but seemed on edge.

"How 'bout some coffee?"

"Bar coffee's not known for its quality. Why don't you treat me to a good cup at that little coffee shop a couple doors down the street?" She gave him a forced smile.

Vincent wasn't sure what was happening, but he would go along with it—whatever it was.

"Sure, let's go."

It was a short walk, and the drizzle had let up. Once seated, they ordered coffee and were treated to some great-smelling brew served in oversize ceramic cups. They both sipped at their drinks and smiled. The shop was cozy and warm, but the mood wasn't.

"I'm hearing you've made some enemies," Nancy said. "The sheriff and Detective Sanchez, mostly."

"Yeah, that's true. Seems as though for some reason they don't want me to be a long-term Santa Fe resident."

"I was afraid of that. Sanchez is an okay guy, but the sheriff is a moron. Sheriff Ortega's answer to a lot of things is to run people out of town. He's a bully, and he's dangerous. I know where this is coming from—it has to do with Stephen Martinez. Tito probably regrets telling you about Martinez and that Hamilton woman—but he did, and it's the truth. Anybody paying any attention could have seen that something was going on. They weren't very private about it. The person who should be run out of town is Martinez. The guy's married, with three kids. My god, what a jerk. But he and his family are very well-connected. You asked me once if I was related to everyone in town. Well, I'm not, but Martinez is. I swear, he really is related to half the town, and his family is friends with the other half, including Ortega. Martinez's father is a big rancher with huge land holdings up by Espanola. The family has a lot of money, and they've backed Ortega in every election, with votes and cash. He's going to protect Martinez even if he doesn't know from what."

"Why are you telling me this?"

"I live here. This is my hometown. Ortega and people like him are clannish. He sees everyone who isn't part of his team as an enemy. His corruption and everything about him goes against what I believe. This is a town all about diversity, and Ortega and his antics just piss me off." Nancy had raised her voice and several heads turned. "Sorry," she said more quietly.

"Thanks for telling me. I don't really matter too much, one way or another. Running me out of town might be their civic duty." Vincent smiled to help ease the tension. "But, Sanchez—and, I guess, the sheriff—are playing a dangerous game by trying to mislead the defense on the Adams case. They're messing with one tough lawyer, who will raise more hell than anything they've ever seen."

"You need to go see Police Chief Stanton. You might not know about our crazy quilt of law enforcement around here, but there's the Santa Fe Police Department, which has jurisdiction over the town of Santa Fe, and there's the Santa Fe County Sheriff's Department. The county's huge, and the sheriff's staff is more than twice that of the police. As bad as Sheriff Ortega is, the chief is that good. Brad Stanton is pretty young, in his late thirties, and he was an assistant chief in Albuquerque. He is a complete professional, the opposite of Ortega. Where the murder happened, and for that matter, where the new B&B is located, are in the county, not the city, so the chief would have no jurisdiction. But he'd still be a good person to meet, and I think he'd be sympathetic."

"Thanks, Nancy. I know it's not easy trusting a stranger. Maybe we could have dinner sometime?"

He hadn't planned the words. They'd just popped out. Nancy stared at him way too long, a neutral, appraising kind of look.

"You're an interesting man, Vincent Malone. But I have a feeling you would be a lot of trouble. Not sure I'm interested in trouble at this point in life." Her look softened, though. "Maybe just once, to see how you behave."

"Yes, ma'am. I understand. I'll be on my best behavior." They chuckled, but there was a serious undertone. They both recognized the danger signs.

Vincent walked Nancy back to the Crown and said he would call. She nodded and went inside. Just a few months ago he'd been a broken man, facing solitude and depression, and now there was romance in the air. Even at his age, you had to stay alert in case, just once in a while, something good came along—life could surprise you. He walked briskly to his car.

Vincent waited in the reception area of the SFPD, hoping to see Chief Stanton. He decided he'd give it another ten minutes, but he wasn't going to sit there all day. Just then a tall, distinguished-looking man with prematurely white hair walked out.

"Sorry for that delay, Mister Malone. Please come in." Stanton shook Vincent's hand firmly, then directed him toward an office.

"Thanks for seeing me. Sorry to just drop in, but I wanted to introduce myself."

"Well, Mister Malone, I happen to know who you are, and I'm glad you dropped by. While not in my jurisdiction, I'm aware of the Adams case, and very interested in how it goes. We don't have a lot of murders here. So, when one of our prominent residents gets killed, even a part-time resident, it gets a lot of attention."

Vincent had already decided, based on Nancy's recommendation, to be honest with the chief about his circumstances, and after meeting the man, his own instincts were telling him this was someone he could level with. He explained the fluke that had led him to get involved with Tucker on the Adams case, giving the chief a condensed version of his background.

"I wasn't looking to be an investigator here. I just was more or less biding my time as a driver when this happened. Thought I could be a help to Tucker, and he agreed. But I did want to stop by and introduce myself, just in case my nosing around a bit was stepping on someone's toes." Vincent wasn't very comfortable soft-pedaling things so much, but he was trying to be on his best behavior.

"I don't see a problem with you asking questions and helping out a lawyer. But there's a requirement in New Mexico for anyone who wants to be a private investigator to register with the state and get a license. Might want to look into that just to cover your bases."

"I'll get that done, chief. I was registered in Colorado, and I think that license transfers to New Mexico without any conditions, but I'll make sure it's all squared away." Vincent took a deep breath. "Look, I've ruffled a few feathers. Mostly Detective Sanchez, and I guess, indirectly, Sheriff Ortega."

"I've heard those rumbles. My opinion is that Sanchez is a good detective, but dominated by the sheriff, who's a little over the edge. We all have to work together, me and them, so all I'll say is that you should be careful around the sheriff. He can be impulsive." The chief leaned forward in a conspiratorial manner. "He runs the sheriff's department with an iron fist, and he definitely doesn't like outsiders."

"Well that fits with what I'm seeing. I haven't actually met the sheriff, yet. All my dealings have been with Sanchez. The problem is connected to one of your leading citizens—Stephen Martinez. I picked up information that indicated he might have been having an affair with Ann Hamilton, the wife of the guy who was killed. At that time, Martinez was acting as co-council with Peter Tucker, representing Dave Adams. Tucker asked me to notify Martinez he wasn't welcome in court as part of the defense team, and from there things got ugly."

The police chief smiled, chuckling to himself.

"Yeah, I had heard about some of that, including the affair. I'm guessing your contact was Tito Alverez."

"Yep. I paid him for the info. He thinks I told Martinez where I heard about the affair, but I didn't. Anyway, now Tito's mad at me—I guess Martinez confronted him. How are they connected, anyway?"

"You may think this isn't fair, but even though it's okay for me to get information from you, I can't give you information about the citizens here."

Vincent chuckled.

"Yeah, well, that's not only not fair, it's not true. You and I both know you can tell me anything you want, but you don't want to at this point because you don't know if you can trust me."

"You're a thoughtful man, Mister Malone. Who knows how we may be able to work together in the future? For now, though, I should tell you that Tito is more than he seems. Living on the street is his choice—if he wanted to, he could probably have a very nice house in Santa Fe. And in some distant past, he might even be related to Martinez." The chief grinned. "Tito's originally from San Francisco, but he settled down here. I've heard that Martinez has had Tito work for him in various jobs, mostly related to his real estate business."

"Not sure I'd want to live in a town where most everyone is related to me. I'm more comfortable being anonymous. Maybe that's just a nice way of saying I'm sneaky."

"Or maybe you have a guilty conscience?"

Vincent held up his hands in surrender. "You got me, chief."

They shook hands and agreed to stay in touch. The chief reminded Vincent to make sure he registered with the state, and gave him the name of the agency that would take care of it. Vincent stopped by the licensing bureau, and they were able to locate his Colorado license. With surprising efficiency, and for only a small fee, they transferred it to New Mexico and gave him a letter with his brand-new New Mexico PI license number. The whole thing seemed to him like a bureaucratic waste of time, but it was still oddly reassuring to have the state recognize him as a real PI. With a new bounce in his step, he headed to his car.

Next stop was something he was dreading. He'd looked up the address for an urgent care clinic and it was time to stop in and see if they had some kind of medication he could take for his gout. Luckily, he hadn't had a serious attack since Denver, but it couldn't last. The wait at the clinic was brief, and soon he saw a doctor, a small, round woman who smiled altogether too much.

"Gout, huh? Well, there are several things we could do. First, you can change your lifestyle. Stop drinking alcohol, eat more vegetables, cut back on red meat, and exercise more. That should reduce the incidents over time." When he stared at her blankly, she went on. "Okay, well, something else we can try is a medication that will reduce the uric acid in your system. It's a maintenance program, so you'd have to take it for the rest of your life. The first approach is healthier and cheaper, though. What do you think?"

After a quick medical exam, Vincent paid his bill and left with a prescription for a lifetime of medicine.

It looks like my stupid macho avoidance of doctors was counterproductive. I could have been taking medication back in Denver, and not had gout, and kept my clients. What a dumbass. Maybe it's okay, though. I was burned out, doing the same thing for the same client, over and over, my life going nowhere in particular each day—except that much closer to dying. Plus, the way I was drinking back then probably would have made the medicine useless, anyway. Smile and be happy, you dumb shit—life's not so bad.

19

Hi Ho! Hi Ho!
It's Off To Court We Go

Vincent woke up early from a restless night's sleep. He'd been thinking about Nancy, the case, the police chief, his medicine—everything seemed to be changing at once, and it made him nervous. He was someone who liked routine—Mister Rut.

"Morning, Vincent."

"Morning, Tucker. Is the status hearing this morning?"

"Yep. Might be good if you're there. The new local attorney will be there—you might want to meet him. Also, I requested through the judge that Sanchez be present. The DA filed an objection. But I have a feeling the judge sided with us on the issue."

"Adams going with you?"

"He's not required to be present for this kind of hearing, and he doesn't want to go. Might be for the best. The guy's getting surlier by the day."

"Okay, just let me know when you're ready to go. I'm all set." Vincent went and got himself some coffee and what appeared to be a blueberry scone. He joined Bud and Vickie Turner, who were just finishing.

"How're you feeling?" Vincent asked Vickie. He hadn't seen her in several days. Bud had said she wasn't feeling well, but he hadn't given any details. She answered shyly.

"I'm fine. Thank you." Then she stood and left. It was a little abrupt, but maybe she was still ill.

"Sorry," Bud apologized. "My wife still isn't a hundred percent. I think we'll head home tomorrow. I've already made the other arrangements, but could you take us to the airport in the morning? We need to be there about ten."

"Sure, shouldn't be any problem. How's your arm?" Bud had been using a sling the last few days.

"Oh, it's fine. Just a stupid accident—bumped into the door. Everything's fine now." He got up to leave.

"You were pretty upset with Hamilton when he told everyone about the missing money, almost as much as Adams. Did the cops talk to you about where you were the night he was killed?"

Anger flashed in Bud's eyes, although he kept his expression neutral.

"I don't have to answer your questions, asshole."

"Did Vickie get her money back?"

"Piss off." Bud started to leave.

"Why are you so mad at me?"

Vincent wasn't goading. He actually wanted to know. But Bud left. Vincent went over to Tucker's table and sat down. "Guy's not very friendly."

"Yeah. Seems a little over the top. Could be he just doesn't like people asking him questions. But, before you showed up, he and his wife were having a very quiet, whispered argument. I think it was about leaving. If looks could kill, they'd both be dead. Might want to find out a little more about them."

"Yeah, will do."

"I'm going to my room. We should be ready to leave in about thirty minutes."

Tucker left, and Vincent took his dishes into the kitchen. Jerry was busy preparing what looked like a Bundt cake.

"You're turning into a damn good baker. Your scones are absolutely delicious."

Jerry beamed. "Thanks. Mary's actually the chef around here. I made those, but she showed me how."

"Bud Turner asked me to take him and his wife to the airport tomorrow, need to be there about ten. That okay?"

"Sure. What's happening today in court?"

"It's a status hearing. The judge basically asks both sides how everything's progressing, to see if there are any problems. Tucker's going to raise hell about discovery because someone's not giving the defense everything they should—either the sheriff's department or the DA. It took them days to give us what we should have had within hours, and nothing since then. The judge may explode and threaten the prosecutors and their lackeys, or he could tell Tucker to shut up and be patient. If you don't know the particular judge, it's hard to know which way they'll go. We think this judge is going to lower the boom on the DA, but that may be wishful thinking." Vincent smiled.

"Is Dave going?" Jerry looked worried.

"No, he doesn't have to be there and he decided he didn't

want to go."

Jerry eyed Vincent. "Don't know whether you or Mister Tucker know this, but Dave's about ready to explode. My impression is that he's wound up tight, and the slightest thing could set him off."

"Is he causing any trouble?" Vincent was concerned for Jerry and Cindy. He knew Dave was a tragedy waiting to happen, but it hadn't occurred to him before that Jerry and Cindy might end up being collateral damage.

"No real trouble. Matter of fact, he and I have sort of become friends. I'm not worried about us, so don't change anything on our account. But I can see that he can't take much more uncertainty. He could even take off. Not sure he's thinking straight."

"Well, that would be a huge mistake. We're following up a lot of possibilities about who might have killed Hamilton. If he does something stupid, it'll create a real mess for him. He'd be violating his bail, and it would make him look guilty. Maybe I should talk to him."

"No. Let me. What you and Tucker should do is keep him more informed. I get the feeling that his uncle's so concerned about his state of mind that he's not telling him much, but that's just making things worse. He may not know you're working on stuff, or that you've got other potential suspects. It'd probably help him to know that."

"You're right. I'll talk to Tucker. Thanks, that's very good input." Vincent nodded and Jerry smiled.

As he and Tucker were driving into Santa Fe, Vincent

explained what Jerry had told him.

"Probably need to give Dave more info so he can see that things aren't completely hopeless."

Tucker looked sad.

"Yeah, that's my fault. He's so hard to talk to. He's angry all the time, and maybe I'm too sensitive regarding his state of mind. Need to treat him more like a normal client and stop worrying about his feelings. It's kind of amazing, really. The guy is this huge, badass pitcher, but sometimes I treat him like a baby. I've tried to shield him and Linda from all of the details to protect them, but I guess that's not the right way to go. They need to know what's going on. So, we'll start tonight, give them a full update on everything."

"Good."

There was an unusually large crowd for a status hearing. Of course, a murder trial, even a status hearing, wasn't usual. As they entered, Vincent spotted Detective Sanchez in the back, giving him the evil eye. Martinez was there, too, but he avoided any eye contact.

"Mister Tucker, my name's Curtis Howard. I'm a partner at Martinez, Howard and Fitch. I'd be pleased to act as the local attorney in this matter, if that works for you."

Tucker looked hard at Howard.

"Curtis, I don't know you and I don't really give a shit about you or your firm. Your partner handled this badly, and I can cause him problems if I want to. The main reason I don't isn't because he deserves a break. It's because it would be a waste of my time. If you being here is part of some scheme to cause me or my client some kind of trouble, you can fuck off and I'll discuss local representation with the judge. It'd cause a little delay while I bring in someone else from Albuquerque, but I can live with that."

Howard looked offended.

"I can stay or leave, that's up to you. I have no reason to interfere with you or this case. I'm here because our firm agreed to assist you in this matter."

Tucker looked at him without emotion.

"So, stay."

The DA entered, nodded toward Tucker, and took his seat. The bailiff called for everyone to rise, the judge stalked in, and court was called into session. The judge covered some court scheduling details, then asked Tucker if he had any issues he wanted to raise.

"Your honor, I very reluctantly must request your assistance in getting the discovery we need to prepare our defense. I have no idea if it's just incompetence on the part of the sheriff's department, or some strategy by the district attorney's office to interfere in our defense, but it's ridiculous."

The DA had shot to his feet as if there were a spring in his seat, then waited, red-faced, for his turn to speak.

"Your honor, I object very strenuously to Mister Tucker's characterization of things."

The judge held up a hand, demanding silence from both men.

"Give me the details, Mister Tucker. No need for hyperbole."

Tucker explained when they'd received the initial discovery. Then he handed the judge a list of items and details they hadn't received yet—it was extensive. The judge reviewed the information while everyone waited.

"Mister Carlton, I know you to be a capable attorney and very professional. Can you explain why this information hasn't been given to the defense in a timely manner?"

DA Carlton stood, slowly this time, and began a long explanation that seemed to be centered on a lack of staff. He also claimed that he hadn't been aware that the sheriff's department hadn't been following his explicit orders, but from the look on the judge's face that wasn't going to do him much good. Before he could finish, the judge interrupted.

"There are no acceptable excuses. I will hold you, and I mean you, personally, Mister Carlton, in contempt if you do not deliver to the defense *today* all the information that should have already been forthcoming from the sheriff's department and your office. I'll name the sheriff, too, if there's any delay. Is that clear?"

Carlton looked unhappy, and it seemed to Vincent, from his body language, like he might genuinely not have known about the lack of disclosure until now. There was going to be some serious trouble behind the scenes after the hearing.

"I will ensure that it's done today, your honor."

"Anything else?" the judge asked.

Tucker was back in action. "Your honor, I'd like to request assistance in serving a subpoena on Ann Hamilton, the wife of the victim. We've tried on numerous occasions to make contact with her to arrange a time to conduct a deposition, but she hasn't responded. She's returned to L.A., and we don't have the resources available to track her down. We ask for the assistance of the court in compelling her to come to Santa Fe for this deposition, which we consider critical."

"Mr. Carlton, are you in contact with Mrs. Hamilton?"

"No, your honor. We've tried to contact her, as well, to conduct an interview, but she hasn't responded to us, either. We join in the request that she be ordered by the court to make herself available in Santa Fe. In that regard, your honor, it should be noted that she owns a house here, and is a part-time resident, so the court has jurisdiction to require her to travel here for any matters related to the trial."

"So ordered. Anything else, gentlemen?"

"To ensure things move quickly," Tucker rose to reply, "we have a list of people we'd like to depose in advance of the trial. Two are obvious: Mrs. Hamilton and Ryan Lewis, who are both, as far as we know, in Los Angeles. Neither has shown any interest in participating in this proceeding. I believe a deposition is the best way to preserve their testimony for trial. Our other request is unusual, and we ask for your indulgence. We'd like to depose Detective Sanchez. We find the information provided by the sheriff's department regarding statements taken during their investigation to be incomplete, and we're concerned that there may be an attempt to withhold critical information."

Carlton was back to his feet immediately.

"Objection, your honor. Seriously. We may be running a

little behind schedule on discovery, but Mister Tucker's hinting at some kind of wild conspiracy to withhold information. That's outlandish—there's simply no evidence to support such an extreme accusation."

"It *is* a little strong, Mister Tucker. What's the basis for your request to depose the detective?"

"We've been able to interview some of the people involved, and what they've told us doesn't line up with the documentation from the sheriff's department. We believe they're omitting salient facts, whether deliberately or through incompetence. The sheriff's department has been openly hostile to our inquires, threatening to run my investigator out of town for simply doing his job. We need to have complete information regarding the night of the crime and any subsequent investigation. The easiest and quickest way for us to resolve any issues, without creating delays once the trial begins, is to depose the detective."

"Mr. Carlton, conspiracies aside, that sounds reasonable to me. Any objections you may have to their questions; you can raise at the deposition. What's the basis for this request for Ryan Lewis?"

"Ryan Lewis was Mister Hamilton's attorney. He was the person who hired the financial advisor who stole money from Hamilton's clients, creating the environment in which Hamilton's death occurred. We believe his testimony is critical at trial, and he hasn't responded to numerous requests from us to arrange a meeting. He resides in Los Angeles, but we believe that if he were ordered to by the court, he would come to Santa Fe."

"Unless you have some objection, Mr. Carlton, I agree regarding Lewis." The judge paused and looked at Carlton, who shook his head. "Fine, then. Without objection, I'm ordering depositions from Ann Hamilton, Ryan Lewis, and Detective Sanchez. Hamilton and Lewis will be served summons. Anything else?"

Both sides indicated they had nothing more.

"Good. Court is adjourned."

Vincent watched Sanchez leave the court room. It was obvious he wasn't pleased. No detective wanted to be deposed, and he had been called out in open court for threatening a member of the defense team. There would be no cease-fire in hostilities with the sheriff's department.

20

Everybody Lies Sometimes

Tucker was in a good mood as they headed back to the Inn.

"Short and sweet. I think we got everything we wanted today. Did you see that detective? He looked like he had just slammed his hand in a door or something. That guy is not going to be your buddy, Malone."

"We were never going to be pals, anyway. Seemed like the judge was on our side."

Tucker nodded.

"It did, but that kind of thing can be deceptive. We were in the right today, and they'd screwed up, so it's not really that he was on our side, it's just that this time the issues were on our side. Next time that could go the other way. My feeling is this judge will be in control and will be fair, and in a trial, that's about all you can ask for."

"Bud and Vickie Turner are leaving tomorrow. I'm taking them to the airport early in the morning. Not sure I can get anything, but don't you think I should try to talk to them?"

Tucker thought for a minute.

"Yes, you should. Not sure you'll get much, but we have to try anything that might help untangle what's going on. Bud in particular seems to have a problem with the whole thing—or maybe just with you."

Vincent's feelings were not hurt. "Do you want to be involved?"

"No, you go ahead. I think they're probably not involved in any material way with the case. They seem to be having some kind of couple's problem, probably because Bud's a big pain in the ass. See if you can get them to go over what they remember, tell them that if they don't do it now, they might be called back for an official depo. Might motivate them."

"I'll do that. You know, we both pissed off the sheriff's department, you in court and me on the street. There's a city police department that has jurisdiction over Santa Fe, and I met with the chief. Much more reasonable sort of guy. He could be an ally, if anything comes up within his jurisdiction. And on that point, you should be aware that the Inn is in the county, not in the city. While I may think the sheriff is a good ol' boy who might do just about anything, I can't believe he would go so far as to challenge the judge or cause a major conflict within this case. But, just in case, it might make sense for you and your client and his wife to stay somewhere other than the Inn, like somewhere inside Santa Fe proper."

They rode in silence for a while as Tucker considered what Vincent had said.

"That's good information, and we may do something later. Right now, I'm very concerned about Dave's mental state, and I don't want to do anything that might give him even more reason to feel paranoid and agitated. You think the sheriff and his department are covering something up?"

"It could be something as simple as they don't like outsiders—people who aren't in their comfort zone. That would be us and Dave, but Hamilton, too. They could be pissed that some rich white guy got himself killed in their county and it's created a bunch of extra work." Vincent was actually sure that the sheer bother of dealing with the murder accounted for at least a small part of their hostile attitude—maybe more than a small part. "If there's anything more sinister than that, then I'd bet it has to do with Martinez, your ex-co-counsel. I think there's some chance that he was not only involved with Ann Hamilton, but that he has something to do with the death of Mark Hamilton."

"You think he could be the killer?" Tucker asked with renewed interest.

"I don't have any evidence of it, but it's possible."

"Would the sheriff and Detective Sanchez lie for Martinez?"

"The sheriff has a very bad reputation. According to some people, he might do just about anything—lie, cheat, even kill. Sanchez has a good reputation, and most people think he is an honest man working for a thug. But, who knows?"

"Keep digging. I need to show that there's a reason Martinez's testimony is critical to the trial if I'm going to try to depose him—some reason other than that the defense needs someone else to be the killer. If we can convince the judge to allow us to depose Martinez, maybe we can catch him in some way."

"Right now, we have nothing tying Martinez to the murder. Even the stuff about the affair with Ann is more rumor than fact. I've had one person tell me Martinez and Ann were having an affair, but that was a street person I paid to give me information. I've had another person, someone fairly reliable, say that she *thought* there was something going on between them because of the way they acted in public. But that's just someone making an educated guess, not proof—not something you'd want to present to a judge. Martinez admitted the affair to me, but we can't ask him about it under oath unless we're already deposing him, and the whole point right now is to find enough evidence to convince the judge to order a deposition."

"What do you think?"

"I believe both my sources, especially the street guy."

"Get something else. We need more. Something we can use in court to get a deposition."

"Thanks for meeting with me." Vincent smiled in an effort to reduce the obvious tension.

Bud wasn't having it.

"Yeah, well, threats work. What the hell do you want from us?"

"Tell me what you did after Hamilton told you about the money, and tell me where you were when he was killed."

"This is so much bullshit. We told all that to the cops. Are you accusing us of something?"

Vickie reached over and put her hand on Bud's arm.

"Let's just tell him what he wants, and then leave. No reason to get angry."

Bud glared at her as if to say there were plenty of reasons, but he stayed quiet while she answered the question.

"We took one of the SUVs and went into Santa Fe, and had dinner. It was some place close to downtown. We parked and walked around a bit, just looking at stuff, window-shopping or whatever, and then we saw this little restaurant and decided to eat. I think we both had enchiladas. Once we finished, we came back to the Inn and went to our room. We didn't leave again until the next morning when you woke us up because the detective was here."

"Thank you. Vickie. Do you remember the name of the restaurant?"

"No, I don't."

"It was a Mexican restaurant," Bud cut in. "'Cantina' something. And what she's not telling you is that I started drinking as soon as we got there, and by the time we left, I was completely shit-faced. She drove us home, and she was furious with me because I got too loud at the restaurant. The whole damn day had been miserable. But I did not kill the sonofabitch, even though I thought about it." Bud made an ugly face, as if, given the opportunity, he might kill someone right now.

"Did you see any of the other guests when you got back to the Inn?"

Vickie shook her head, but it was Bud who spoke.

"Well, she didn't, but later I was out back, just thinking,

and I saw Troy and Terry. They were smoking weed, and I gave them some shit for that, then I went to bed, just passed out."

Vincent nodded, making a mental note.

"Why did you pick Hamilton to be your agent? He mostly represented football and baseball players. No one else in the tennis world."

Bud threw up his hands.

"That's enough of this crap."

He left the dining room and for a moment the room was silent. Vickie stared at her hands. Vincent was reluctant to interrupt her—she seemed fragile.

"Sorry, this is a problem for Bud. He's very jealous of just about everyone I come into contact with, but especially Hamilton. I knew Mark in college, and he and I dated for a time. I was probably in love with him. We broke up, but I carried a torch for years. When I started having some success on the tour, I contacted Mark and asked him to be my agent. At the time I pretended it was because I knew him and he'd become a successful agent, but in my heart I knew I wanted him back. After Bud and I met and got married, he kept asking me to drop Mark. He knew all about my past with him. But I didn't, and it's been an issue with Bud ever since."

"Why didn't you get another agent?"

Vickie looked sad and she spoke in a whisper.

"I think I still loved him."

Vincent thanked her for talking to him, and apologized for having upset her. She told him she was fine and apologized again for her volatile husband's behavior. After she'd left, Vincent went outside, still thinking about the Turners. They both seemed so terribly unhappy. What the hell happens to people? They want to get married, and then in just a few years they seem to hate each other.

"Hey, Mister Vincent. How's it going?"

"Hey, Hector. Kind of a mixed day—some good, some bad. How 'bout you?"

"Well, got lots of weeds to take care of and trash to haul off, so I guess that's good and bad. I really don't want to do it, but it's good that I have a job." Hector laughed.

"Hector, how long have you been married?"

"Oh, I guess about thirty years. Mary would know exactly, but I don't keep up with things like that."

"How can you stay married that long and still be happy?"

Hector gave Vincent an appraising look. "Not sure I would know."

"What would Mary say?"

"Oh, she'd probably say we're happy because that is who we are. Got to get to those weeds now. See ya."

"Yeah, see ya." Happy people are happy, unhappy people aren't. Mary was one smart woman.

"Jake, how'd you like to make a hundred bucks for doing almost nothing?" Vincent had driven into Santa Fe to the Plaza Cantina on the assumption that it was the restaurant that Bud and Vickie had visited.

"What are you some, kind of cop?"

Why did everybody think he was a cop? "Nah, not a cop. I do investigative work for attorneys." Vincent described the time frame, and told him what Bud and Vickie looked like, and explained that he was interested in knowing if Jake remembered them. He laid a hundred-dollar bill on the bar.

With the efficiency of someone who had a fair bit of practice scooping bills off of the counter, Jake made the money disappear.

"How do you know my name?"

"I was in here a while back and sampled one of your best-in-Santa-Fe margaritas."

"Yeah, I thought I remembered you. And I remember those people. The guy got drunk in record time and was yelling at his wife—and anybody else who even looked at him. I asked him to keep it down, or he would have to leave. I got a bunch of brave back-talk, but no action. His wife gave me a nice tip when they left, said he'd had a hard day. She seemed nice, but he was a jerk."

"Jake, it's been my experience that bartenders know more than just about anyone else on the planet. Any chance you know who killed Mark Hamilton?"

Jake looked alarmed, not the reaction Vincent was expecting—he'd been bullshitting, kidding around. "I don't know anything about that," Jake said, then retreated to the other side of the bar to assist a customer who didn't actually need any assistance. What the hell was that about? Vincent signaled him again, and Jake returned, but reluctantly.

"How 'bout a Coors in a bottle?"

Jake turned his back on Vincent and got the beer from a cooler. Placing the beer in front of Vincent, he spoke softly.

"Look, I don't want any trouble, okay?"

Vincent pulled out another hundred and placed it on the bar. Jake looked scared. He turned and headed into the back-room. Vincent waited. After about ten minutes—with some customers complaining loudly—a female bartender appeared. She made the rounds of the customers, taking orders and quieting the complaints.

"Sorry about that, pal. The other bartender had an emergency and had to leave. What can I get you?"

Vincent grabbed the hundred, which still lay on the bar. "Nothing, right now."

He gave her his best smile and left. Outside, he decided he would walk the few blocks to the Crown Bar and have another beer, maybe get to talk to Nancy—that was a happy thought. Santa Fe is an old town with very narrow streets, and numerous, even narrower, alleys. Many of them are brick or cobblestone, and throughout the maze are businesses tucked away here and there. One problem this creates is that every street or alleyway looks very much like any other. After a short walk, Vincent decided that he'd passed the street where the Crown was located. He stopped, and was turning, when two large men walked up to him.

"You need to leave Santa Fe and not come back, got that asshole?"

"You friends with Jake?"

"What the fuck are you talking about? Stop asking questions and leave people the fuck alone."

A fight was unavoidable, so Vincent moved first, stepping into the closest guy real hard, with his knee jammed into the man's balls followed by his elbow breaking the guy's nose. The blood and obvious pain were gratifying. The man screamed and buckled, and the other one ran. The first man was throwing up, now, and bleeding all over the charming little street—quite a mess.

"Who sent you?" Vincent asked.

"Fuck you."

He grabbed the man's hand and bent one finger back much further than it was made to go, until the man howled in pain.

"This will only get worse. Who sent you?"

"Tito."

Vincent stood up. That wasn't at all what he'd been expecting. He walked away.

That makes no sense. Why would Tito send thugs to beat me up? And those guys weren't street people. Did Tito pay them? Or maybe the creep lied, and it wasn't Tito at all. Lots of people know Tito's name. I need fewer questions and more answers. And goddamn it, now my elbow hurts like hell. Still, that wasn't bad for an old man. Vintage Malone—mess with me, and you suffer. Unless, of course, it's one of my bad days, and I can't get out of bed.

21

The Ups and Downs of Life

The drive to the airport was silent. At first, Vincent tried to talk to Bud and Vickie, but neither was interested, so he shut up and just drove. He helped them unload their luggage, and they walked off without a word. Vincent was having trouble making friends. He decided that he had to say something before Bud left—he needed to plant a seed.

"Bud, can I talk to you for just a minute?"

Bud gave Vincent a dirty look, and was probably about to tell him to fuck off, when Vickie spoke up. "Just go see what he wants. I'll wait in the terminal." It sounded a little like an order.

"What the hell is your problem, Malone?"

"You and Vickie can run and hide—not much I can do about that—but somebody killed Hamilton, and I don't believe it was Dave. I don't quit on a case until I solve it. That means it's a process of elimination. You go one by one through the suspects and eliminate the innocent until only the guilty are left. You should know, I won't give up until I can prove who killed Hamilton."

"Fuck off, Sherlock. You leave me and my wife alone." Bud headed toward the terminal, giving Vincent the finger as

191

he went.

When you don't have the facts on your side, you have to shake every tree and see what falls out. Vincent's goal was to make as many people nervous as possible. He thought he'd succeeded with Bud.

Vincent stopped in a gun store just off of the highway and purchased a small pistol. Once the paperwork was completed and approved, he walked out with a little more confidence. He still had his large revolver, which was in his locked suitcase, but he'd decided it was a little too obvious for his current situation. If he was going to have thugs accosting him, he could no longer just rely upon his cat-like reflexes and the hope that if he beat up one bad guy then any others would run away. Vincent was no Second Amendment evangelist—if he'd had his way, he'd ban all guns except his, of course.

His earlier attempt to visit the Crown Bar had been interrupted, so he decided to stop by and have lunch—and hopefully chat with Nancy. He wanted to ask her to dinner. Before he entered the bar, though, he took care of a last piece of business—sending a text message to Terry Carter.

Need to talk. Have been unable to leave VMs, no response. This is important—call this number back or send me a better contact number for you. If you do not respond, we will be forced to ask the court for a summons. We just need to talk.

Vincent had no reason to believe Terry Carter had anything to do with the murder. He was the least likely suspect of all the guests. But it seemed strange that the number he provided didn't have voice mail. Vincent had used the internet to track Terry to an address in Orlando. Using that, he had tried to get another number, but was unable to find another listing. What had originally started as a call just to touch base now felt more important.

The Crown was in the midst of the lunch rush, and there was a small line to get a table. Vincent headed to the bar instead. A male bartender with long, flowing hair, and muscles that bulged prominently under a very tight shirt, asked what he wanted to drink.

"Tecate." He held up his hand to indicate he wasn't done. "Is Nancy here today?"

"Haven't seen her, but she's almost always here. I'll check in the back in a minute." He headed off to fill orders.

Malone had his back turned to the bar when he heard the bartender set down his beer.

"Hear you're looking for me?" Nancy was smiling, but she didn't look well.

"Hello. You okay? Look a little ragged."

"I'm sure 'ragged' is a nice way of putting it. Must have a cold or something. Just came in to work on the books a bit, and they said someone was looking for me. What's goin' on?"

"Nothin' much. Thought I'd see when you might be available to go to dinner—of course, at this point, I guess you have to recover first."

She let out a soft laugh. "Give me a couple of days. After that, dinner sounds great. Did you have someplace in mind?"

Vincent might have been the only person in New Mexico who didn't like green chilis, so he was reluctant to pick a local restaurant. "I'm the senior transportation manager for the Blue Door Inn, so how about I make dinner there?"

"Senior transportation manager?"

"I drive the van." If he'd had a chauffeur's cap, he would have tipped it.

Nancy smiled and tilted her head. "I wouldn't have figured you to be someone who cooked." She said it in a skeptical tone that Vincent heard a lot.

"It won't be real fancy, but I can manage some things. How about it?"

"Friday okay?"

"Sure, want me to pick you up?"

"Nah, I can drive. See you Friday at about seven." With that, she turned and left.

Vincent was excited, but now he had to find something he could actually make—he was a lousy cook. He ordered a bowl of chili and enjoyed his beer. He was heading back to the van when his phone rang. "Vincent Malone."

"Malone, there is no damn reason to threaten me with some kind of summons. My phone has been out and I wasn't getting messages. So fucking sue me. I was not trying to avoid you or anyone else."

Terry Carter was pissed, and maybe he had a right to be. *If he's telling the truth.*

"Sorry about that, Terry. Didn't mean it to sound threatening. That's just what the lawyer said he'd do if I couldn't connect with you. I was just giving you facts."

"Whatever. What do you want?"

"Fill me in on what happened the day of the meeting with Hamilton."

"You know I've told the cops all of this, right?"

"Yep, I know. Sorry to have you go over it again, but it's important."

Terry sighed. "Nothing much happened at all. We hung around the B&B most of the day. When it got close to evening, the lady at the Inn asked if we wanted her to arrange a car, or a cab, so we could go into Santa Fe for dinner. We opted for a cab in case we wanted to have some wine, and the lady gave us a couple of restaurant recommendations. Once the cab got there, he made a few suggestions, too, and we arbitrarily picked The Coyote Cafe. It was okay—damned expensive, though. The cab guy gave us his card and said to call when we were done, which we did, and we rode back to the Inn at maybe ten or so. Tina was tired and went to bed."

"Don't suppose you remember the cab company?"

Terry sighed again and Vincent was pretty sure he was getting a dirty look that he couldn't see.

"Why would I? Shit, maybe Santa Fe Cabs, I don't know. That lady at the Inn probably knows, though."

"Okay. I'll ask her. What else happened?"

"Look, this gets into something that we didn't mention to the detective, for obvious reasons that have nothing to do with any murder. He didn't ask us about it directly, and it seemed like he'd already decided Adams was the killer, and really just wanted to know if we'd seen Adams that night, which we hadn't."

"Who's we?"

"After Tina went to bed, I spotted Buster and Troy sitting outside. I went out and joined them. They had a bottle of scotch, which was damn near gone, and they seemed to be a little drunk. I went back in, found some wine and a glass, and went back out. We sat out there for some time, drinking and talking. We talked a little about the missing money, but mostly just about sports and sportswriters and some of the crap we put up with as professional athletes. After a while, Buster said he needed to go to bed before he passed out, and he left. Troy asked me if I wanted to smoke a little weed, and showed me he had some in his coat. I'm sure the reason he didn't mention it earlier is that everybody knows Buster thinks drugs are the devil—he'll drink like there's no tomorrow, but he's really down on anything else. Anyway, we lit up and just mellowed out."

"Anything happen during that time?"

"Yep. We were pretty high, and that guy Bud shows up at the table and starts yelling at us. Saying shit about what kind of losers we are for doing drugs out in the open, didn't we know that shit was illegal, and on and on. I mean, my God, it's not like we were smoking up at a major intersection in broad daylight. We were out in the middle of fuckin' nowhere in the middle of the night. I don't know, he was way overboard—a little out of his head, if you ask me. We told him to fuck off and go to bed, and just like that he left. I don't know if he told anybody about that or not, but that's it. After Bud left, the buzz was gone, so Troy and I went to our rooms."

"Thanks, Terry. I have not seen anything about weed in the police report, so I guess Bud didn't say anything. Do you think he was drunk?"

"I wasn't in any shape to evaluate him. But now that I think about it, he almost had to be. He was acting so strange."

"Who do you think killed Hamilton?"

"The guy made a lot of enemies in the last few years, treating everyone like shit, so the list is long. You're not going to like this, but of the people at the Inn, I'd say the most likely really is Dave Adams."

Vincent closed his eyes and took a deep breath. The truth was the truth, and Adams—with his flaring temper and loud threats—was the obvious choice.

"Thanks, Terry. If anything comes to you that might help us, give me a call. Once again, sorry if I was rude."

Vincent headed back to the Inn. His next critical task was to find Mary and see if she could train him to be a chef in a few short days.

⎯⊙⎯

Police Chief Brad Stanton wound his way through the maze of emergency vehicles, amidst the flashing lights. The activity was several blocks from the Plaza, but it had still attracted a sizable crowd. It was late, and some of the gawkers—clearly from nearby bars—were a little too rowdy. The chief spotted his deputy. "What the hell's going on?"

Deputy Police Chief Wood looked up from his phone.

"Nothing good. We've got a body. Looks like he was stabbed." Wood paused, seeming reluctant to say more. "It's Tito Alverez."

"Shit." The chief stopped, staring in the direction of the body. His breathing was labored and all color had gone from his face.

"You okay, chief?"

"Get some men over there and disperse that crowd. This is not goddamned entertainment for a bunch of fuckin' drunks."

The chief walked to the spot where his friend lay dead. He greeted some of his men, and they parted so he could come closer. He was full of grief, but determined not to show it. The scene was surprisingly tidy, with little blood, and he didn't see a knife. He stood still for a few moments, then turned and walked away, needing privacy.

The police chief had known Tito Alverez since college, when they'd both attended the University of New Mexico, where they'd been great friends. Brad had been the perfect student: Dean's Honor Roll every semester, elected to several leadership positions in his class, the ultimate over-achiever and straight arrow. Tito, not so much. He'd been more attuned to a rebellious, anti-establishment point of view, and any list his name appeared on was probably not one you wanted to be part of.

They'd met in a philosophy class they'd each taken as an elective option to complete their degrees. They represented the opposite sides of every argument, disagreeing and arguing with great intensity in class, which eventually led to after-class discussions that often appeared heated to anyone on the outside. But it was through this unlikely connection that they became friends. Each man grew as a result of exposure to the other's deeply held beliefs, and they began to respect the other's point of view.

When Stanton told Alverez he'd decided to pursue a degree in law enforcement, it was like declaring that he was going to live on Mars. To Tito it was unthinkable, an absurdity. They'd argued a lot about that decision. Brad had argued that if none of the good people became police officers, the world would go to hell. That struck a chord with Tito, and he got past the unnerving fact his friend was going to be a cop.

They graduated in the same year—Brad with a criminal justice degree in law enforcement and Tito a with a degree in philosophy. By graduation, Brad had already interviewed with the Albuquerque police department, and expected to be accepted to the next class at the police training academy.

Tito, on the other hand, was headed home to San Francisco. By this time, he'd already told Brad his horrible secret—his family was absurdly rich. His father was an investment banker worth millions. He'd gone to school in Albuquerque in an attempt to hide the fact that he was the son of a famous multimillionaire. His father's family had deep ties to California, and owned vast amounts of land in the Central Valley. In large part due to Brad's influence, Tito was considering a career in counseling within the criminal justice system. They found the choice ironic, funny, and fitting, all at once. Tito wanted to help the poor, especially street people.

Only weeks after he returned to California, tragedy struck Tito. His father had invested heavily in a new startup, a high-tech company with promising developments in biotechnology, led by a genius CEO. He'd borrowed huge sums of money, using the family land as collateral. Shortly afterward, the genius was talking on his phone on the freeway and failed to see a pileup in front of him until it was too late. No more genius, no more company. And it quickly became clear that the genius had also been a fraud, his discoveries fake. The world was full of lawyers, and the one guy left standing, who was both associated with the company and had deep pockets, was Tito's father. The lawsuits began. He was going to lose most of his fortune, and might face criminal charges, too. One night, alone in their mansion, his father killed his mother and shot himself. A philosophy degree just can't bulletproof you against that kind of tragedy.

Tito had returned to New Mexico, looking for solace in drugs and a life with no purpose.

22

Santa Fe Blues

Vincent walked into the dining room looking for coffee, and maybe a muffin. He'd sampled a lot of Jerry's sopaipillas, and felt like he'd gained ten pounds since he started working at the Inn. Mary was a great cook, and Jerry was always insistent that whoever passed by the kitchen had to sample his latest concoction—and of course, Vincent didn't want to be rude. Today he would limit himself to a single banana-walnut muffin. He was sure it had to be low in calories.

"Vincent, glad I caught you," Tucker seemed in an unusually good mood. "Just got word from the DA that Detective Sanchez will be available tomorrow morning for a deposition. It's not required, but I sure would like for you to be there."

"Sure, no problem. You seem especially cheerful this morning."

Tucker grinned. "I know. I think it's this place. The case causes a lot of stress, like any case—maybe more, because it's family—but I feel better than I normally would. Don't say anything to Jerry, or he'll raise our rates."

"Did I hear that I should raise your rates?" Jerry was standing in the doorway.

"Lower! I said, 'lower.'" Tucker chuckled. "You and Cindy have a great place. You're going to be very successful, I'm sure, once you start getting more normal guests."

"Thanks." Jerry paused with a worried look. "Just heard some bad news. No real details, and nothing official—this came from the delivery guy bringing eggs—but he said that a street person was killed last night just off the Plaza. Said the whole town is upset. Apparently, the guy was something of an institution here."

"Wait," Vincent said. "Did he tell you the person's name?"

"Tito—he didn't say a last name."

Vincent was stunned. He knew Tito lived in a dangerous world, but never expected he would come to some harm.

"I'd better go into Santa Fe and see what I can find out."

"Does he have something to do with the Hamilton murder?" Tucker asked. "If so, maybe I should go with you."

"I don't think so. He was the source for my information about Martinez. And I thought he knew more, too. He was an unusual person, and he was someone I wanted to get to know better. It could be a coincidence, and have nothing to do with the Hamilton murder, but it seems awfully suspicious. As soon as I find out more, I'll call you."

Vincent went to his room before leaving—this was a day he wanted to be armed. He wanted to find out more about Tito, but really didn't know where to start. He decided Santa Claus was his best bet.

"Mister Collins around?" Vincent asked the guy passing out coffee.

The server didn't look up, but called out to no one in particular.

"Anybody seen Butch?" There was no answer. "Guess he ain't here."

Vincent walked toward the Plaza thinking that he'd wander around for a while, then come back and see if Santa Claus had resurfaced. Many of the bars and restaurants would be closed until later, but several breakfast spots had lines waiting to get in, and as he passed them the aroma was enticing. Some of that had to be the green chili, which always smelled great, but every time he'd tried the New Mexico staple, he had somehow gotten the hottest chili on the planet. As he entered the Plaza, he could see police vehicles blocking one of the narrow side roads. He approached a bored-looking patrolman leaning against a cop car.

"What's going on?"

"Nothing, right now. Had some action back there last night, and the forensics guys are doing their thing. Nothing to worry about, we should be done in a few hours."

The cop eyed Vincent suspiciously, the way all cops seemed to do. Maybe it was his size.

"What kind of crime?"

The cop suddenly looked more alert. This wasn't some tourist asking about a blocked street. "What's your concern, pal?" This was said in a typical cop tone—one Vincent had tried over the years to describe, though he'd never quite got it right. It wasn't exactly rude, but it sure wasn't polite either, and there was an implied threat in the delivery. Apparently, every policeman, everywhere, had been trained in its use.

"No concern, just curious." Vincent tried his best innocent smile.

"Well, we're not giving out any information at this point, so just move along."

Crowd control, even if the crowd was only one guy, was an important police function. Vincent headed back onto the Plaza. He chose a shaded bench facing a sidewalk, where numerous vendors were laying out their wares. It was mostly jewelry of various kinds. Many of the vendors were Native Americans or, as the less sensitive kids would say, Indians. Vincent thought about the way humans labeled other humans, dividing them into groups that more often than not carried a reference to their social status. Americans liked to think of the United States as somehow status-free, but that was a joke. Try to step up in status and see what happens to you.

After sunning and people-watching for a little while, Vincent noticed that the Plaza Cantina had opened, presumably to catch the morning drinkers. In a tourist town, that would be a sizable market.

"Hey Jake. How 'bout a cup of the greatest coffee served in Santa Fe?" Vincent grinned but sensed that he'd annoyed Jake.

"That would be over at La Posta, the breakfast bar across the Plaza."

"Wow, honesty from a bartender. What's the world coming to?" The wiseass game seemed to thaw things a little. Jake poured Vincent a coffee, then went on with the prep work he'd been doing. "What's going on over there with the cops?"

"A street guy got killed last night. There not sayin' much about it, though. Most likely another homeless guy killed him. That's usually what happens—fightin' over booze or drugs or even cigarettes."

"Know who it was?"

"Nah. Some of the guys in the back probably know, but it'll cost you twenty." Jake was clearly a highway robber *pretending* to be a bartender. Vincent handed over two tens, making it easy for Jake to keep half. He was back in a few minutes.

"They say it was some guy name Tito. Seems he was well known around here."

"Anything else?"

"One of the cooks says he was a friend of the police chief. Sounds like bullshit to me, but what do I know?"

Vincent decided not to answer that question. He also calculated that it would make no sense to ask Jake why he'd disappeared the other day—he'd just lie. He waved so long and headed out.

It was only a short walk to police headquarters. Vincent asked to see the chief and was asked to wait. He found a chair and closed his eyes. He wasn't tired, so much as he just wanted to shut the world out for a minute. He thought about his ex-wife, someone he hadn't talked to in twenty-five years or so. She was probably still lovely. For some reason that made him smile.

"Sir. Sir? The chief will see you now."

He opened his eyes and stood up. Time to get to work.

He followed the patrolman to the familiar office.

"Thanks for seeing me, chief. I know you must be busy."

"What can I do for you?" He was much less friendly than he'd been the previous time they'd met. Maybe this visit wasn't such a good idea. Based on the chief's demeanor, he decided on the fly to try a different tack.

"We're setting up depositions with several key people in the Hamilton murder. Tomorrow we'll be talking to Detective Sanchez. I'd come into town today to talk to a man named Tito about doing a deposition for us, but found out he's just been killed. Not sure how or when, but I was wondering if you could give me some information."

"What would Tito have to do with the Hamilton murder?" The chief's annoyance was heading toward anger.

"He was a source. He gave us information that led us to believe that Stephen Martinez might have been having an affair with Ann Hamilton. We wanted to see if he would talk to us under oath about how he knew that."

The chief was quiet for a long moment, and Vincent waited.

"Tito Alverez told you that Martinez and Hamilton's wife were having an affair?"

"Well, not exactly. He told us they *might* be having an affair. At the time, Martinez was co-counsel with Peter Tucker, so even a possible affair was a serious problem. I confronted Martinez about it, and he admitted it was true. As I'm sure you know, one of our objectives in defending Dave Adams is to offer believable options to the jury about who other than

Adams might have killed Hamilton. The affair might have played into that." Vincent wasn't sure, but it seemed the chief had tuned him out a few sentences ago. He was thinking hard about something.

"Yeah, yeah. I can understand how the defense would consider that important. Look, Malone, I don't want to give you the bum's rush, but I have a meeting I need to get to. Let me think about what you've told me, and see if I can think of anything that might help you. Give me your number and I'll call you later, okay?"

Vincent nodded. He knew the chief had to check some things before he would say anything more, but something was bothering him. "Sure, that'd be great." He gave the chief his number. He walked back toward his car, but stopped in at the clinic to see if Butch Collins had turned up. He was sitting in his usual spot, drinking coffee.

"Sorry to hear about Tito. I was just talking to the police chief. He seemed pretty upset."

"Yeah, they were friends going back to college. I considered Tito a friend, too. This is really—" He broke off, not finding the words. He looked a mess.

"Any idea what happened?"

"Nah. I don't even know how he was killed. Do you know?"

"No. Probably find out later. Chief said he would call me. I'll let you know what he tells me."

"Thanks."

"Do you think this could have something to do with Martinez?"

Collins looked up and frowned. "Well, Martinez was upset that Tito had told you about him and that woman, but half the town knew something was going on between Martinez and the rich lady. If Tito hadn't told you, somebody else would, and Martinez knew that. I think he was angry because he and Tito had become friends. He was trying to get Tito a job with the chief as some kind of counselor or something. I think more than anything they were trying to get him off the street. Both the chief and Martinez worried that he was at risk being homeless. Plus, he was already basically a counselor, anyway, but for free. When he would show up here, people would go to him and ask him to help with all sorts of things. And he always took time to listen to people. He cared."

"Doesn't sound like a man anyone would want to kill."

"Yeah, well, he didn't have any enemies among people who knew him. But there's lots of people moving through Santa Fe every day. Most of the street people have to be hypervigilant, always on the lookout for danger. It's unavoidable, given the world they live in, given how vulnerable they are, but it means they can overreact—even be violent, sometimes. And, of course, some have mental health issues, and that doesn't help. There may not be any real reason."

An emotional Collins got up and left the room. Vincent retrieved his car and drove a short way to the offices of Martinez, Howard and Fitch. The receptionist eyed him suspiciously, but told him to wait and she would let Mister Martinez know he was there. Vincent waited. After a much longer wait than seemed necessary, given the empty reception area, Martinez appeared and showed Vincent into his private office.

"I'm not talking to you. I know that idiot judge is allowing you to depose me, but I'm filing an objection today and I have nothing to say, so please leave."

"Did you kill Tito?"

"Are you insane? What a stupid question. He was my friend. Get the fuck out of here." Martinez started forward in a way he probably hoped was threatening, but he paused several steps away when Vincent didn't move.

"That's not an answer. Did you kill Tito?"

"No!"

"Did you kill Hamilton?"

Martinez glared at Malone for a long moment. "You're crazy," he snarled. "I didn't kill anyone. Now leave immediately, or I'll call the police."

Vincent left. It had been a confusing morning. It was obvious that Martinez was covering something up. If the affair with Ann Hamilton was common knowledge, did that mean Mark Hamilton knew about it? If so, how would he have reacted to that kind of news? And how the hell was Tito involved?

He dropped in at a nearby coffee shop, and against his better judgment, ordered a green chili bagel to go with his regular coffee—the very cute young woman behind the counter insisted they were great. Sitting in his car, he tried to give the bagel a chance, but it had to be one of the worst things he'd ever tasted. The coffee, thank goodness, was great. He headed back to the Inn, feeling like he hadn't accomplished anything.

23

Deposition Times One

As a result of Vincent's visit to Martinez's office, as well as the fact that they wanted to depose their former co-counsel, Tucker was notified that the Martinez law firm was no longer interested in having anything to do with him—and especially with Vincent Malone. They would need a new co-counsel licensed to practice in New Mexico, and a new place to conduct the depositions, which had previously been scheduled for the Martinez law offices.

Tucker got on the phone, and quickly arranged for the Albuquerque law firm of Johnson, Johnson and Hill to be their new co-counsel, led by the best-known lawyer in New Mexico, Jack Hill. Hill and Tucker were contemporaries, and had been adversaries before, never on the same side of a case. Hill said he would arrange for a conference room for the depositions, setting things up at the downtown Santa Fe Hilton.

"You know this guy Jack Hill?" Vincent was driving the van, heading into Santa Fe—a now familiar trip.

Tucker looked up from some notes he was reading and smiled. "Yeah. We butted heads on three cases, all of which I won. I wouldn't say we're friends. After the last case, my guess was that, given the opportunity, Mister Hill would have gladly stabbed me with his gold Mont Blanc pen."

Vincent laughed. "And this is the guy you're calling in to join your team?"

"We're not pals, but I don't need a pal. He's the best legal mind in New Mexico, and that's exactly what I need. I almost expected him to say no, and not too politely. But he's heard about the case, and I think he's curious. Anyway, one way or another, he's willing to get involved. This is the biggest murder case in his state in a long time, so it won't hurt his reputation any to be on our team—or his ego, for that matter. As long as one of us doesn't kill the other, he'll be an asset. And in case it comes up, he's very politically connected in this state. Might come in handy."

"Yeah, it might." Tucker was full of surprises.

The Santa Fe Hilton, a luxury hotel just a few blocks from the Plaza, was huge, but the giant, hacienda-like structure didn't look like any Hilton Malone had ever seen. They parked and entered through an impressive lobby, where signs pointed them to the correct conference room.

Detective Sanchez was already there, as was an assistant DA named Matt Moore. Those who didn't know each other introduced themselves and shook hands. Sanchez was nervous, but that was normal. Even under the best of conditions, giving testimony under oath can play hell with a person's nerves. Soon the court reporter showed up, and they all settled in. The court reporter swore in Sanchez, and they began. Tucker started after everyone had identified themselves for the record.

"Detective, as I'm sure you know, this deposition is an extension of the court process, and operates under the same rules as a court of law. If at any time you feel you need to discuss matters with the assistant DA before answering, you may call for a recess. The objective of this deposition is not to try and cover new ground, but to provide documentation for matters that you'll testify to in court. If you're ready, we'll begin."

Tucker took Sanchez through some housekeeping matters, establishing his professional credentials, his training, and his experience. He also had Sanchez document his employment history and his current status on the job. "If you could, give us an accounting of the night that Mark Hamilton was murdered."

"The 911 call came in about eleven thirty. They—"

"If I can interrupt, who made the 911 call?"

"We don't know. The call was recorded, but the sound was muffled, so we're not sure if it was a man or a woman. They said someone had been shot and gave us general directions to the location which they identified as the Hamilton residence, and then they hung up."

"Did you trace the call?"

"No. Even if we'd had equipment to do that automatically, which we don't, they weren't on the line long enough."

"Did you ask the neighbors if they had made the call?"

"We talked to all of the neighbors. They said they did not hear anything and for sure didn't hear a shot. Those houses are on huge lots so they are pretty far from one another. Plus, with air conditioning running in those heavily insulated, expensive homes you don't hear much."

"Go on. What happened next." Tucker was taking notes.

"The first person to arrive was Deputy Cole. Based on his report, he immediately saw the body in the yard and checked to see if the person was alive, but he wasn't. He went to the door and rang the doorbell, but no one answered. He returned to his patrol car and called in that information, stating that an unidentified man had been shot and killed, then waited for more deputies to arrive. I arrived at the scene at twelve-fifteen and conferred with Cole. Like him, I tried ringing the doorbell, but got no answer. By then, other deputies had arrived, and I instructed them to secure the area. I called in for the coroner's people and our forensics team. At about twelve forty-five, we were all going about our various duties when Ann Hamilton appeared at the door. She seemed to be in a daze."

"Had you made an attempt to enter the house apart from ringing the doorbell?"

"I'd had someone check all of the doors and windows to see if anything was open or broken. Nothing was. We hadn't made a forced entry—we would have needed a search warrant for that."

"You didn't suspect that Mrs. Hamilton was inside?"

"No. We don't have a lot of information on part-time residents, especially in the more upscale neighborhoods. The information we received from dispatch was just that the house was owned by Mark Hamilton—there was no mention of a wife. The man in the yard didn't have identification on him, but it was our operating assumption at the time that it was

Hamilton. Our focus up to the point Ann Hamilton appeared had been on the yard and the surrounding area, securing it and protecting any evidence."

"Before we go on, you did say he'd been shot?"

"Yes. He had been shot in the chest. A gun was lying next to the body."

"What kind of gun?"

"It was a Ruger 9mm handgun."

"Is that a pretty common handgun?"

"Well I don't know the numbers, but I'd guess there are a lot of them made."

"Did you find anything else relevant in the yard?"

"Yes, there was a baseball bat."

"Was there any indication that the bat had been involved in this incident?"

"There appeared to be a small amount of blood on it, but at that point we saw no indication that Hamilton had been hit with it. Forensics later discovered—"

"Objection," Assistant DA Moore spoke up. "The forensics people can provide direct evidence of their findings and analysis. Detective Sanchez should limit his testimony to things he personally saw."

Tucker smiled at the young DA. "Sure, that's fine. Tell us what occurred with Mrs. Hamilton."

"She immediately became upset when she saw her husband in the yard. She was close enough that she could easily see it was him and that he was dead. We took her back inside and tried to calm her. We called for medical assistance and tried to make her comfortable. She didn't say much until the medical people arrived and they gave her something to calm her nerves. It was probably thirty minutes or more after she opened the door when I was first able to ask her some questions."

"So, during that thirty minutes she said nothing?"

"Well nothing that really made sense. She kept saying things like, 'why' or, 'how did this happen.' She was crying most of the time, and some of what she said we couldn't make out."

"So, what did she tell you after she calmed down?"

"She said she wasn't aware of anything at all after she went to bed at about ten. She took some prescription sleeping pills and didn't wake up until she came to the door and saw us. I asked her if anything had happened that day that was out of the ordinary. That's when she described the meeting with her husband's clients, and the scene that took place when he told them that their money was missing. She said all the clients were upset, but that two in particular were very angry. Those were Dave Adams and Bud Turner. She told us Dave Adams had threatened to kill her husband. She said that after the meeting, she and her husband returned home, and he got on the phone and was mostly yelling at people, threatening them with legal action if something wasn't resolved regarding the missing money. She indicated that, as the afternoon went on, her husband started drinking, and he became increasingly angry. She said she decided to leave him alone, since he didn't seem to want anyone around. Eventually she tried to talk to him, but by then he was very drunk, and when she tried to get him to come to bed, he pushed her and she fell against a chair.

She said that he was scaring her, and she left and went to the guest room and locked the door. She said she could hear him yelling and breaking things in the living room. Eventually, she got her sleeping pills, took some, and then was out completely until something woke her and she found us in her yard."

"Could she identify any of the people he talked to on the phone?"

"I don't know. I didn't ask her that." Sanchez looked worried.

"Go on."

"She said she wasn't feeling well, so she went back to her bedroom. The forensics people were there by then, and I asked them to run a check on the gun. I decided I would go to the Blue Door Inn and see how the clients would react to the news that Hamilton was dead. That's what I did next."

"About what time is that?"

"It was about three-thirty. I called dispatch and asked them to get a number for the Inn. I called and talked to the owner, told him I wanted to come and speak with the guests. I let him know that Hamilton had been killed. I arrived and conducted interviews with everyone except Dave Adams and his wife. I can go over each interview if you want."

"No need, we can read your report. You left at that point—why did you leave?"

"I got a text message that the gun we'd found was registered to Dave Adams, so I left to get an arrest warrant. I arranged to have the Inn surrounded with deputies, then went and woke a judge to get the arrest warrant for Adams. When I got back, several deputies and I entered the Inn just as Adams was apparently leaving. I arrested him and read him his rights."

"Did you or anyone else interview Adams?"

"No. We tried to talk to him a couple of times, but all he would say was that he wanted a lawyer. I think your assistant may have had something to do with that."

Sanchez gave Vincent a dirty look. Tucker ignored the reference and the look.

"Did you have any further discussion with Ann Hamilton?"

"After booking Adams, I returned to the Hamilton's residence, and the deputy on the scene told me she had left in a cab about fifteen minutes before I got there. I later learned that she had gone back to L.A. We have tried to contact her, but so far she hasn't responded."

"Let me digress a bit. When the first deputy arrived on the scene, did he say the front door was closed or opened?"

"I don't think he said. But when I arrived, it was closed."

"Did you check to see if it was locked?"

"No."

"So apparently Hamilton went into the front yard for some reason and shut the front door behind him, is that correct?"

"Objection. That calls for speculation by the detective." Assistant DA Moore was paying attention.

"I'll withdraw the question. Do you know Tito Alverez?"

"I've heard of him."

"He was found dead a few blocks from here. Do you know

anything about what happened?"

"Objection, relevance." Moore was glaring at Tucker. "I don't know what that has to do with the matter at issue. I'd need to know some relevance to allow that line of questioning."

Tucker simply moved on.

"Do you know Stephen Martinez?"

"Yes."

"Did he talk to Dave Adams?"

"Yes. He said he was his attorney, and he met with him in the county jail."

"Did you talk to Martinez?"

"I briefly talked to him when he asked for my help to get in to see Adams. I told him there wasn't much I could do until after the hearing, which was scheduled for the next morning. That was it, he left."

"Did you know that Martinez was having an affair with Ann Hamilton?"

"Objection! What's going on here? You know the rules as well as I do Mister Tucker. I'm not going to allow Detective Sanchez to answer questions based on rumor or speculation."

"It is not rumor or speculation to ask him if he knew. How about if I put it this way. Were you aware of anyone living in Santa Fe who was having an affair with Ann Hamilton?"

Moore looked annoyed, but also uncertain. While he was thinking about it, Sanchez answered. "No. I didn't know anything about any affairs involving Mrs. Hamilton."

"Thanks. We're done."

The court reporter had everyone sign a document related

to the deposition, regarding date and times. Once done, everyone left but Vincent and Tucker.

"Sounds like Detective Sanchez didn't do a very good job investigating Ann Hamilton," Vincent commented.

Tucker looked up. "Well that's a fuckin' understatement. She started crying and he left. He didn't even ask her for her prescription bottle. Just unbelievable what women can get away with."

"You mean; what men will fall for. Of course, the big question we can't answer is, how did Adams's gun get there?" Vincent hated to state the obvious, but it was going to have to be explained.

"Yeah. I don't have an answer for that yet. Not even one I can believe in, much less sell in court. Where are we on the depositions for Ann Hamilton and Ryan Lewis?"

"Both summonses have been served and they're required to respond by tomorrow. At this point we have no idea if they'll show up or head for the hills."

"I've been thinking maybe I should move Dave and Linda somewhere else, maybe here. They'd be a lot more anonymous and the change might do them some good. Do you think Jerry and Cindy would be offended?"

"I think Jerry and Cindy are great people who want to concentrate on their new business, not some court case. They would never ask you to leave, and might even be a little hurt if you do, but that's exactly what you should do—and what Jerry and Cindy need. The Adamses can't stay there during a trial, because we can't provide the security they're going to need once the inevitable horde of asshole reporters shows up. So, move them now and let them get comfortable in a new place. Have you heard anything about them getting their investment back?"

"Yeah, they got everything. It never left the U.S. at all. And that's another weird piece in this whole, big puzzle: that guy Jackson getting killed. I have no idea at all what he was doing—he just moved all of that money from one of his accounts to another in the same bank. Technically, it wasn't even illegal because both of them were trust accounts for his clients. So, all the money has been returned to the clients. Dave said he even made some money, because it was invested in bonds while it was supposedly missing. Very strange."

"Well, we've got the deposition with Martinez tomorrow. Let's hope he confesses to everything and we can celebrate. What do you think Mister Mason?" Vincent was smiling.

"I think you are full of shit, Mister Drake."

One nagging aspect of this case that I can't get a handle on is, why did Hamilton ask his five clients to come to Santa Fe? Obviously, it wasn't to tell them their money was gone—there are better, safer ways to do that—so why? Need to ask his wife this question. I think it's important.

24

Work and Play

Tucker and Vincent returned to the conference room at the Hilton for their scheduled deposition with Stephen Martinez.

"What do you expect to get from this guy?"

Tucker looked thoughtful. "Not sure. It may be nothing more than a way to find out more about the wife. I know one thing, though—Mister Martinez has gotten himself into some sticky ethical issues by representing Dave, even briefly. If it's true he was having an affair with Ann Hamilton—and I guess it is, since he told you as much—then no way in hell should he have agreed to represent the guy accused of killing her husband. That's 'Conflict of Interest 101.'"

"He must have known that."

"I don't know. Lawyers who don't deal too much with the criminal side of things can lose their bearings when it comes to ethics. The business lawyers are always on the verge of conflicts in almost everything they do. But he definitely screwed the pooch on this one."

A Hilton hostess stuck her head in the door. "Mister Tucker?"

"Yes."

"There's a phone call for you at the front desk. Do you want me to transfer it in here?"

"No that's fine, I can take it out there." Tucker left, returning just a few minutes later. "Martinez has cancelled the deposition. I talked to his new lawyer, who said that he was no longer available for a voluntary deposition. Guy was not friendly, very abrupt. Hung up before I could even ask him anything."

"What now?"

Tucker pulled out his laptop. "I'll file electronically with the court and ask them to compel Martinez to provide a deposition. They'll probably object. So, most likely we'll have a hearing soon." Tucker began to work.

Vincent spent most of a day doing chores for Jerry. It was calming to have tasks to do that didn't have life-and-death stakes. He took the van and had it serviced and washed. On his way back, he stopped off at the restaurant supply house and picked up an order that Mary had phoned in. Very routine and non-threating.

It was still early days for the team at the Blue Door Inn, but with each day that they were able to practice on actual guests, they became more comfortable in their various tasks. They were starting to want to step things up.

"Any new business on the horizon?" Vincent asked, as Jerry helped him unload the van.

"We've had some inquires, and we've actually turned down some business. Mister Tucker is paying for all of the rooms, so it would be cheating to let someone else stay."

"I talked to Tucker. He's thinking it might be better for Dave and Linda if they moved into the Hilton. It's close to court, and it's easier to provide security there. He's concerned it might hurt your feelings if they left—would it?"

Jerry grinned.

"No. I like Tucker, and especially Dave and Linda, but we're ready to have more normal guests. Should I say something to him?"

"I'll let him know. My guess is that he'll move everyone in a couple of days."

Jerry sighed. "I'm worried about Dave. He seems to withdraw more each day. How long is it going to be before the trial?"

"The trial is still a few months out. That maybe another reason for them to move. At least it'll be a change."

"Yeah. Might be the best for everyone." Jerry sounded sad, all the same.

Vincent went outside and found Hector trimming some trees. He asked if he could help, and Hector asked him to gather the cut limbs, showing him where to put them. He seemed pleased to have the help and company, and they chatted about trees, the weather, Santa Fe, world politics. It was nice to do physical work and talk about things that were neither personal nor earth-shaking. Of course, he soon got tired. When he'd finished collecting the branches, he went back inside.

Tucker was sitting at one of the dining room tables working on his computer. Vincent interrupted. "I think you should ask the judge to issue a summons for Bud and his wife Vickie to appear for a deposition."

Tucker looked up.

"Why the interest in them?"

"The alternate suspects that we know about are the five clients and their spouses who were staying at the Inn, plus Martinez, Ann Hamilton, and Ryan Lewis. Obviously, there might be others who we don't know about. But based on motive and opportunity, the five clients have been our focus. Three of them were supposedly together drinking and smoking during the time when Hamilton was probably killed. That leaves two, Dave and Bud—or Linda, Vickie Turner, and Tina Carter, I guess. Call me a sexist, but I don't think it was one of the women. Which means we need to talk to Bud."

"You know, more than likely the DA is going to object. He'll say that we're just trying to muddy the waters with a fishing expedition."

"But this isn't a fishing expedition at all. We can show that Bud was outside and not accounted for at about the time of the crime. He approached Troy and Terry while they were smoking some weed, and bitched at them for using drugs. Troy said he was acting weird. I think Troy would sign an affidavit to that effect, maybe leaving out the weed part, which would mean Bud had opportunity as well as a motive, because of the money. I think the judge will give us some latitude so long as it's someone connected to the case. He knows the sheriff and his deputies made up their minds early on and never did an adequate investigation. These are things the detective should have covered. And the judge, maybe better than anyone, knows the weaknesses of the sheriff's department."

"I'm going to need an assistant if there are many more of these filings." Tucker sounded annoyed and pleased at the same time. He began typing.

"Okay, what'll I fix?"

Mary looked at Vincent like he smelled bad. "You can't wait until the last minute to decide what to make, Mister Vincent. This is not like a restaurant, where you walk in and order your food, and it's brought to you in a few minutes. First you have to decide what you're going to prepare, and then you would go to the store and purchase what you need. Then you make sure everything is cleaned and prepped. You do all that before you actually start cooking the food."

"Yes, master."

Mary gave Vincent a smirk—it was her way of calling him a wiseass, since she didn't use that kind of language. "I knew you wouldn't think ahead, so I bought two small filets. A little expensive, but you can afford it, now that you're working. I also prepared a salad. So now you have to start the filets."

"Isn't it early?"

"Yes, it is. You are going to start them at a low tempera-ture, and then once your guest arrives you'll be able to get ready very quickly. At this low temperature you can cook the food for quite a while without burning it." Mary seasoned the filets and put them in a skillet, then placed them in a low-heat oven. "Now, when you're ready, you can take them out and put them on the stovetop on a high temperature and sear them."

"Is that like, burn them?"

"Sort of." She grabbed a covered bowl. "This is the salad, which you can just place on the table and you can each serve yourselves. It already has a red-wine vinaigrette dressing, so you don't need to do anything. The bread is in the warmer. You're all set." Mary smiled.

"I owe you one, Mary."

"You owe me two, Mister Vincent." She left the kitchen, smiling.

Cindy came in.

"Vincent, your guest has arrived."

"Oh, thanks, Cindy. And thanks again for letting me do this." Cindy gave him a smile and a thumbs-up. Vincent felt like a teenager. He went to the dining room. "Welcome. You look lovely, Nancy. Would you like a glass of wine?"

She looked more than lovely. She'd always been attractive, but now she was beautiful, with the hair done and some carefully applied make-up. Vincent restrained himself from cheering out loud, but she looked wonderful.

"Thank you, a glass of white wine would be great."

Vincent went to the bar and poured them each a glass. He directed Nancy outside, to the gazebo. The evening was summer cool and very pleasant. Nancy looked around the grounds.

"This is really a lovely place. I didn't even know it was here."

Vincent gave her the short history of how Jerry and Cindy had acquired the place and remodeled it into a B&B. "I might as well confess right at the beginning. I don't know how to cook much of anything. Not sure why I said I could. Maybe I thought you'd say no, so it wouldn't matter. Mary, who's the nicest person on the planet, has more or less prepared everything. I'm supposed to take the steaks out of the oven and sear them on the cooktop. I didn't want Mary to know I'm a compete idiot, so I said I could handle that much. But honestly, I'm not sure I can. Can you help?"

Nancy laughed and smiled. Vincent laughed and smiled. It was going to be a good evening. Watching Nancy prepare the meat, Vincent realized that he could have done it—he just hadn't been sure what it was Mary had wanted him to do. Afterward, they sat in the dining room with their steaks, salad and bread along with a bottle of red wine, and talked about nothing personal.

Eventually, the subject of Vincent's past came up. He could have pleaded the Fifth, but she was a nice lady and deserved to hear the ugly facts, straight from the horse's mouth. He gave her the short version, but he didn't sugarcoat it—he'd made a lot of mistakes in his time. When he was done, Nancy told her story, too.

"My husband was a cop. He liked to drink and hang out in bars. He invested all our savings in the Crown Bar, said it would be our retirement. But I knew and he knew it was because he enjoyed being in a bar and drinking. He was usually smart about it, and didn't mix drinking with the job. He was on call one night, and maybe he forgot that he was, but he'd been drinking. A call came in about a robbery in progress. He responded, and he opened a door that a sober cop wouldn't have—got shot dead. I know a lot about good men who do stupid things."

Vincent wasn't sure what to say for a moment. "I'm sorry about your husband."

"It was years ago, but it took a long time to heal. There was a time when I thought it never would, but it has." She quickly wiped away a tear. "You going to stay in Santa Fe and keep on being 'Transportation Manager?'" She forced a smile.

"Not sure. I like it here. Not sure Jerry and Cindy can justify having a part-time van driver, and I'm not sure if I can get more investigative work in Santa Fe. But I'm not ready to quit. I thought I was, but doing this work with Tucker on the Adams case has made me realize that I like doing something I'm good at. The gout thing had me thinking I was physically done, but now the medication seems to have that under control. So, the big question for me is whether I can make things work here. If I can, then I want to stay. It felt like I'd really lost my mojo, but I've found it again in Santa Fe."

"Got your mojo workin', huh? You're an interesting man, Mister Malone."

"I've enjoyed getting to know you, Nancy McAllen." Vincent leaned over and kissed her on the cheek. She did not pull back, and she didn't scream—both good signs.

"I should be going. Can I help clean up?"

"Oh no, I'll do that."

"You're not going to make Mary do it, are you?" She gave him an amused frown.

"No. I'll do it myself."

He walked her to her car and said good night, then went back inside and cleaned up.

My god, now what? She's attractive, smart, and owns a bar—it's like striking oil. Very romantic, Vincent, you heathen. Can I do this, be an almost normal person? Have a relationship with someone I respect? Can I stay in Santa Fe and find investigation work? I'm an old man. Maybe I should just go somewhere warm and watch TV. No way. My god, this is great.

25

Deposition Times Two

Vincent and Tucker took their usual path to the Hilton for Ann Hamilton's deposition.

"Let's hope this one actually happens."

Tucker looked up from his notes.

"It should. Her attorney, guy named Frank Taylor, notified the court that they would be here today. So, we'll have her attorney, DA Carlton, assistant DA Moore, and our guy, Jack Hill. That many lawyers in one place, there are bound to be a few objections."

The gathering began, people greeting each other as they arrived. The court stenographer set up her equipment. After a while it became obvious that Ann Hamilton and her attorney were late. No one said much about it, but they didn't have to—everyone wanted to get on with things, and they were all concerned that she might not show. Ten minutes late, she appeared.

She didn't just come in, she made an entrance, like a movie star would, nodding to people with a loftiness that wasn't usual at a criminal deposition. She was dressed all in white, with a large, striking red belt. The stenographer glared at her, while the men seemed a little in awe. There was no question who the star of this show would be.

After some procedural matters were resolved, and Ann Hamilton was sworn in, her attorney made a statement.

"We want it made clear for the record that Mrs. Hamilton is appearing at this deposition voluntarily. She was served a summons, but that wasn't necessary. Due to the recent tragedies in her life, she hasn't been answering her phone and has gone into treatment for anxiety. If she had been aware that she'd been requested to come back to Santa Fe for this proceeding, she would have done that without being compelled to do so. She wants more than anyone to resolve her husband's murder and see justice done."

It sounded nice, but Vincent knew it was legally meaningless.

The stenographer asked Ann to state her name, address, and occupation. She did—giving her occupation as "none." It seemed an odd choice. She might have said wife, or homemaker, or something similar. Tucker looked at Ann Hamilton with those cold, steady eyes, and smiled.

"Why did you leave Santa Fe so soon after your husband was murdered?" He was starting fast, hoping to shake her out of her comfort zone.

"I was very upset, obviously, and I wanted to get back to my main home in Los Angeles so I could get medical assistance and begin healing." It was clearly a practiced answer, and the lovely smile that went with it seemed out of place.

"Did the police question you before you left?"

"Yes."

"For how long?"

"I don't remember. I was very upset, crying."

"Detective Sanchez, the leading investigator, has said that he didn't question you much because you were distraught. That he left the house after you went to your room, planning to question you more later, but that you left before he could. Do you dispute that?"

"Well, I did talk to him. I don't know how you want to define 'question,' but I didn't ignore him. I was upset and I needed some time. He left me alone, and after a while, I decided I needed to go home. I was not trying to avoid him—he wasn't there."

"Have you talked to him or to any other investigator since that night?"

"No."

"So, to be clear: your husband was murdered in the front yard of your Santa Fe home while you were present, and you haven't talked to the police, other than a brief exchange that night, about what happened?" Tucker's tone was skeptical.

"Objection. She's answered the question. Mr. Tucker is just making a statement." That came from Carlton, but Ann's attorney Taylor was halfway to his feet, presumably to say something similar.

"Withdrawn." Tucker was frowning and shaking his head, showing his disbelief, but he moved on. "Were you involved in your husband's business as a sports agent?"

"Not in any official way. I was supportive of my husband

and his business. I would attend events with him and join him when he was socializing with his clients."

"There was a meeting of five of his clients scheduled for Santa Fe, did you make the arrangements for that meeting?"

"Yes, I did. Normally I wouldn't do that sort of thing, but Mark wanted to hold the meeting in Santa Fe rather than L.A. I spend more time at our house here than he did, so it was natural for me to take care of it."

"How did you decide on the Blue Door Inn as a venue?"

"We got some promotional material at our house about the opening of the new place. I liked it because it was close by."

"Was it important that the guests be close to your home?"

"Not really. It was just convenient for Mark."

"How far is your house from the Inn?"

"Maybe a mile or so?"

"Is that by car or walking?"

Ann thought about it. "Not sure. I've never walked it, but it would be closer walking, since the road twists around some. I would say it might be only a half-mile or so walking, if you cut through the wooded area."

Tucker paused while he shuffled some papers. "The meeting at the Inn ended up being about the missing investment funds—money that belonged to the clients who were there—is that correct?"

"Yes, that was the main thing we discussed."

"But your husband wasn't aware of the fact that the funds were missing until the day before the meeting, correct?"

"Yes."

"So, what was the original purpose of the meeting?"

Ann glanced at her attorney, but only for a split-second.

"A week or so before, Mark had finalized a deal to sell his business to VMG. He organized the meeting with his top clients to tell them about the change and how it would benefit them to be part of a larger organization."

"Were the clients aware of this sale beforehand?"

"No. He was going to tell them at the meeting."

"What's VMG?"

"It's a large sports agency in Los Angeles—a competitor, up until the sale."

"What do the initials stand for, VMG?"

"Victory Media Group."

"Who owns that company?"

"I'm not sure, it may be a public company. The CEO is Victor Lorenzo."

Tucker was making notes and didn't look happy. "I'd like to take a short restroom break, if that's agreeable to everyone."

No one seemed to believe the reason he gave, and Ann Hamilton gave Tucker a dirty look, but no one objected. They agreed on ten minutes.

Tucker and Vincent huddled in the lobby, Tucker speaking in a whisper. "I need you to get online and find out about VMG and Victor Lorenzo. That name means something to me from my past. This may bring a whole new element into this case. I want to have some information before I finish with her, if possible."

"Sure, can I borrow your laptop?" Vincent hadn't realized

he might need his computer at a deposition, and had left it at the Inn.

"Yeah. I won't need it. If you have any underworld contacts, you might make some phone calls and ask about Lorenzo and his L.A. business. Also, I need to know if it's a public company. If it is, there should be some kind of filing related to the purchase of Mark's agency." Tucker had a renewed energy. He gave Vincent a wink. "Guess I'll go to the restroom just for show—I don't want them to accuse me of lying."

When the ten minutes were up, everyone took their seats. The stenographer noted the break and restated who was being deposed. Then she nodded to Tucker, indicating he could start.

"Mrs. Hamilton, could you please walk us through the events that occurred at the Inn, and then later at your house, on the day your husband was killed?"

Ann resettled herself in the chair and looked directly at Tucker. "We arrived about eight-thirty at the Inn. Mark greeted everyone briefly, and then we all went into the conference room. He immediately told them about the missing money. Almost before he could finish talking, people were upset and started yelling at him. He got them to be quiet for a bit, so he was able to give them some details, but then everything got out of hand. Dave Adams, and also Vickie's husband Bud, were yelling nonsense at Mark, like this was his fault, calling him names. He tried to tell them that he'd lost all his money, too, but they wouldn't listen. Dave Adams was being really vulgar. He stood up and stormed toward the door, and as he was leaving, he threatened to kill Mark if the money wasn't returned immediately. He left, and Linda—that's his wife—went after him. I think Bud said something about not understanding why they had been brought all the way to Santa Fe to hear this news. One of the guys, I think it was Buster, said he would support Mark in any way he could to help get the money back. Eventually they all left, and Mark and I went home."

"You said Adams threatened to kill Mark. What exactly did he say?"

"I'm not sure I can quote it exactly, but it was something like 'if this isn't fixed, you'll be dead.' Something very close to that. I think it was pretty clear to everyone in the room that he threatened to kill Mark."

"What happened after you got home?"

"Mark was angrier than I'd ever seen him, almost out of control. He was yelling about 'that asshole Adams,' throwing a fit. I went to the kitchen to fix some tea, just to get away from him. He really seemed like he was having some kind of meltdown, and I wasn't sure what to do. When I came back, he was on the phone, yelling at whoever he was talking to. I left his tea on the table and went to the bedroom. I shut the door, but I could still hear him yelling. That went on for the whole afternoon. I was worried that he'd have a heart attack or a stroke if he didn't calm down. And to make matters worse, toward late afternoon he started drinking. There was a point when I heard him yelling obscenities, and I don't think he was even on the phone—he was just losing it. At some point, I decided I had to go and see if I could calm him down, maybe get him to eat something. He was pacing like a madman, and he yelled at me to leave him alone, and he gave me a look that actually scared me. I didn't think he would hurt me, but it was like looking at a different person. I knew I should do something, but I had no idea what. I definitely didn't want to call the cops and have him crazy the way he was—there was no telling what might happen. So, I decided to hide. I got my prescription sleeping pills and went into the guest room and locked the door."

"What time was that?"

"I'm not absolutely sure, but it must have been around seven-thirty or so, maybe even closer to eight. When I went to the guest room I didn't hear him yelling. He was talking to someone, but calmly, so I thought that maybe the worst was over."

"Was there any way for you to know who he was talking to?"

"No. Of course, I could only hear his side of the conversation, and now that he wasn't yelling I couldn't make out what he was saying. I didn't hear him say anyone's name."

"Okay. What did you do then?"

"I laid down on the bed for a while. I was completely exhausted by then. But I was so anxious, I knew I wouldn't be able to sleep. So, I took one of my pills and that put me to sleep."

"And you think that was about eight?"

"Yeah, or a little before."

"When did you wake up?"

"Something woke me in the middle of the night. I don't know what it was. I got up and looked at my phone—it was about twelve-forty-five. I listened for sound, but didn't hear anything. I went into the living room, but Mark wasn't there. While I was standing there, I thought I heard something outside and I went to the door and opened it. There were cops everywhere. I just stood there for a bit, staring at them, and that's when I saw Mark lying in the yard. I screamed, and suddenly all these men were running at me. I started to run to Mark, but some guy caught me and said I should go back inside. I could tell he had to be dead—there was blood all over him. I think I may have passed out for a few moments. That detective brought me into the house and put me in a chair. He was asking me if he could get me anything. I just sat there for some time, trying to get everything straight in my head. I was telling the detective about what had happened at the meeting that morning when I started shaking and I think I must have gone into some kind of shock or something. The detective helped me into the bedroom, and he said he would be back. I laid down for what seemed like a long time—it had to be hours. When I got up, there was no one in the house. I could see outside that police cars were still scattered around on the drive and in the road. I waited some more, but when no one came, I called a cab. I just wanted to get out of there. Maybe I should have gone to a hotel or something, but I wanted to be far away, and I wanted to be someplace where I felt at home. I had the cab driver take me to the Albuquerque airport, and then I had to wait for a few hours before I could get a flight to LA. At LAX, I took a cab home and went to bed. I think I slept for almost two days. I called my therapist, and she signed me in at a clinic. I spent several days there."

"We'll need to get the cab company name, name of the airline, your therapist's name, and the name of the clinic, but we can take care of that later. Based on what other people have said, it seems likely that Mark had been told that afternoon that the money had been recovered. Maybe by one of the people you heard him talking to. If the money had been recovered, why do you think he was still angry?"

"I don't know. Maybe he was worried that all the bad press that would come out of this mess would cause a problem with the sale to VMG."

"Had he been paid by VMG?"

"Yes, I believe so."

"Do you know Ryan Lewis?"

"Yes, of course. He and I used to date before I married Mark. He was Mark's best friend, and I think he was his main attorney."

"The man who supposedly stole the money, a guy named Larry Jackson—was it Lewis who introduced him to Mark?"

"Yes."

Carlton spoke up.

"Might be a good time for a lunch break. Shall we say, one hour?"

Everyone nodded. Tucker went into the hall to look for Vincent but couldn't find him. He went to the front desk and asked if anyone had seen a very large man working on a computer. The woman at the front desk directed Tucker down a couple of doors, to a small work area for guests. Vincent was there working intently on the computer.

"What have you found?"

"You probably know, or knew, this guy's father. The VMG guy is Victor Lorenzo Junior, but you may have known Victor Senior. Junior is supposedly a respectable businessman, but dad was suspected of being a hitman for the mob. One of your buddies?"

"Sonofabitch. That's one bad family, I don't give a shit what people say about Junior. If he's the son of the Victor Lorenzo I knew, he's almost certainly one very bad person."

26

Evil Woman

They started the deposition up again.

"Did Ryan Lewis want to harm your husband?" Tucker was studying his notes, not looking directly at Ann.

"No. At first, when I started dating Mark, he was upset, but that was a long time ago. We were all friends."

Tucker looked up. "Do you know Stephen Martinez?"

"Yes. He's an attorney here in Santa Fe."

"We're you having an affair with Mister Martinez?"

She dropped the movie star smile and gave Tucker a threatening look. "He and I would go to local social events, and maybe we had a little fling. But it was nothing. My god, he's married. And I would never have left Mark—it was just some casual fun."

"Did the casual fun involve having sex?"

She turned to her lawyer. "Can this bastard ask me that? What does that have to do with anything? Object or something."

The attorney looked like he wished he was somewhere else. "Objection."

But it was too late—the façade of the devoted wife had

fallen. Tucker continued. "For the record, we believe the question to be relevant, but we'll move on." He had showed that Ann was willing to lie, which was his main goal. As a bonus, he now knew for sure that she hadn't coordinated her testimony with Martinez, who'd admitted the affair, while she'd tried to deny it and minimize it. "Mrs. Hamilton, are you aware of any affairs that your husband had since you married?"

"This is just more bullshit. He didn't have any affairs." She glared at Tucker.

"Are you familiar with the security system in your Santa Fe house?"

"I know it's there and how to turn it on and off." She looked like she thought it was a clever answer.

"Did you turn the system off on the night of your husband's murder?"

"No."

"How much money did your husband sell his company for?"

"Is that really something I have to answer?" Her lawyer nodded, looking unhappy all over again.

"I'm not sure of every detail, but I believe it was fifty million."

"Fifty million dollars?"

"Yeah." She couldn't help herself—she actually smiled.

"And now that's your money?"

She shrugged.

"Please answer."

"Yeah."

"Does Ryan Lewis get any of that money?"

"Mark used a different law firm for the business deal. I don't think Ryan even knew about it."

"Did you know a man named Tito Alverez?"

"Nope, never heard of him."

"Have you met Victor Lorenzo?"

"My husband and I had dinner with him about two weeks ago. Seemed like a very nice man."

"VMG isn't a public company. It's owned entirely by Mister Lorenzo, who's the son of Victor Lorenzo Senior. The father was believed to be part of a Mafia family in New York City, and was killed in a suspicious car accident about ten years ago. At that time, Lorenzo Junior moved to California and started a business, which later became VMG. Were you aware of Mister Lorenzo's family history?"

"No. He didn't seem like a mob guy to me."

"Did your husband know anything about the rumors that his money came from organized crime?"

"If he did, he never said anything to me about it."

"Could that be an explanation of why your husband was still so upset even after finding out the money had been recovered?"

"I don't know. He never told me the money was recovered."

"If these clients—the ones he'd invited to Santa Fe—were unhappy with how Mark had handled the missing funds, and if they decided to drop your husband as their agent, do you know if VMG would have had any recourse? Could they have undone the purchase, or reduced the price?"

"I wouldn't know."

"Has Mister Lorenzo contacted you since your husband's death?"

"He left a message, but I haven't talked to him."

"Were you and your husband heavily in debt?"

"Mark handled all of the financial matters."

"So, you don't know how much debt you and your husband had?"

"No, not exactly."

"How about ballpark?"

"No, I just don't know. Okay?"

"You said your husband closed the VMG deal and was paid some time ago. Is that money in your account?"

"I don't see what any of this had to do with his murder. How come this guy's allowed to ask me about my finances? It isn't right. My god, I just lost my husband and now it's like you're accusing me of being involved in something or other. I don't know anything about the money, can't you understand that?" She began to cry, the ultimate refusal to answer.

"Let's take a break."

The DA didn't look pleased. He knew her response was bullshit. Ann got up quickly and left the room, her attorney right behind her. Jack Hill came over to Tucker and Vincent.

"Well, Tucker, you won't see her back today. Sounds like you were headed in the right direction. Somehow or other, this is about money—a lot of money. My guess would be that Ann Hamilton knows down to the penny where the money is, how much she owes, and what the downside on the VMG deal is. I guarantee you she has better money management skills than most CPAs." He grinned at Tucker.

"Yeah. She's only stupid when she doesn't want to answer."

"Hello, I'm Vincent Malone." Vincent extended his hand to Hill.

"Heard a lot of stuff about you, Vincent."

"All good, I hope."

Vincent couldn't decide if Hill was a good guy or a bad guy. For his part, Hill looked at Vincent a bit too long before answering.

"Well, more like a mixed bag. But Tucker thinks you're okay, and that's what counts."

Vincent put Hill into the "bad guy" category for the time being. "I think Hill's right," he said. "She's not coming back."

Tucker shrugged. "I got almost everything I wanted. I think I'll tell the DA, when he comes back, that we're done with her, let him notify her attorney. Our next priority is to get Martinez to agree to a deposition or have the judge order it—I think he's going to punch some holes in her story. And Ryan Lewis is a nagging itch that I can't quite scratch."

Hill asked. "Just out of curiosity, Peter, why do you think Dave Adams didn't do it?"

"We should be getting a statement today from the Jackson investment firm giving us the exact timing on when they told Hamilton the money had been recovered, but it was somewhere around seven o'clock. Long before Adams was supposedly there. Adams threatened Hamilton all right, but the threat was 'unless you get the money back.' He didn't hate Hamilton, like a lot of people did. He just needed his money back, lost his cool, and made an empty threat. If you had a large, angry man at your door, and you knew that the reason for him being so angry no longer existed, wouldn't you tell him? And of course, that is what Hamilton did. That was after the two drunk men struggled a bit with Hamilton's bat, and he got clonked on the head with it in the process. Now, you can argue that Adams didn't believe him, and killed him anyway, but that wouldn't make sense at all. Adams would have said, 'Okay, if it's not in my account by next week then I'm going to kill you'—something like that. That was all he wanted—the money. He was already done with Hamilton, although Hamilton didn't know that. With the injuries he had, there weren't going to be any more contracts to negotiate. Whoever killed Hamilton more than likely did it because they hated him, and that's not Adams."

"That still leaves the number one question, though," Hill said. "How did his gun get there?"

The annoying thing was that he was right.

Vincent waited outside the Hilton while Tucker made arrangements to move himself, Dave, and Linda there. It was going to be expensive, but if you had more money than you could count, what did it matter? He was thinking about how different Tucker seemed to him now, as opposed to when he'd first met him, when his thoughts were interrupted—his phone was vibrating.

"Vincent Malone."

"Mister Malone, this is Brad Stanton."

"Well, hello, chief."

"Wanted to give you a heads-up on the death of Tito Alverez. The coroner's report indicates he died of natural causes, specifically a heart attack."

"I wouldn't have guessed that. He seemed pretty healthy, and he was young."

"Yeah. The officers at the scene jumped to conclusions because he was a street person. They account for a substantial percentage or our violent crimes, whether as perpetrator, victim, or both. Plus, there was the blood. The forensic people say they believe he stumbled and fell against a broken part of the fence and cut himself, but it had nothing to do with his death. He suffered a massive heart attack and died almost immediately. The doctor said he could see that Tito had very advanced heart disease. Without aggressive treatment, this kind of thing was inevitable. He said it was probably hereditary."

"Well, I'm sorry he died, but I'm glad it wasn't murder. I liked Tito."

"Me, too. He was a good friend." The chief was silent for a moment. "You should know that Tito was working odd jobs for Stephen Martinez. He and Martinez had become friends. When he had the heart attack, he was very close to Martinez's office, and I believe that's where he was headed. Martinez has done some really stupid things in his life, but this latest, getting mixed up with Mark Hamilton's wife, is the worst. That said, I'm pretty sure this was just a guy being an idiot for sex—I don't think he was involved in Hamilton's murder. What I'm hearing is that Martinez fell pretty hard for Ann Hamilton. Seems he lost whatever good sense he had at that point."

"I've seen her, so I guess I understand. She's gorgeous, but it's more than that. She's regal, as if she were some kind of queen—I can imagine that could become addictive." Vincent had a theory about people that was more biblical than he would like to admit: some of them were just evil. He was pretty sure Ann Hamilton was one of them.

"He's in a tough spot with his family and his career," Stanton said. "Not sure how it'll turn out. I've talked to him at the request of the sheriff. As I've told you, the sheriff's a bit of a buffoon, but there's no one more concerned about the people he thinks of as his extended family, and Martinez is part of that. I advised Martinez to give your buddy a deposition and not to fight it, which is what his attorney wants. Martinez has screwed up plenty because of Ann Hamilton, but if he wants to fix it he has to start by taking responsibility for his actions. And the first step is to provide to you anything he knows about the killing of Hamilton. If you call him, he'll come, no matter what his attorney says."

"I think you gave him good advice. He's got some issues with his license regarding Adams. He should never have represented him, and should never have agreed to be Tucker's co-counsel. But if he cooperates, then I'm sure Tucker will use his influence to try to lessen the consequences."

"I hope so. I'm going to tell you something, but you can't use it as coming from me. You have to find another source. Agreed?"

"Chief, I'm not real sure what I'm agreeing to here. You wouldn't ask me to withhold evidence, would you?"

"Once you know what I have to say, you'll know exactly who can confirm it. I'm just asking that you confirm it before you say anything about me."

"Okay, I'll buy that."

"It was Tito who made the 911 call reporting the Hamilton murder."

"Tito. But how?"

"Think about it some, and I think you will see how. Goodbye, Mister Malone."

I believe in people being evil. Not bad—evil. There is probably a psychological term that describes the pure evil in words that don't sound so terrible, but the ones I've met are just plain rotten. Ann Hamilton has all the signs. She's sure that she's entitled to whatever she can get, and no one else matters. Did she kill her husband for the money? It'd make sense, because I'm guessing money and power are all she cares about. You have to feel sorry for Martinez, despite everything. He was way out of his league, and there'll be a price to pay.

27

Moving On

"Morning, Vincent." Jerry came into the kitchen from the back yard just as Vincent was getting a cup of coffee.

"Hey, Jerry. Looks like no one's up yet."

"Well they are. They all had coffee, but that was it. They're leaving this morning. I hear Mister Tucker's rented an entire floor at the Hilton. That ought to keep everyone secure. Maybe you could pull the van around so they can start loading."

"Sure. Boy, that was quick. Tucker told me he'd made arrangements, but didn't say anything about moving this fast."

"I think they only decided late last night. I suspect Dave's having panic attacks, or something along those lines. I don't have all the details, but Linda said this morning that she'd decided it was best to move, that it would keep Dave occupied for a while. She seemed very upset."

"Yeah, I'm sure it's been tough on them. Maybe this is for the best. I'll go get the van, then check with Tucker and see if I can help." Once outside, he took out his phone and called Tucker. "Man, this is sudden. Did something happen?"

"No, not really. Somewhere in the night I guess Dave had some kind of emotional attack. Linda called and I went to their room. It took almost an hour to get him settled down. Linda and I talked and decided we'd go ahead with the plan to move downtown. Going to the Hilton might be the best thing for him. Change of scenery might give him something to think about other than the trial. Plus, she's arranged for a doctor to see him later this afternoon to see if he can get something to help with the anxiety. So, yeah, it's abrupt, I guess, but I think this is the right thing to do. Your friends can get back to trying to run their new business without all of this gloom and doom hanging over them."

"I hope it helps. In a bigger place, Dave should feel a little more anonymous, I guess—not so much the center of attention, and that has to be an improvement. I'm sure he'd love to go home, but for now this is probably the best you can do. I'm pulling the van around now, so I can help with anything you need."

"Thanks. We'll get the luggage into the dining room in a bit, and then we'll be ready to go."

Vincent cleaned up the van a little, then went inside. There was luggage in the dining room and he began to load it into the van. Soon everyone came into the dining area. Jerry and Cindy said goodbye like they were relatives, with hugs for everyone. Mary and Hector said more restrained, but still heartfelt goodbyes.

Vincent noticed all over again how genuinely nice Jerry and Cindy were, and wondered to himself if they could really be successful in business with such good hearts. He hoped so. With everyone loaded up, they headed off to Santa Fe. Vincent remarked on the great weather, but got no response. So, after that, he just drove.

⊸—

On his way back to the Inn, Vincent was running the van through a car wash when his phone vibrated.

"Vincent Malone"

"Malone, my name is Sheriff Ortega. I'm not sure why you're fucking with me and my people, but I want to talk to you about it."

"That's not a very friendly way to begin a conversation."

"You want friendly, go talk to the nicey-nice police chief. Look I just want to talk, not bash your head in or anything. Can you come by the office?"

"Since you asked so nice, sure. Be happy to talk to you."

"You really are a wiseass, aren't you?"

"It's a condition I have."

The sheriff gave him directions and hung up. Vincent drove over, parked in front, and then hesitated. He felt in his pocket for his pistol. It gave him what was almost certainly a false sense of security, but it was a comfort, nonetheless. He didn't really think the sheriff would hurt him, but better safe than sorry. It would actually probably be best of all to just leave, but he was curious about what the blowhard wanted, so he went in—but armed.

The sheriff was a huge man, about Malone's height, but maybe a hundred pounds heavier. He looked angry, but it seemed entirely possible the guy always looked that way. They went into his small, cluttered office, the two bulky men filling the room to capacity.

"I don't like private dicks. I don't want amateurs investigating anything in my town. I don't give a shit if you have a license or not, understand?"

It was decision time. Was it "yes sir" and leave, or "fuck you"? "I believe in the law and I believe in due process, whether it's in Denver or Santa Fe or any fuckin' place in this country. I will not be steamrolled by some two-bit sheriff who throws his weight around like he's living in a goddamn banana republic." Vincent got up to leave.

"Fuck, man, sit down." The sheriff gave him a sideways glance. "Okay, maybe that was a little strong, but I don't like people snoopin' around trying to do our job. You got some kind of problem, you should have come to me."

"Ortega, I had no indication from anyone that you would be open to a visit from me about the operation of your department. I'm still not sure about it even now. But I'll tell you this for free: you and your department made mistakes investigating the murder of Mark Hamilton. I can list them if you want."

The sheriff crossed his arms and leaned back in his chair. He didn't speak, but it seemed to leave room for Vincent to continue—so he did.

"No one interviewed Mrs. Hamilton after her brief initial statement. She was right there in the house the night he was murdered. They'd been fighting. She had apparently been involved in an affair that was public knowledge, maybe more than one. I'd think it was pretty important to get her information about what happened."

Ortega shrugged. "We had the killer, the murder weapon was his gun, found at the scene of the crime. End of story."

"Okay, let's see how that plays out. First, he fought with Hamilton and it was recorded on security video. Somehow the video gets mysteriously turned off, and he comes back and shoots Hamilton, then leaves his gun next to the body. He wipes his prints off the gun, even though it's registered in his name, so it's going to come back to bite him with or without prints. Is that your killer?"

"I didn't say he was smart."

"I have no problem with what Sanchez did that night. I would have done pretty much the same. He had the most likely suspect, with pretty good evidence, and he arrested him. That's good police work. But then you stopped, Sanchez stopped, the whole goddamned case just stopped. That's not how it should work. There should have been more interviews and follow-ups. There were additional tests that should have been run. More investigation of every kind. Why? Because the guy you arrested said he didn't do it, and there was evidence that at least raised questions about whether he might be telling the truth. Besides the issue of leaving his own gun at the scene—after carefully wiping it clean of his prints—who called 911? Who turned off the security video when it had been working earlier the same night? These are holes you have to fill to have a complete picture of what happened, and you didn't."

"Do you have answers to those questions?"

"Nope. I can guess at some of them, but I don't have definite answers. But unlike this department, I haven't stopped looking. Even if the answers are bad for my client, I want them."

Vincent was getting steamed, and he fought to get his temper under control.

"You're not the law Malone, I am. You had your Colorado license transferred to New Mexico—one call from me, and it'll be revoked."

"Why the fuck would you do that?"

"The law isn't a fuckin' game, that's why. And you've been interfering with our ability to perform our duties."

Vincent smirked. "You don't believe that—there's some other reason. I'm doing investigative work for Peter Tucker and Jack Hill, both respected attorneys with lots of pull in Washington and the state government here in Santa Fe. You want to test your political connections against those guys, go right ahead. Neither of them will back down from a fight."

"Jack Hill, huh? Yeah, I know Jack Hill. Maybe I should just leave you alone and let you fuck up this whole case so everyone can see what a jerk you are."

The sheriff still had a mean look on his face, but he seemed to have shrunk a little at the mention of Hill.

"I don't want to fight with you sheriff, I just want to do my job. If I learn anything that you should know, I'll tell Detective Sanchez immediately." *Here, asshole, take this graceful exit.*

"Yeah, you better."

Vincent was back in the Inn parking lot when he called Tucker and relayed the gist of his conversation with the sheriff. "Why would he be so concerned about Jack Hill?"

"There's no one in this state with more political pull than Jack Hill. He's a major contributor to the Republican Party—and the Democrats, too, when it suits him. But my guess would be that the sheriff knows the other Jack Hill, the street fighter. He made his reputation in law and politics as a no-holds-barred tough guy. Anyone with a memory from that time would probably be afraid of Mister Hill."

"Is he crooked?"

"Vincent, he's our co-counsel and a gentleman. But don't fuck with him."

Vincent had found Hector in his favorite spot—the vegetable garden. Hector had told Vincent some time ago that his dream had always been to be a farmer.

"Hector, how's the garden?"

"Going great, Mister Vincent. We should start to have some crops real soon. It will make all of Jerry's and Mary's cooking so much better." He smiled broadly.

"I've heard that there's a path that runs from behind the Inn all the way around where the Hamilton's house is located—do you know about that?"

"Oh sure. It's been there for years, long before these houses were here. The road cuts the path, but it picks up on the other side. It actually goes for a long way, maybe twenty or thirty miles, almost to the Tesuque Pueblo. It is a beautiful walk if you ever have time. I told Vickie Turner about it—she seemed real interested. I think she's a runner, so it would be perfect for her."

"Do you know where the Hamilton house is?"

"I think so. Vickie mentioned that you could see their house from that little rise over there. If it's the one I think it is, it's only maybe a ten-minute walk from here on that trail."

"When did you talk to Vickie about this?" Vincent kept his tone light, not wanting Hector to guess why he was asking.

"Had to be the first day they were here. Everyone was resting, but she came out and asked about some place she could run. I pointed out the trail and she headed off. I was still outside when she came back, and she told me she could see the Hamilton's house from the hill—I guess she had been at their house before. At that time, I really didn't know who she was talking about, so I kind of just ignored it."

"Thanks, Hector. Can't wait for those fresh vegetables."

Vincent sat down in the gazebo, called Tucker, and filled him in on what Hector had said.

Some days you're good, some days you're smart, and some days, you're just plain lucky.

28

Two Timers

Vincent headed into Santa Fe in his Mustang, planning on hitting Pasqual's for breakfast. He knew there would be a line, but it didn't matter—he wasn't in a hurry. He would meet Tucker around ten at the Hilton to discuss the case, and was looking forward to some alone time in a bustling restaurant filled with delicious aromas. A busy restaurant was calming to him—all that activity, none of it his responsibility.

The line was longer than he'd expected. It made him pause for a moment, but he decided he had nothing else he had to do. He went in, left his name, and picked up a *New York Times*. They were delivering hot coffee to the patrons waiting outside, and he made himself comfortable.

He glanced at the headlines and groaned. He wasn't interested in politics, though the thought nagged at him that it meant he was a lousy citizen. He should care more than he did, but it seemed to require more effort than he was willing to part with. If everyone would just tell the truth, then he thought he could just about deal with it, but it was an idiotic game where everyone lied—some more than others, but no one was exempt. How could you decide anything important if all your information was bullshit? He turned to the sports section.

He followed the Denver teams, and was an avid Rockies fan. He thought baseball was a smart game, played more or less according to rules. Football, by contrast, seemed like chaos, with victory often being decided by penalties for breaking rules that were subjective and poorly administered. It was as if the government was in charge of football, with all of its bickering and clowning, while baseball was run by the best fourth-grade teacher you ever had, the one who ensured that everyone played by the rules or not at all, and if you weren't polite, there were consequences. He wasn't sure where basketball fit in.

Somewhere in the back pages, there was a small article that caught his eye.

NYPD spokesperson Daniel Davis released a statement announcing that an arrest had been made in the murder of Larry Jackson, a New York City financial consultant and hedge fund manager. Mr. Jackson's body was discovered in an alley in SoHo. Late yesterday, the Los Angeles Police Department arrested Ryan Lewis, a prominent L.A. attorney who had a business relationship with Mr. Jackson. An arraignment is scheduled for this afternoon on the charge of first degree murder. Mr. Jackson was struck in the head with a heavy object, but the police report indicated that all of his belongings were intact, so police ruled out robbery.

Ryan Lewis arrested for the murder of Larry Jackson—that was interesting. He thought about calling Tucker, but he would see him soon and he wasn't really sure how Lewis fit into the murder of Hamilton, anyway. He was part of the puzzle, but Vincent didn't know how that piece connected to everything else. He suspected Lewis had been having an affair with Ann Hamilton, but that was because he suspected that just about everyone was having an affair with Mrs. Hamilton.

He really didn't think Lewis had anything to do with Hamilton's death—he was just the guy behind the missing investment funds. He'd hired Jackson, maybe even tricked him into moving the funds to create a panic. That sounded like something an asshole attorney might do to an old buddy to teach him a lesson. But killing Hamilton? That would be a surprise. Most of the top-dollar attorneys he'd met would never get their hands dirty actually killing someone. They were much more likely to frame them for some misdeed.

"Malone, table is ready." The waiter yelled into the gathered crowd. If you weren't Malone, you ignored him, but Vincent jumped up with a little happy dance.

It was hard to order anything in Santa Fe without running into the ubiquitous green chili. In a daring move, Vincent decided that if he was going to live in New Mexico he couldn't ignore the local staple. He ordered a green-chili breakfast burrito. When it arrived, he was sure it was meant to be a dish for two, but he ate the whole thing. And it was wonderful. The chili was mild, and the taste was fantastic. He was a convert. If he'd been alone, he would have leaned back and moaned.

After such a massive breakfast, he decided to walk to the Hilton. His car was in a comfortable spot, and the hotel wasn't that far. The uniqueness of Santa Fe was both charming and off-putting. How many little artsy shops did one town need? The answer seemed to be, "lots."

He entered the Hilton lobby and immediately spotted Tucker, who was leaning back in a large stuffed chair with his eyes closed, apparently asleep.

"Tucker."

The lawyer opened his eyes. "Not sure what it is around here. I eat all the time and can't get enough naps. Not all bad, but I shouldn't fall asleep in public—not good for my sharp-as-a-tack reputation."

"I won't tell. Want to go into the conference room?"

"Nah, let's go upstairs. I'm renting a whole goddamn floor. We've got plenty of room."

They took the elevator to the fourth floor and got out.

"Very nice."

"Yeah, not bad. It's not really a whole floor. The hotel has three wings off the central core, so this is the entire floor in the third wing. I think it's eight rooms, the guy said. Anyway, I had them set one up as a meeting room, down here."

All the bedroom furniture had been removed and replaced with a conference table and eight chairs. Everything seemed to be first-rate.

"I read in the *New York Times* this morning that Ryan Lewis has been arrested for the murder of Larry Jackson," Vincent said.

"Yeah, I got a call from my FBI contact. They charged him with murder and think they have a good case. They can place him in New York at the time he was attacked, and they have several witnesses who saw them together not long before Jackson was killed. No weapon so far, according to NYPD, but they're working on it. Being a lawyer, Lewis has given them nothing. Any chance he could have killed Hamilton?"

"I guess there's always a chance. I have yet to talk to him, so I don't know about his alibi, but my guess is that it likely wasn't him. I think he was bitter about Hamilton stealing his girlfriend, and he probably orchestrated the whole investment fund problem. But the fact that the money was just moved to another account seems to suggest that it was a very ugly little prank. I'm pretty sure he meant to hurt Hamilton, but not by killing him."

"Do you think Lewis killed Jackson?"

Vincent paused a minute.

"Yeah, I actually do. There's always the chance that he was killed in some kind of unrelated event, but my guess is he had no idea what Lewis was up to until it happened, at which point he probably was really pissed that he'd been dragged into it. So, he was either threatening to go to the authorities and confess, or he was threatening Lewis in some way—maybe blackmailing him for money or something. If that happened, I can see Lewis losing it, hitting the guy in the head on impulse with the first thing he found. A brick, a trash can—hell, an old toilet seat someone put out with the garbage. You can kill someone with a lot of old junk. So, maybe he just reacted—a reflex, with no thought at all. I bet they have some forensic evidence that links him to the murder weapon, even though officially they're saying no weapon has been found."

"I asked Dave if he wanted to go to the hearing today, but he didn't want to. No matter what I say to him, he acts like he's going to jail. I flat-out asked why he was always so low, and he said he's afraid of jail. I tried to tell him that I thought we already had enough to give the jury good alternatives, and I didn't think they had sufficient evidence to convict him. He looked at me like I was lying, and said he didn't know, just walked off."

"You might want to look into getting him some help for his mental health. Do you think he'd talk to someone?"

"Hell, no, not a chance. We've got to get this thing settled, now."

The court came to order. The judge looked tired and irritated—not what you want to see just before you ask for a favor. "You say in your filings that the number of depositions in this case is due to the inadequacy of the investigation by the sheriff's department. I'll need you to be more specific, Mister Tucker."

"Your honor, the sheriff's department didn't bother to interview Mrs. Hamilton when they had the chance and failed to locate the person who phoned in the 911 call. They haven't provided us with interview transcripts for the guests at the Inn, or anything from Stephen Martinez, and only preliminary forensic information from the crime scene. I'm not saying they haven't done anything, but it's very little. They arrested my client and then just stopped investigating."

The judge peered at the DA. "Mister Carlton, haven't we already had this conversation?"

"Yes, your honor. All I can say is that there doesn't seem to be extensive files from the sheriff's department's investigation. We're prepared to agree to any reasonable number of depositions that the defense feels are necessary to overcome this shortcoming."

"I see that Mr. Martinez responded to the summons and refuses to appear for the deposition. What are you requesting on that issue, Mister Tucker?"

"Mister Martinez's attorney advised us that he wouldn't appear for the scheduled deposition, but since then we've been advised by a reliable source that Mister Martinez has changed his mind and wants to have the deposition rescheduled. At this point we think we should reschedule and see if he shows up."

"I agree. Please schedule that as soon as possible. If he doesn't show up this time, I'll hold him in contempt of court and issue an arrest warrant. Anything else, Mister Tucker?"

"We believe that the Turners, who were guests at the Inn, may have critical information regarding the night of the murder. They're no longer in Santa Fe. We would like you to issue a summons to them, requiring that they return immediately for a deposition."

"You're not just fishing here, are you?"

"No sir. I think my filing gives sufficient reasons to conduct those interviews."

"Mister Carlton, have you read the defense filings in support of this deposition of the Turners?"

"I have, your honor, and we do not object."

"Very well, so ordered. If you will make sure that we have

the latest and best contact information for the Turners, we will immediately get these summonses out and will ask the local authorities to serve them ASAP."

"Yes, sir, we'll make sure you have all the contact information we have. Your honor, I'm sure you've been notified, but I wanted to mention on the record that Mister and Mrs. Adams have moved from the Blue Door Inn to the downtown Hilton, all of which was coordinated with pretrial services."

"Thank you for the notification, Mister Tucker. May I ask, why the move?"

"As we get closer to the trial, I thought the downtown location made more sense in terms of convenience and some aspects of security."

"Yes, I'm sure that will be more convenient. I've given you a lot of latitude regarding this phase of the trial, but once these two depositions are done, I'm going to tighten up the schedule for the trial. I'm hoping we can begin the trial in about three weeks, so keep that in mind, gentlemen. Anything else?"

Tucker and the DA both said there wasn't.

"Then this hearing is adjourned."

Everyone filed out of the courtroom.

"Do you think we should contact Bud and Vickie?" Vincent asked Tucker.

"Probably not, just now. Let the court do its thing, that'll have more impact. We'll give it some time and then, if we haven't heard anything, you can get on their trail. Something you can do now, though, is contact Martinez. Let's get that set up as soon as possible. You headed back to the Hilton?"

"No, my car's down by the breakfast place, in the other direction."

"Okay, see you later. You hear anything about anything, let me know."

They headed in opposite directions.

About a block down, Vincent took a detour and headed for the Crown Bar.

"What can I get you?" Yet another bartender. Maybe Nancy was difficult to work for.

"Tecate."

Vincent looked around at the sparse crowd. It was early, and Nancy didn't seem to be there. The bartender brought the beer.

"Is Nancy working?"

"No, I don't think she's in. I think I heard she had a date or something."

"Okay, thanks."

A date! What the hell was that about? Vincent suddenly felt nauseous. A date? They were practically engaged! Okay, they'd had only one date, but he'd kissed her on the cheek. Didn't that count for something? He downed half his beer and left. It was a long, lonely walk back to his car. He headed home so he could go to bed early—old men need a lot of rest.

What was I thinkin? Women! At my age? Attractive, successful women aren't going to have anything to do with me. I'm just some old drunk—it's not like I have a future to offer.

He made it to his room, but he was considering finding some whiskey to drown his sorrows. His phone vibrated.

"Vincent Malone."

"Hey, did I miss you at the bar?"

"Yeah, I dropped by. No big deal, you were busy."

"The new bartender, Charlie, he described you—said a handsome older guy. Said he told you I was on a date. Did you think I was two-timing you, Malone?"

"What? No. Of course not. You don't owe me anything. That's great you were on date, or whatever."

"Why are all men such little boys? The 'date' was my women's book club. Hell, we don't even read romance novels—it's all serious stuff. Come by and see me tomorrow night about seven, and I'll treat you to dinner, okay?"

"Okay. That would—that would be really great." He hung up and realized he was smiling.

Tucker had said not to contact Vickie or Bud Turner, but his gut told him otherwise. He decided to make a quick call to Vickie, but it went directly to voice mail. No big surprise.

"Vickie, Vincent Malone from Santa Fe. Just wanted to chat with you a little bit. I was talking to Hector, the gardener at the Blue Door, and he mentioned that he told you about a direct path to the Hamilton house from the Inn. Need to talk to you about what he had to say. Give me a call." He left his number. He knew he was fishing, but at least he had bait.

29

Lewis In Wonderland

Vincent was headed into Santa Fe to meet with Tucker. He couldn't stop for a big breakfast this time, even if he was starved—his waistline was becoming global in both shape and proportions. With a budding romance, he was going to have to improve his eating habits, even exercise a little. The thought made him smile, for more than one reason.

The summer months had arrived, and the traffic around the plaza was horrible even at this early hour—people everywhere. Generally, tourists are a pretty cheerful bunch, trying to enjoy their holidays, but for some reason they seemed to operate in a bubble when it came to cars. With apparent disregard for the obvious risks involved in a contest between a fragile human body and a ton of metal, they would step into the road without looking even perfunctorily for danger. Vincent narrowly missed two older ladies who were chatting—no doubt about something of vital importance—and walked right out in front of his car. He stopped abruptly and got a double dirty look for his trouble. He was going to have to find a saner path to the Hilton.

"Got a call from my FBI contact," Tucker told him.

"Sounds like Lewis is spilling his guts to anyone who will listen. He claims he didn't kill Jackson, even though he'd thought about it. He told the L.A. cops that it was all just a big joke that went off the rails. It was his way of getting back at Hamilton for hiring another law firm to represent him when he sold his business to VMG, which cut Lewis out of some huge fees. The plan was for Jackson to move the money to another trust account, and then have some friend notify Hamilton that the money was missing and Jackson was, too. He would no doubt call Lewis immediately to find out what was going on and Lewis would stall him while the money was transferred back into the correct account. That way, when Hamilton showed up at his office, he could torment the guy for a while, and then eventually tell him the truth. Just a rich-kid prank."

Vincent chuckled and nodded his head in disbelief. "Well, it sure turned into a prank on a whole lot of people. What went wrong with all the innocent fun and games?"

"Apparently, Jackson misunderstood what he was supposed to do. Of course, no one knows for sure since Jackson is dead, but according to Lewis, Jackson thought he was supposed to disappear and not answer his phone for twenty-four hours. Lewis says he told him *four* hours, and that he was supposed to take calls from Lewis no matter when they came. Up until then, the joke was going just fine. Hamilton called Lewis in a panic and was headed to his office. Lewis tried to call Jackson but didn't get an answer. He tried a few times more with the same result. Lewis says that at that point he was worried that Jackson had pulled a fast one and taken the money for real.

He called the investment firm, but all he could find out was that the funds were missing. Apparently, Jackson hadn't shared their little secret with any of his employees. Nobody knew that the cash was in the other trust account the whole time. Then Hamilton shows up raising holy hell. Lewis tries to calm him down, but inside he's starting to panic, too. He says he told Hamilton that he'd already contacted all sorts of people, and they were tracking the money, and everything was going to be okay, but actually, he hadn't contacted anyone yet."

"This is starting to sound Shakespearian, like a comedy of errors—and then the ending turns tragic."

Tucker nodded. "Exactly. Lewis was trying to find out what had happened with Jackson, while Hamilton went into full panic mode. It wasn't just the sports clients who were going to be up in arms—he was going to have to deal with Victor Lorenzo. Hamilton wasn't stupid. He knew Lorenzo's background, and had heard all the rumors about how he did business. Piss off Lorenzo, and it would likely be the last thing you ever did. He had to be in complete melt down over that, and meanwhile, he had to go to Santa Fe and face this hostile crowd. Must have felt like the world was closing in on him."

"Weird. You have to give the guy credit for even showing up in Santa Fe. Not sure I wouldn't have just headed to Tijuana, or something."

"Well, there were millions of dollars involved. My guess is that he thought he could calm the clients down and put them on hold while he tried to recover the money. He needed the clients to be quiet if he was going to keep Lorenzo from killing him—and just going to Tijuana wasn't going to save him, anyway. Lorenzo could get him there just as easily—maybe even easier."

Tucker paused to gather his thoughts and look at some notes he had taken before going on. "So, Lewis says he decided he had to go to New York City and find Jackson—that's where his offices were. He jumped on a redeye flight and arrived in New York early the next morning. As soon as he landed, he called Jackson for the umpteenth time, and this time he answered because the twenty-four hours were up. They talked about the misunderstanding, and that Jackson had to put the money back into the account where it belonged. Jackson said he'd take care of it, and they agreed to meet later that day at a restaurant in SoHo. Lewis contacted various people he knew, including an FBI agent and the New York DA. He gave them all a false story but assured them that the money had been recovered, and no crime was involved, just a bookkeeping error. He didn't do this until later in the day, once Jackson had confirmed via text that everything had been put right."

Vincent shook his head. "So, this whole fuckin' mess was just some stupid joke and the money was always in the very same bank where it started out? There was never any risk to the clients' money. And all this pain was to punish Hamilton for not paying a fee to Lewis? That's horseshit. This is about Ann Hamilton. This is driven by hate, and that's powered by lust. Greed may be a factor, but I bet you my bottom dollar that this is about Hamilton stealing Ann from Lewis."

"I think you're close." Tucker looked tired. "Lewis also

admitted to the cops that he was having an affair with Ann Hamilton—I know, what a shock. Ann appears to be a very active girl. He told the cops he wanted Ann back, but she wouldn't leave Hamilton because of his money, especially now that he'd sold the business for a huge pile of cash. Lewis said that may be what triggered his anger."

"So, Lewis meets the financial guy for dinner in SoHo, and he's killed in an alley in the same neighborhood, just a short time after they finish their meeting, but Lewis had nothing to do with it. Seriously? That's his story?"

"That's what he says. They met and argued about who was at fault, and threatened to sue one another, but they parted, and everyone was alive and he didn't see him again. He also said that during their meeting he had Jackson call his office to instruct one of his managers to call Hamilton and tell him the money had been recovered and was back in the account.

"My FBI friend said he thinks NYPD may have jumped the gun, because there's very little forensic evidence at the scene to tie Lewis to the crime. What they have is the situation in the restaurant, where the men were arguing—there are quite a few witnesses to that—and the fact that Lewis doesn't have an alibi. He says he walked back to his hotel, which is several miles away, and at one point stopped in a park and sat on a bench for some time, just thinking. He can't remember exactly where—says he was just wandering and trying to figure things out. They can't find anyone who saw him. His DNA was on Jackson, but that could be just shaking hands or some kind of shoving match. They have an eyewitness who puts him in the area of the alley, but the FBI guy said Lewis told them he went the wrong direction at first from the restaurant and had to double back. Anyway, it's a circumstantial case—may or may not stick."

"Well that's all very interesting. But from our point of view, it does nothing except eliminate Lewis as a suspect in the Hamilton murder, since apparently he was in New York at the time."

"You're right, Vincent. It doesn't change much of anything for us. One item the FBI guy mentioned is that Lewis said he thought Ann Hamilton might be crazy, and that it wouldn't surprise him a bit if he found out that she killed Hamilton."

"I guess their affair is over," Vincent said, smirking.

They took a break and both got coffee. Vincent picked out a bagel and added a large dollop of cream cheese. Diet be damned—he was starving.

Tucker was sipping his coffee and reviewing his notes. "Do you think we should try to depose Lewis?"

"Probably not. He might give us some good gossip, but I don't see how he helps us with Dave's defense. We already have plenty of dirt about Ann Hamilton's character—bringing in more that's not directly related to the case might seem like we're piling on. As for the background about the missing money and the business deal with VMG, it might muddy the waters some as to who wanted Hamilton dead. But for the most part, Lewis seems like he's outside the things that are relevant for us. A bigger question might be, should we try to depose Victor Lorenzo?"

"Good point. Any more information on him?"

"Not really. He's never been charged with a crime in New York or California, but it seems to be an accepted fact that he started his business empire in L.A. using mob money. Now, maybe that just makes a good story and people are sticking with it until something better comes along, but it's the generally held belief. No question that with his wealth and background there'll be a whole team of lawyers ready to fight any sort of deposition, especially one in New Mexico."

"Yeah, might not be worth the battle. This doesn't feel like a mob crime—not even close. Way too many loose ends. Those guys are pretty good at killing, and this feels like amateurs."

"How's Dave doing?"

"Not in a good place. If it wasn't for Linda, I think he'd have ended it all. I get the fact he has been charged with murder and can't go and do what he wants to do, but I don't understand the depth of his depression."

"He's never been in trouble with the law before, and that first time can be an eye-opener. Most normal people don't even understand the power the system has. It looks like everyone is against you: the police, the DA, the judge, the guy who booked you. Everyone seems to be assuming you're guilty and treating you that way. It's shocking to someone who thinks the system actually works. If you're the typical guy going in and out of jail, you know it's all bullshit, but for someone like Dave, this is mind-blowing. This is a guy who's used to strangers loving him and cheering him, and now he's subject to the whims of some moron assistant DA who is only interested in his own chances of advancement."

Tucker knew the weaknesses in the justice system better than most people. Some of the flaws had benefited him when he'd taken advantage of the screwed-up process to get the guilty released. Now his client was innocent.

"You're right. The system is a mess. The state has all the power. If you don't have money, nobody gives a shit. The state can put hundreds of officers on a case to find evidence that seems to say you're guilty, but if you're a normal guy, you can't afford to hire even a single investigator to go out and find evidence of your innocence. The system is supposed to work because even the prosecutors are supposed to be after justice—if someone's innocent, they're supposed to want to know about it—but that's a load of crap. They're looking for one thing: a win. I've bumped into more DA's than I can name who should be locked up for the crimes they've committed against innocent people, just because they could get away with it, and justice be damned. The only reason the system is still in place is because most people never see what a fucked-up mess it really is."

Vincent was looking grim. "Guess there's not much we can do about that, huh?"

"Probably not. Two past-their-prime old guys sitting around complaining won't change much. But we need to do something, anyway. Stir the damn pot a little, try to make a difference. I've never been much of an activist, except for myself—maybe that should change."

"Sounds like a good cause for someone who has more money than god."

30

Depo Time

The deposition of Stephen Martinez had been moved to a room in the courthouse. Carlton had consulted with Tucker about it, and all sides had agreed that a more secure area was required. People who regularly dealt with the carnage caused by guns weren't comfortable just walking into some conference room somewhere, without proper screening for weapons.

The new venue was larger and more ornate, but there weren't any refreshments. Vincent wasn't sure the tradeoff was worth it.

The people were the same—the DA, assistant DA, court stenographer, Jack Hill, Vincent, and Tucker. Martinez, apparently, would be showing up without an attorney. No one thought that was a good decision, but it was up to him.

Just before things were scheduled to begin, Martinez arrived, but he looked awful. He appeared not to have slept for some time, and he didn't look anyone in the eye. If he'd been Vincent's client, there was no way in hell he'd be at this deposition—he was clearly not physically well enough to deal with the grilling he was likely to get. Vincent looked at Tucker, who shrugged. The court stenographer took charge, stating the purpose of the gathering and named the participants for the record. She swore in Martinez and sat back, nodding to Tucker.

"Mister Martinez, a lot has happened over the last few weeks, much of it I'm sure very difficult for you. Do you believe you are up to giving testimony today?" The old bastard did have a heart—plus he was buying a little insurance, just in case someone later claimed that Martinez hadn't been competent to testify.

The shaken lawyer took a sip from the water in front of him. "I am. This whole thing has been hard on me, and on my family, because I've messed things up very badly. I want very much to testify today so I can try to get all the facts on the table. I don't think I'll be able to rest or recover until I do this, so let's start if we can."

Tucker nodded to him. "I want to ask you about Ann Hamilton, the wife of Mark Hamilton. How long have you known her, and what was the nature of your relationship?"

Martinez let out a deep sigh, his eyes down, staring blankly at the surface of the table. "I met her about six months ago. She contacted me about helping her on some zoning issues she was dealing with regarding a deck expansion she wanted to add to her house. The zoning board had turned it down, because it exceeded a standard for the relationship between the size of the house and the size of any exterior deck. I told her that this was the type of thing I did, and that I'd be happy to help her."

"How did she find you?"

"I'm not sure she said, but a lot of people in city government know me, so if there was an issue and she was giving them trouble, they might have suggested that she call me to see if I could help. Anyway, I went to see her the next day."

"Were you able to help with the zoning?"

"Yeah. We agreed to change the shape a little by moving a portion of the deck so that it wouldn't be visible to her neighbors, and after that, it was approved. I'm sure it was the neighbors who had objected in the first place."

"Did you see her after that?"

"Yes. We started going to charity events together. Her husband rarely came with her when she was in Santa Fe, and my wife hated those events, but she and I both enjoyed them."

Tucker smiled a fatherly smile. "Were you having an affair?"

Martinez repositioned himself in the chair. "Yes."

"How long did the affair go on?"

"It started within a week after we first met. And I guess it just ended."

"Were you in love with her?"

"I don't know. She was absolutely gorgeous and so sophisticated. I had never been with someone like her, and I think I was star-struck. I'm not sure about love."

"Was she in love with you?"

"No, I'm sure she was using me. I knew that pretty much from the beginning. She didn't like being alone, and her husband left her alone a lot. I think what she wanted was someone who adored her. I have really no idea how she felt about me."

"Did you know a man named Tito Alverez?"

"Yes."

"Did he work for you?"

"Sometimes he would do odd jobs for me, mostly things related to my real estate business. He would take the pickup and go out and install for sale signs or pick them up when the house was sold. He just did odd jobs, and I paid him in cash."

"Was he homeless?"

"Yes, but it seemed to be by choice. He might have been the smartest man I've ever met, and there were rumors that he actually had money."

"On the day that Mark Hamilton was killed, did you receive a call from Ann Hamilton?"

"I did."

"What was the call about?"

"She was at her house and said her husband was very angry and drunk and she was scared. She told me he had just had a fight with one of his clients in the front yard and when he came back inside, he started breaking up the furniture. She was really worried about what he might do next. I asked her if she wanted me to call the police, but she said no. She said she would be worried that if the cops showed, given how he was acting, something really bad could happen. She said she wanted me to come and get her."

"What did you do?"

"I hesitated. I wasn't sure this was something I wanted to be involved in." Martinez paused and put his head in his hands. He seemed to be thinking about what to say next. "Eventually, I decided that I couldn't just hang up. Either I had to go out there and get her, or I had to call the cops. I probably didn't make the right decision, but I decided to go get her. I told her I would be there, that it would take about twenty minutes. She said she would turn off the alarm system."

"So that's what you did, you went to the Hamilton's house alone?"

"No. I was worried about the husband. If he was acting the way Ann described, what was he going to do when I showed up? So, I decided to see if Tito would go with me. I drove down to the free clinic, where he hangs out a lot, and found him. I told him what was going on and asked him to go with me. He told me I was stupid. I asked him, sarcastically, if we should let the husband kill the wife, or if it would be better to call the cops and have them kill the husband. He didn't like it, but he eventually said he would do it for five hundred bucks. It pissed me off, but I said okay. He got his knapsack and we headed out."

"Describe what happened after that."

"Once we got close, we parked in the street and approached the house on foot along a path in the woods. I called Ann and she came out. Tito stayed in the background, though—she didn't know he was there. She said she had decided to stay until morning, that her husband had passed out in the living room and she didn't want to just disappear on him. She said she was going to take a sleeping pill and deal with her asshole husband in the morning and that I should leave. I got mad, after I came all the way out there to help her, especially when I really shouldn't have, and she just says go away. We exchanged nasty words and she goes back inside. It was just so bizarre. I knew right then that I had to get away from her, because she was just nuts. I went back and found Tito, and told him she wasn't coming. He said that since he took the five hundred, he'd stay there in the woods for the night just in case something happened. I thought, 'Well, he's nuts, too,' and I left."

"Did anything else happen that night?"

"Yeah. Tito called me sometime around eleven or so. He sounded out of breath, like he'd been running. He said he wanted me to pick him up at the gas station on the highway, down the hill from where we were. He told me he'd just seen two people kill someone at the Hamilton's house and he thinks the guy they killed was Mark Hamilton. I was stunned. It just sounded so wild. I asked him if Ann was involved. That's the first thing that crossed my mind—maybe the husband woke up and attacked her or something. But why would they be outside? Anyway, he said no, he was sure it wasn't Ann. I told him I'd be there as soon as I could."

"Was Tito the person who called 911 that night?"

"That's what he told me. When I got to the station it seemed like there were cop cars everywhere, and they were headed up the hill toward the house, so obviously someone had called 911. I pulled up and he got in. He told me he'd made the call, just in case the guy was alive. He said he didn't go check because he saw that there were security cameras. I asked him what he saw. He said that he'd gone to sleep in his sleeping bag, but he was woken up by people yelling. He looked up and saw two men screaming at one another. One was in a robe, so he figured that was Hamilton. They were obviously very angry, and Hamilton shoved the other guy, who fell down. Hamilton picked up a bat that was lying in the yard and hit the other guy really hard on the shoulder. The guy was trying to crawl away, and Hamilton swung the bat back, like he was going to hit him again. Tito said it looked like he was going to hit the guy right in the head. Then there was a shot, and Hamilton looked stunned and then fell. Tito said he looked dead. At that point, another person ran into the yard with a gun. The shooter was dressed in a dark hoodie; he didn't know if it was a man or a woman, and he couldn't see faces. More as a reflex than anything else, he said he stood up and yelled at them to drop the gun and stay where they were. He knew the second he did it that it was stupid. But the people *did* drop the gun—and then they ran. He said they took off toward the trail that leads back to the highway. He stood there a minute, not sure what to do, and then he took off as fast as he could. About halfway down the hill he called 911, and then he called me."

"What did you and Tito do?"

"We drove back to Santa Fe. Tito wanted to call the police. He's friends with the police chief, and said that was what we should do. I told him no, it would just lead to trouble and we hadn't done anything wrong. He argued with me and we said some pretty ugly things. But eventually I let him out in the area of the clinic and I went home."

"What was your fear about contacting the police?"

"I guess the honest answer is that I was afraid for my reputation. By now it's pretty much mud, but that night I was worried that if something got out about my relationship with

Ann Hamilton, it would damage my business and my family. I just wanted it to go away, and I never wanted to see Ann Hamilton again. I knew I'd made a major mistake getting involved with her, and now, way too late, I was worried about my wife and kids." He lowered his head again and began to cry.

"Let's take a short break."

Tucker watched Martinez for a few seconds and then got up and left the room, the others following. There was little conversation in the halls. Martinez remained in the conference room and everyone looked somber. Only when Tucker returned did everyone else re-enter, at that point the clerk re-started the process.

"Mister Martinez, why did you become Dave Adams's attorney?"

"Bad judgment—again. Jerry, the guy who owns the Blue Door Inn, asked me if I could help out one of his guests who needed an attorney. Jerry is a great guy, and I just said yes without thinking it through very carefully. Obviously, it was wrong. I thought I would just help get him released, and then someone else would show up and take over. I couldn't really represent him, anyway, because I'm obviously not experienced in criminal law."

"Did you want to know what was going on with the investigation? Was this a way to find out?"

"No, no. I didn't even think about that. I knew Tito and I hadn't done anything wrong, so I somehow rationalized it, thinking I could help Jerry out—that's who I was focused on. I know it's dumb, but that's the truth."

"Have you talked to Ann Hamilton since that night?"

"No."

"Were you involved in Hamilton's death?"

"No."

"We're you involved in Tito Alverez's death?"

"No."

"Do you know who killed Mark Hamilton?"

"No."

"Some goons attacked my investigator—they said it was Tito who sent them. Do you know why he would do that?"

"No. He and I had a big argument because he told your investigator about my affair with Ann. I think he did that because he believed we should have gone to the police, so he was forcing the issue through your guy, Malone. The goons might have been the same thing—pushing Malone, provoking him, so he would look harder at me and Tito. I think Tito was going to see the police chief the night he had his heart attack. He was having a lot of trouble with his conscience about the fact that we hadn't told the cops what we knew. I'm really sorry I ever got him involved."

"Thank you, Mister Martinez. We're done."

Martinez was the first to leave. Maybe he could get some rest now. His troubles weren't over, but at least he'd begun steering things in a better direction.

"I'm headed back to the hotel. I think I need to go to sleep and dream about happier things. What about you, Vincent?" It had been a long day and Tucker was showing his age.

"Think I'll head to the Crown Bar and say hello to my

At the bar, he had a Tecate in front of him the moment he took a seat.

"I know you change your drinks once in a while. This okay?"

"Cold and wet—perfect." He took a sip and smiled. "I just listened to a man who destroyed his life because of a beautiful woman, whom he now hates. The whole process took just a few months. Are women ever that stupid?"

"This must be a trick question, because I know you know the answer. *With depressing regularity.*"

Vincent's phone vibrated and he retrieved it. "Vincent Malone."

"Got a call from Carlton. Bud and Vickie Turner just flew into Santa Fe airport. Bud called Carlton and said he wants to do his deposition in the morning. I agreed. I have doubts about this, but I think we should go through with it. I was surprised the DA agreed, but I think he wants answers just like we do. See ya tomorrow." Tucker hung up.

"Looks like an early morning tomorrow. Okay if we skip dinner? Better go home and get my beauty sleep."

Nancy walked him out and gave him a real kiss. "Let's try again tomorrow night."

"It's a date."

31

Tell Us What Happened

It was a cool, rainy morning in Santa Fe, and Vincent was headed into town from the Blue Door Inn. He felt anxious, and the low-hanging, dark grey clouds didn't help. What would happen today was anyone's guess. Tucker had called earlier and said that the DA wanted to meet before they got started, to go over a few things. Vincent was developing an admiration for Tucker. The man he'd first met had been angry, lashing out at everyone. Tucker 2.0 was calmer and much more in control. The brash, bitchy Tucker had been an interesting character, but it was today's Tucker he wanted as a friend.

As Vincent passed through security, he spotted Tucker standing in the hall, chatting with the ADA. When Vincent walked up, the ADA nodded and left, disappearing into an office. Tucker smiled at Vincent.

"The DA has met with Vickie and Bud. Vickie wants to go first. It'll be structured as a statement under oath, not a deposition—no questions from us. She's been read her rights and has agreed that we can be in the room. The DA will conduct the interview. They're already in the room and she's been sworn in, so they're ready when we are."

"Well hell, enough mystery. I'm ready."

"Something you should know Vincent. The DA said they came back because they thought you knew what happened. He said Vickie indicated she could not live with the guilt she was feeling. Do you know what that's about?"

"Nope."

"Well, I guess we'll find out soon enough."

They entered to find Vickie sitting at the table, her head down. She looked somehow like a child. Vincent hadn't noticed before just how small she was, and how delicate. Her manner was subdued. Bud wasn't in the room, just the DA, the ADA, and the stenographer. The DA spoke.

"Shall we get started? For the record, I'll note that Vickie Turner has been advised of her rights and has freely agreed to make this statement, without any pressure by anyone involved in this case. She has also agreed to the presence of the defense team, consisting of Peter Tucker and his investigator, Vincent Malone." The DA paused, then looked directly at Vickie. "Tell us what happen the night Mark Hamilton was killed."

Vickie looked sad, on the verge of tears. She straightened her posture in the chair and looked directly at the DA.

"The short answer is, I shot him. He was attacking my husband, Bud, and I killed him."

She lowered her head a little.

"Can you give us the details of how this happened?"

She smoothed out her skirt in a nervous tic. She looked again at the DA and smiled, as if there were no one else in the room.

"Yes, I can give you the details. It really began several months ago. I came here, to Santa Fe, to talk to Mark about dropping him as my agent. I expected it to be a bit confrontational, but nothing like what happened. Bud wanted to come with me, but I didn't let him. This was all complicated by the fact that, at one time, I'd been in love with Mark. Bud was extremely jealous of Mark, and that was a big problem in our marriage. It was the main reason that I wanted to change agents. I loved Bud, and I needed Mark completely out of my life. It was a strange scene at his house."

Telling the story seemed to take Vickie over, as if she were living it all over again, rather than telling it to someone else. She seemed mostly unaware of her surroundings, looking at no one in particular as she spoke.

32

Details Remembered

"Vickie you're looking great. I really like your hair that way."

Hamilton tried to give Vickie a kiss on her cheek, but she backed away. "I half expected Bud to be with you. He seems to track your every move lately." He chuckled.

She smiled. Why the hell did she smile? He was acting like this was just a friendly visit. She had to concentrate, remember what she'd come to say. "I want out of my contract, Mark, and I want my investment money returned to me today." She was determined to be assertive and not let Mark talk her out of anything. She wanted him gone, out of her life. Hamilton looked at her with a wry smile—he seemed to be enjoying himself.

"What the hell are you talking about? This is that asshole Bud talking. This isn't you, Vickie. We've worked together for years. We're partners." Hamilton paused, his expression darkened. "You were nothing when I started handling your career, and now, all of a sudden, you want to leave? Have you lost your goddamn mind? No way that's going to happen, understand? No fuckin' way in hell."

What had she expected? That he'd just say okay and wish

her well? She felt powerless, the way she always did around him, but she had to resist it. She had to be strong—she would be, no matter what. But she also realized, too late, that it had been a mistake to come by herself. "You can't force me to use you as my agent. Our past has complicated everything for too long, and I've had enough of it. Whether you agree or not, I'm cancelling our contract and hiring a new agent. I need you to return the money I invested, and I want it done immediately."

"You want it done immediately." He mocked her attempt to sound commanding. "I don't give a shit what you want immediately. It's not going to happen, sweetheart. You should hire a lawyer, let them look over your contract. I decide when you go, not you—unless you want to forfeit your investment."

"You can't do that. That can't be legal. Why are you such an asshole?"

"Why are you such a bitch?" His expression had been mocking before, but now anger seemed to turn him into someone else entirely—he was losing control. "I work my tail off for you people, and just when I'm getting ready to cash in, you come along and say, 'Please let me leave, Mark, so I don't have to deal with my idiot husband, who thinks we're still fucking.' No. That's not happening. You're going to leave now and go back to doing what you do. I'm your agent. You don't get a choice."

"That's crazy. I'm not your slave. Have you lost your mind?"

Vickie decided to leave. Mark looked unstable, and it scared her. She turned and headed toward the door. He followed, grabbed her by her hair, and dragged her into the living room, where he threw her on the couch.

"Stop this. My god, stop," she screamed, as he pushed her onto the couch.

"Shut up bitch."

He hit her, then hit her again. He tore at her clothes until she was half naked, then raped her. When he was done, he got up and walked out into the yard, staring off into the woods.

Vickie was hurt, physically and mentally. She felt herself wanting to shut down, to curl up into a ball, but she knew she had to get out before he came back. She was afraid for her life. The pain was intense, but she managed to get up. She stumbled some, but she got her things and went out the back door. She snuck around to her car, then left. As she drove away, she looked in the rearview mirror, almost expecting to see him behind her, a monster chasing after her, but there was no one.

She was crying, and had trouble seeing the road. There was too much adrenaline in her system, and she was in pain, all of which made her drive too fast, hitting curbs, but she managed to make it to the highway. Once there, the driving smoothed out—she seemed to go onto autopilot, and she stayed that way all the way to Albuquerque. It seemed to take forever. She debated stopping and calling for help, but she was too afraid to stop, to lose her momentum. If she paused, she might really fall apart, and not be able to get going again. And she was humiliated. She pushed away the thought of talking to the police—no one could know.

In Albuquerque, she finally allowed herself to stop and, to her surprise, she was able to compose herself a little. She took out her phone, found an urgent care clinic, and went to get treatment for her cuts. She found a blanket in the car to cover herself and went inside. They told her she had two broken ribs, which they wrapped tightly. The staff wanted to call the police, but she said it was just her boyfriend, that she was leaving him and didn't want the grief of filing charges and following up. The women in the clinic understood—her story was hardly unique. They fixed her up as best they could, gave her some clothes to wear, and she went on to the airport.

She wanted to keep everything to herself, not even tell Bud, but she knew she had to. She wanted to put it behind her, but he was going to want revenge. God, she just wanted to forget. She couldn't help it: this felt like it was her fault. No matter how she argued with herself, that was how she felt deep in her gut. Sitting in the lonely airport, she thought about suicide. Everything in her life was wrong—maybe it would be best if she just ended it. But making the decision, and figuring out the practicality of how to do it, was too much for her just then. By default, she flew home instead.

33

Details For The Record

Breaking the trance Vickie continued. "I got home and Bud went ballistic. He wanted to kill Hamilton or have him arrested. He had to be punished. We spent several days plotting ways to make him pay for what he'd done. Nothing worked though, because he was still holding all my money. I convinced Bud that even though it was crazy, we needed to act like nothing happened until I could get my money back. We talked to a lawyer about my contract, and she said it was probably void, that it might even constitute fraud for Hamilton to have written a contract the way he did. She was completely comfortable with us just ignoring it, operating on the assumption that it was a nullity—that's what she called it. But she wasn't so confident about the money. We could sue, but that was going to take a long time, even assuming we won. She suggested we try to talk to him, reason with him, and see if he might give us the money voluntarily. Of course, I hadn't told her about what he'd done when I went to see him, so I'm sure that seemed sensible to her."

"Rape is a crime, and the urgent care center could have corroborated your account of what happened. Why didn't you go to the police?" Carlton sounded genuinely interested.

"I was humiliated, embarrassed. It was all so personal. I think even on the plane going home, I was starting to just suppress it, push the memory away. I just wanted it to not to have happened. The money he was holding was an issue—if the police became involved, how would I get it back? But it was mostly my own shame. I didn't want anyone to know."

Carlton spoke. "Go back to that day of the meeting at the Inn. How did you end up with Dave Adams' gun?"

"While we were trying to decide what to do about the money, and how to punish Mark somehow for the horrible things he had done to me, we got the invitation to Santa Fe for a meeting with him to discuss the future of the agency and how it would impact us. It was *so* strange. His world had just gone on like normal, while we'd been living in hell for weeks. We were even more angry after that, and convinced he had to be stopped—punished. But I couldn't imagine seeing him again.

"Bud was the one who got me through that time. He insisted we had to go and confront Mark. He even said we should threaten him with criminal charges for what he had done to me if he didn't return the money. If we could get the money back, then we could decide what to do. After that, our hands wouldn't be tied anymore. Eventually he convinced me that we should go.

"We got there, and he didn't show up at first. It was so *maddening*. Bud tried to be sociable, as best he could. I more or less just hid—I didn't want to talk to anyone. That first evening,

Bud was talking to Dave Adams and someone else, and Adams was talking about how he didn't go anywhere anymore without his gun because of aggressive fans. He said some of them were really nuts, so he kept his gun in his room, no matter where he was.

"The next day was the meeting. We were shocked that the money was missing. It seemed almost too convenient. We were convinced that Mark had something to do with it disappearing. Bud was furious, and threatened to sue Mark, or worse, and stormed out of the room, taking me with him. We went to our room and fumed, but we didn't know what to do. We knew the Adamses, who's room was next door, had left. Bud said he was going to see if they'd left the sliding door open—people were doing that because it felt so safe out there—and if they had, then he was going to get the gun. I begged him not to do it, but he went next door and came back in only a few minutes holding the gun. He said they hadn't even tried to hide it, just left it sitting in the dresser drawer. He hid it under our bed. After a few hours, we decided we couldn't just stay cooped up any more, so we went downtown to have dinner.

"Bud was drinking the whole time we were in the restaurant. We came back to the Inn, and he got a bottle from the bar in the dining room and brought it back to our room and just continued drinking. I was worried sick. I could see he was getting ready to do something. I watched TV for a while, but Bud just drank and stewed. A little after ten, he got up and got the gun. He said we couldn't let this go on any longer. He was going to talk to Mark, and if Mark didn't make things right, he'd kill him. He was drunk, and I knew something bad was going to happen. I grabbed the gun and pushed him. He fell to the floor and hit his head on the dresser. He didn't say anything, just got up and ran out of the room. I stood there for a while in a daze, and then it dawned on me that he was going to Mark's. When we'd first arrived at the Inn, I had gone for a run on a trail that the gardener had shown me, and I knew it passed Mark's house. And I'd told Bud about it. I grabbed a black hoodie, put on gloves, and wiped all the prints off the gun. I had no idea what I was going to do exactly, but something bad was going to happen and I had to get over there, be ready to deal with it.

"Out on the trail, I started running. It only took me a few minutes to get to Mark's. As I approached the house, I saw Bud and Mark fighting. Mark had a baseball bat and was going to hit Bud, and I thought he would kill him. I had to shoot. I really didn't have any choice. Then the most bizarre thing happened—some guy stood up in the woods and yelled at us. I dropped the gun. We just ran. I was so terrified.

"Bud told me to go in through our patio door, which we'd left unlocked, and he would go in through the back door. Not sure why he did that—might have been to have someone see him enter and establish that he was alone, since the witness had seen two people, I don't know for sure, because we didn't talk about it. He told me afterward that he ran into Troy and Terry sitting out in the yard smoking weed, and he yelled at them some, but he didn't really remember what he said—he just felt like he had to say something or it'd seem weird.

"We thought that at any minute the police would show up and arrest us. We just sat in our room and waited. But nothing happened. We must have eventually gone to sleep, and then they woke us up and said the police were there and wanted to talk to us. We knew for sure what it was about. But once we got out there, we could see right away that they didn't know it was us—they were focused on Dave. And, of course, we knew why: the gun.

"After a few days, we went home. We still expected that soon, at any moment, things would change. Dave would be released and eventually the police would focus on us. We were never going to let Dave actually go to trial, and we felt horrible about him every day, but we couldn't agree on what to do. Bud and I fought. He wanted to be quiet and wait, see what happened. But I knew we had to tell the police what had happened that night. I couldn't stand it that Dave was in jail for something I had done. But I understood Bud. It seemed completely impossible that the police would continue to hold Dave. There was the eyewitness, whoever he was. He might not know who we were, but no way could he have mistaken either one of us for Dave. Plus, we figured there was security video.

"After a day or two at home, we decided we were going to come back here. Bud wanted to confess, not to have me involved at all, but I couldn't—it was just wrong. I shot Mark, not Bud. We argued a lot about how to handle things, but we knew we had to act quickly so everyone could see Dave was innocent, and he'd be cleared. Then we got these messages from the van driver at the Inn. He sounded like he knew what happened—we were sure he knew, which meant it was only a matter of time. The local police showed up at our door, and we thought, well, here it is, but they were just delivering a summons. But that was it—even Bud had had enough. As soon as we saw it, we decided we would fly to Santa Fe and explain what had happened."

Vickie slumped in her chair. There might be more to tell, but she was done for the moment. The DA nodded to the court stenographer, who began packing up her machine. The DA went to the door, and an officer came in and asked Vickie to go with him. Tucker got up and went over to speak, very softly, to Vickie. She nodded her head several times and then was escorted out by the officer.

Bud Turner was called in next. In a shorthand version, he corroborated everything Vickie had said. He seemed defeated and exhausted, with no real life in his eyes. "That bastard deserved to be dead. I don't regret that part at all—I'm glad he died. What he did to Vickie was unthinkable."

The DA asked Bud why they started fighting so quickly.

"I rang the bell and Mark answered immediately. He looked horrible. As soon as he saw me, he pushed me into the yard. He came out and shut the door. He said he had had enough shit for one day, and somebody was going to pay. He went and picked up a bat in the yard and started to attack me. I hadn't said anything. He acted like a wild man. I thought he was going to kill me." Bud shivered a little bit and put his head into his hands.

The DA nodded, and said that was enough for today. An

officer came and escorted Bud from the room.

Vickie was charged with first-degree murder and Bud with obstruction of justice.

Vincent walked into the hall with Tucker. "What did you say to Vickie?"

"Told her she should let me represent her. And not to talk to anyone, ever, about this case without me or some other lawyer present. I'm sure the DA will change the charge to manslaughter without us having to do much. I know a jury will look very favorably on the whole thing. She may spend some time in jail, but I bet it won't be much."

"Mark Hamilton, the man who had everything. Famous sports agent, filthy rich, gorgeous wife, multiple houses. He had it all and still couldn't stop being an asshole. What does that say about the human race?"

"Little too deep for me. You're the philosopher, Malone. So, you tell me."

Vincent chuckled.

"I think we're all flawed—some only a little, and some fatally."

34

Another Day

Tucker immediately went to the Hilton to give the news to Dave and Linda, who both broke into tears. Within minutes, they were planning their departure home. Over a celebration dinner, Tucker told them part of the story about Vickie, and how Hamilton had treated her. It softened their anger at Bud and Vickie for not coming forward sooner. Mostly, they were happy to finally be free of fear, and were eager to put the whole experience behind them.

"I owe you a lot, Uncle Peter. I know I haven't been easy to deal with during all this. Thank you for helping me."

They hugged—not a normal practice for either of them. Tucker sighed. "I'm glad it worked out. If the cops had done a better job in the beginning, this could have been avoided, and sometimes mistakes like that cost people their lives. Don't mind telling you, now, that I was a little worried." He chuckled. "Don't tell anyone, though—it might damage my reputation."

"Your secret is safe with me."

Vincent was exhausted. Hearing Vickie tell her story had been emotionally draining. He knew they'd made the wrong decision by keeping quiet—letting Dave live through such a nightmare had been cruel—but he wasn't sure he would have done much better in their shoes. And when it came down to it, Vickie had done the right thing. He still wasn't too sure about Bud.

The person he wondered about the most was Ann Hamilton. Would she figure out a way to keep those millions and avoid being killed by some mob hitman? It was hard to guess. But one thing he was sure of was that she wasn't going to give up the money without a fight. Still, she was in a different league with Victor Lorenzo—he played by much harsher rules than even she was used to. It would be smart to negotiate a deal and give up most of the money if it let her keep her lovely head attached to that gorgeous body.

He entered the Inn, but he didn't see anyone. He left Jerry and Cindy a note in the kitchen saying the charges against Adams had been dropped because Vickie Turner had confessed to the murder. And that he was taking a nap. Details later.

Vincent lay down on the top of his covers without removing his clothes. He wasn't much of a nap taker. He wanted to call someone and let them know about the case, but there wasn't really anyone—except Nancy, and he would see her tonight. What the hell? He called her anyway.

"Hello."

"Hi, got a minute?"

"Sure, what's up?"

Vincent filled her in on the sad tale of Vickie and how she'd gotten her ultimate revenge. As he was telling the story, he realized how important Nancy had become to him. It scared him some. He knew he wasn't an easy man, and he didn't want to hurt her.

"That's sad. But I'm glad for Dave Adams and his wife, and for you and Tucker. You guys going out tonight and celebrate? Maybe chase some women?"

"I thought I was having dinner with you." Vincent actually sounded concerned. Sometimes he had trouble recognizing sarcasm.

"Of course, you are. You really need to cheer up some. Why don't you rest a little and come by the restaurant about five, and then we can decide where to go?"

"I'll be there."

"Thanks for calling, Vincent."

He tossed and turned for a bit, then decided he just wasn't a nap person. His conversation with Nancy had made him sound pitiful, and he didn't like it. All of a sudden it seemed he was worried about all sorts of things. Relationships are hard, and he wasn't real sure he was up to it. He went out back and saw Jerry and Cindy. They waved.

"Did you see my note?"

"No."

He told them about Vickie and Dave Adams, giving them some of the details he hadn't put into the note.

"My goodness. That's great for Dave and Linda, but how horrible for Vickie and Bud." Cindy wanted happy endings for everyone.

"Our first guests, and it turns into a murder mystery. I hope we never have anything like that again." Jerry was shaking his head at the absurdity of recent events.

"Well, you definitely got a trial run with lots of surprises and last-minute changes. You should be ready for almost anything now." Vincent was trying to be supportive.

"What about Ann Hamilton? Is she in trouble for anything?" Cindy asked.

Vincent shrugged. "Not that I know of. She made some very bad decisions, morally speaking, but nothing that's illegal. I suppose she lied under oath about what happened that night, and if the DA had nothing better to do, he could charge her with perjury. I doubt it'll happen, though."

"Some little bird told us that you have been seeing Nancy quite a bit. Is that true?" Cindy gave him a knowing smile.

"A little bird?"

"You can't tell her this, okay? One of the ladies in her book club is related to Mary's cousin. She told Mary that you and Nancy are an item."

Vincent had not seen Cindy's gossipy side before, and it was a little frightening.

"Tell me you're just making this up."

Cindy looked offended. "I would never do that."

Vincent looked to Jerry for help, but he just shrugged and left. "I've seen her a few times since she was here for dinner. As a matter of fact, we're going out tonight. What that means, right now I don't know. But Mary has my permission to confirm to her cousin that something is, in fact, going on."

Cindy grinned. He almost expected her to say thank you.

Vincent's phone vibrated. "Vincent Malone."

"Dave and Linda are leaving tonight. Guess I can't blame them. They want to get home and feel safe again. He wanted me to thank you for everything you did. Not sure this would have turned out the same without your efforts."

"I don't know. I think that no matter what, Vickie and Bud would have eventually come forward. But you wish Dave and Linda the best for the future."

"What's *your* future lookin' like?"

"Guess I'm going to hang around here for a while. My deal at the Blue Door Inn looks solid, so I'll at least have a job driving the van."

"Jack Hill wants to talk to you. Told me he could use someone like you. You know, his firm has just opened an office in Denver. He's got lots of money."

"I'm not sure about him. Am I wrong to be nervous?"

"No. That's probably smart. He's a damn good lawyer, and incredibly successful, but I'm not sure about his ethics. His reputation is that he's a street fighter, like me, but he may not have my charm." Tucker chuckled. "I'm not sure I would turn him down, but I'd be careful."

"I'll give him a call. What are you going to do?"

"Kinda thinkin' about comin' back to the Inn and spending a couple of days. Do you think they have a vacancy?"

"I'm sure they do."

"I need to meet with Vickie and then get her and Bud released on bail. I think the DA is even going to recommend that they be allowed to return home, as long as they have some sort of monitoring arrangement. I'm pretty sure we'll be able to reach a deal on the Turners that doesn't involve much, if any, jail time. After that, I'm not sure. But if I get hold of a hot one, I'll be giving you a call. I think we make a good team."

"Nothin' better than two handsome old gents who absolutely know what they're doin'."

"Maybe we should run an ad."

"Wow, this is a big crowd. Somethin' special going on?"

"Late summer in Santa Fe. Tourist season is peaking about now, so most places are crowded. Where would you like to go for dinner?"

"Hey, I'm the visitor. I should be asking you. Where would you like to go?"

"How 'bout The Shed for fish tacos?"

"Doesn't sound very fancy."

"Not in a highbrow way, no. But it's one of the best restaurants in town. As a matter of fact, we probably couldn't get in if I hadn't made reservations—which I did."

"Smart *and* beautiful. A winning combination."

Vincent was surprised when she blushed, but it was

quickly followed by a large smile.

"First, though, let's have free drinks, compliments of the famous Crown Bar. What can I get you?"

"How about a margarita?"

She brought two full glasses, although much smaller ones than the Plaza Cantina used. She placed them on the bar, came around, and joined Vincent on his side. They sipped their drinks and smiled.

"What do you think happens with Stephen Martinez?"

"I'd be surprised if charges were brought against him, but they could be. He withheld evidence, which can lead to an obstruction charge. But he belongs to the lawyer's club, so it may be ignored. His biggest problem will be that he could lose his law license. That was really stupid, taking on Dave Adams as a client when he knew he had a glaring conflict of interest. And if that happens, then he'll lose his real estate license, too."

"I know his wife. She's devastated. From what I hear, even though they're Catholic, she may be leaving him. That doesn't happen that much in their community. I feel just terrible for her."

"Yeah, it's always the innocent people who suffer the most."

"What do you think is going to happen with us?"

"I thought we could get married, have kids, move to a farm, and raise goats."

"You really are a wiseass."

"Yep. Is that a problem?"

"Nah, I think it's fine."

Epilogue

Peter Tucker

Tucker secured a reduced charge of second-degree manslaughter for Vickie Turner, but was disappointed that he couldn't get her acquitted by arguing self-defense. He told a friend that she was "the nicest murderer" he'd ever defended, although that may not have been much of a contest. He sold his house in Tulsa and purchased a small condo in downtown Albuquerque—the altitude was good for his health, and he liked visiting Santa Fe. He established a non-profit working with several groups to promote change in the criminal justice system. He also began a consulting arrangement with Jack Hill. He's old, but he's not done yet.

Dave Adams

His baseball career was over and he suffered long-lasting effects from the emotionally draining experience of being charged with murder. He became socially withdrawn, mostly speaking only with Linda. They purchased a farm in Iowa, and Dave began raising several crops, including the state staple, corn. He generally worked the farm himself, and soon discovered that most of the aches he'd acquired as a pitcher were gone. He seldom ventured off of the farm, with Linda handling most of the contact with outside people, but he was—in her words, when she described him to his uncle—happier than she'd ever seen him. They had plenty of money and each other, and life was good.

Vickie Turner

Vickie dropped out of professional tennis before her trial began, and never talked about that part of her life again. It took many years for her emotional trauma to subside. The threat of many years in prison had created a lot of anguish for her, but she spent a total of only fourteen months behind bars in the Santa Fe county jail. Her lawyer's attempt to argue self-defense didn't succeed in getting her acquitted, but almost everyone involved in the case believed her version of events, which played an important role in her sentencing. She became a spokesperson for an organization advocating solutions for violence against women. She wasn't happy in the public eye, but she felt she had an obligation to speak out. She'd always been shy, but now generally preferred to avoid people entirely. She became a dog breeder specializing in Yorkshire Terriers.

Bud Turner

All the obstruction charges against Bud were dropped, but he had real difficulty during the time Vickie was in jail, falling into a deep depression. After Vickie was released, they realized that they were no longer in love. Both of them had been emotionally damaged, and for each the other was a reminder of the recent past. Eventually they divorced. Bud wouldn't take any of the money Vickie had made playing tennis, saying he still felt responsible for the bad things that had happened to her. He would sometimes talk to Vickie by phone, but even that contact eventually trailed off.

Ann Hamilton

After the legal issues around Mark's estate were settled, Ann was worth an incredible sum. Soon, though, she heard from Victor Lorenzo, who suggested she had been involved in defrauding him out of millions—though he didn't detail exactly what she'd supposedly done. Now, he said, somebody had to pay. She thought he sounded like a gangster from some old movie and told him so, laughing. The next day her Mercedes Benz 500S caught fire—inside her building's parking garage. The fire was hard to put out, and the car burned until much of it had melted. Two days later, she found a dead rat at her front door. She got the message.

Negotiations weren't easy. Lorenzo wanted the entire amount he'd given Mark, and she no longer had that much. This had been one of Mark's issues with Lorenzo—he'd spent a large amount of the purchase price almost immediately squaring up some very pressing debts. He and Ann had spent money freely for years, which meant that even though Mark was making a lot, they'd accumulated a big pile of debt. Ann debated calling the cops, but when she talked to Ryan Lewis—who had his own problems—he told her she should either give him the money or expect to die. She thought he was being dramatic, but she got the point. She offered Lorenzo eighty percent of the money she had, plus the house in Santa Fe. He accepted, but she was left with the nagging feeling that she wasn't done with Victor.

She had about a million dollars left. Staying in L.A. felt risky, the same town where Lorenzo lived. She sold everything, put the apartment on the market, and went back to Ohio to stay with her aging parents. She had affairs with several men in town, most of them married and none of it very well concealed. When she went so far as to dally with a young minister, her mother asked her to leave and not come back. She left, and her family hasn't heard from her since. Some rumors say that she left the country, while others claim Lorenzo finally took his revenge.

Ryan Lewis

Lewis had legal problems, financial problems, health problems—just about every kind of problem you could name. He was removed as a partner at his law firm and was suing the remaining partners for the value of his interest in the firm. And, of course, there was the big one: he had a murder charge hanging over his head. He hired a well-respected law firm in New York to represent him, but it cost a fortune. His lawyer assured him that the case against him was weak and said he was confident of an acquittal, all the while racking up costly hours. He knew the game. He'd called Ann twice since Mark's death—the second time she told him not to call again. His obsession with an evil woman had turned his life of privilege into an inescapable mire of suffering.

Stephen Martinez

Martinez's world collapsed. He lost his law license and his real estate license. No charges were filed against him for lying or withholding evidence, but few of his friends wanted anything to do with him anymore. His very religious wife defied her own church to divorce him. There was nothing left for him in Santa Fe, and he moved to Las Cruces, New Mexico, taking a job as the night manager in a small motel. As his world went from bad to worse, he began to drink, which led to him being fired from the motel. He moved on again, this time working as a cab driver in El Paso, Texas. During one late night shift he took a passenger to Juarez and was never seen again.

Troy Arenado

Troy was the age where a baseball player, even if he's still good, can usually see that his skills are starting to decline. Against the odds, he somehow had the best year of his career, becoming an All-Star. He had only signed a one-year, prove-it deal, and was ready to cash in as a free agent. He traded in his agent for an industry leader, who negotiated the contract of a lifetime for him with the Milwaukee Brewers. Seven years and one hundred and twenty million dollars. Some people swore he would immediately slump, but he proved them wrong. The next year he was MVP in the National League and in the World Series. He remained an All-Star for most of his career.

Buster Fisher

Recognizing that he was no longer physically able to play football opened a whole new career for Buster. He started making the rounds of the TV and radio sports talk shows, discussing his retirement. It suddenly became clear that, first, Buster knew a lot about football, and, second, he was very likable. He became a sought-after guest, and was offered his own show. One central theme of his show was the power of the people who officiated. From a lineman's point of view, he said, *every* play contained fouls if the refs wanted to call them—it was the refs, he claimed, who had ultimate control over who won a game. The NFL screamed and demanded that he be taken off the air, while fans loved it. He started rating refs and calling out all their mistakes—and was a ratings hit. Talking football and ragging on officials was nothing new to Buster—it was what he'd been doing most of his life—but now he did it as a TV star.

Terry Carter

With declining performance on the field, Terry was traded. The conditions of the trade required testing, and he failed a drug test, resulting in a seven-game suspension by the league. The trade fell through, and his old team cut him.

The drug test he'd failed on was marijuana. Terry tried to make the case that it shouldn't even be a banned substance, but got no traction. Since there was now no team with an interest in signing him, he retired. He moved to Denver, where he purchased a controlling interest in a marijuana dispensary. His football fame, and his much-publicized suspension, boosted his business, and he was soon a successful businessman.

Almost everyone else will return in the next Vincent Malone novel, Blue Flower Red Thorrns—available now. Visit TedClifton.com for details.

About the Author

Ted Clifton has written mystery novels which feature the settings of New Mexico and Oklahoma, places where Ted spent considerable time. One of his books, *The Bootlegger's Legacy*, won the IBPA Benjamin Franklin award and the CIPA EVVY award. Today Ted and his wife reside in Denver, Colorado, after many years living in the New Mexico desert.

Keep in touch

Once a month, I send my readers a newsletter with a little of everything in it: southwest US culture, be it art, recipes, or local sights; my thoughts on writing and reading; book recommendations; updates on my current writing project; and from time-to-time a short story.

To sign up, visit **TedClifton.com** and either wait for the pop-up window, or scroll to the bottom of the page. Everybody who signs up receives a mystery gift, with my compliments.

You can also learn more about me and my latest books by visiting **TedClifton.com** or emailing me at **ask@tedclifton.com**.

Books by Ted Clifton

The Bootlegger's Legacy

(Prequel to the Pacheco & Chino mystery series.)

When an old-time bootlegger dies and leaves his son Mike a cryptic letter hinting at millions in hidden cash, Mike and his friend Joe embark on a journey that takes them through three states and 50 years of history. What they find goes beyond money and transforms them both.

This is an action-packed adventure story that partially takes place in the early 1950s. It all starts with a key, embossed with the letters CB, and a cryptic reference to Deep Deuce, a neighborhood once filled with hot jazz and gangs of bootleggers. Out of those threads is woven a tapestry of history, romance, drama, and mystery; connecting two generations and two families in the adventure of a lifetime.

Winner of the IBPA Benjamin Frankling Digital Awards (2016 Silver Honoree).

"The Bootlegger's Legacy takes the reader on a wild ride through Oklahoma's bootlegging history. It makes for a wonderful escape into a fascinating, dangerous, and strange world filled with characters your mother warned

you about. Most readers will only ever interact with these types in make believe, but while the ride lasts it's a rollicking good time."

—Self-Publishing Review, 4 Stars

"Although the mystery elements in this novel are certainly engaging enough to keep readers turning pages, it's Clifton's superb character development that makes this story a transformative journey of self-discovery. The noteworthy narrative also includes vivid backdrops, brisk pacing, and a meticulously researched, historically accurate account of the Prohibition era in Oklahoma and Texas. A tale with an authentic, immersive setting, inhabited by well-developed, endearing characters."

—Kirkus Reviews

Dog Gone Lies

(Pacheco & Chino Mysteries Book 1)

Sheriff Ray Pacheco returns from his introduction in The Bootlegger's Legacy to start a new chapter as a private investigator, along with his partners: Tyee Chino, often-drunk Apache fishing guide, and Big Jack, bait shop owner and philosopher.

The trio are pulled into a mystery immediately when an abandoned show dog appears at Ray's cabin and the dog's owner is reported missing. Ray and his team pursue leads that bring them into confrontations with the local sheriff, the mayor, and the FBI, while in the meantime two bodies are found—neither of which is the missing woman.

Sky High Stakes

(Pacheco & Chino Mysteries Book 2)

Tired of spending his days fishing, Ray Pacheco takes on his second assignment with his partner Tyee Chino when the state Attorney General asks them to find out just what the hell is going on in Ruidoso, New Mexico. With the town's sheriff in the hospital with a mysterious illness, acting sheriff Martin Marino is running rough-shod over everyone around him.

What seems like a simple assignment becomes more complicated when Marino is found dead, shot at close range while sitting in his patrol car on Main Street. The suspects include most of the town, from Dick Franklin, manager of Ruidoso Downs racetrack, to bar owner Tito Annoya, to members of the local law enforcement.

At the same time, Ray has an uneasy feeling that the AG is withholding critical details about what exactly is going on in Ruidoso—and why the state was so slow to respond.

It all comes to a surprising conclusion with the involvement of a Spanish princess, a drug lord gone mad, and a few other lowlifes . . . and leaves Ray wondering if maybe fishing wasn't so boring after all.

Murder So Wrong

(Muckraker Mystery #1, with Stanley Nelson)

After his first day as a political reporter in 1960s Oklahoma, Tommy Jacks finds himself investigating the murder of a competing reporter at the state capitol. The mystery becomes a story of intrigue, love and tragedy, involving a would-be mentor, a gorgeous lover, a jailed father, an adopted mom, and shocking violence.

Murder So Strange

(Muckraker Mystery #2, with Stanley Nelson)
In an exclusive residential neighborhood, a U.S. Senator's wife has died. Tommy Jacks and his fellow journalists don't believe the police chief's story blaming it on natural causes. It has the smell of a crime. So begins a new journey set in the 1960s involving numerous dead bodies, high-tension political intrigue, police corruption, the drug underworld and unsavory hidden pasts. Tommy has a lot to write about in his My View political column.

Only in his second year as a political columnist, he finds new romance and emotional healing among a chaotic mixture of characters, from his new mother and his recently out-of-jail father to his acerbic journalistic mentor and antagonist and a foul-mouthed lawyer of questionable ethics, all wrapped inside the saga of two competing daily newspapers still at war.

Lurking in the shadows is the powerful and corrupt police chief, who seems to think it might be best if Mister Jacks, even so young, was dead.

Murder So Strange continues the 1960s saga of Tommy Jacks: Muckraker.

And More...

To keep up-to-date on all of Ted's newest books, visit www.tedclifton.com.